NO
SMALL
MURDER

NO
SMALL
MURDER

A Mini-Meadows Mystery

Lena Gregory

LEVEL
BEST BOOKS

Greg, Elaina, Nicky, and Logan: you are my world!

Praise for No Small Murder

"A delightful and determined heroine, a fresh setting, and a slew of worthy suspects make this an enticing start to a new series."—Susan Furlong, *Shattered Justice, New York Times* Top Crime Fiction of the Year

"With an enchanting setting, masterful misdirection, and a surprising twist, *No Small Murder* will delight cozy mystery readers. Lena Gregory has created a well-crafted and fun start to a new series!"—Lucy Arlington, *New York Times* bestselling Novel Idea Mysteries

"Jam-packed with adventure and a touch of romance, Gregory's new cozy series is the epitome of tiny house life. Her amateur sleuth, Emma Wells, and the feisty Granny Rose are enjoying life in Mini-Meadows until a client turns up dead. Emma has to solve the murder to save her business before someone else is 'down-sized'."—Heather Weidner, author of the Jules Keene Glamping Mysteries, the Mermaid Bay Christmas Shoppe Mysteries, and the Delanie Fitzgerald Mysteries

Chapter One

"Hurry up! You're gonna miss the best part." Jade Campbell, one of Emma Wells's two best friends, pounded on the steel wall behind her on Emma's miniature second-story sundeck.

"I'm coming, I'm coming." Emma dumped a second bag of microwave popcorn into the already half-filled bowl and sprinkled a bag of chocolate chips over the top, her gaze glued to the dirt road outside her window. Jade was right, she definitely didn't want to miss the moment Mr. Oh-So-Sure-Of-Himself pulled up to his new tiny home.

Ginger, the orange tabby cat who'd adopted Emma the first week she'd moved in, purred loudly, weaving between her feet.

"You know you can't have popcorn, silly." When she'd first found Ginger, she'd been a kitten, so scrawny she had to have been starving, her fur matted and beat up. Emma had made it her mission not only to fatten her up but to heap all the love and affection she could onto her. She put a few treats in a ball for her, scratched her head, and rolled the ball across the floor.

Ginger took off running after it.

Emma washed her hands and gave the popcorn a quick stir, mixing the melting chocolate.

Her other best friend, Chloe Garrett, opened the front door and peeked in, her hazel eyes alight with mischief. "Libby just called. The moving truck is pulling into the development as we speak."

If the truck had passed Libby's Diner on the outer edge of Mini-Meadows, the community of tiny homes in which the three women lived, it would be there any minute. Emma thrust three cans of root beer at Chloe, grabbed the

1

bowl of popcorn and a handful of napkins, and followed her up the narrow staircase to the bedroom then out the glass sliding door onto the sundeck. "Can you see him yet?"

"You're just in the nick of time." Jade dipped one slim shoulder and swung her long, dark hair behind her, then settled back in her chair, binoculars at the ready. "He's coming around the corner now."

Emma flopped onto her own chair between Jade and Chloe, propped her feet on a rattan ottoman, and set the bowl of popcorn in her lap so they could all reach.

"So…" Chloe dug in for a handful of popcorn. "What do you know about our newest occupant?"

"His name is Tanner Reed." Emma grinned at her. "And I went out to his sprawling, thirty-five-hundred-square-foot ranch, at his invitation, for a free consultation. Three times. And he wasn't happy with my suggestions, so he decided he could downsize on his own."

"Oh, yeah," Jade hooted. "This is gonna be a fun one."

"You know what I don't get?" Chloe narrowed her eyes at the short driveway Tanner Reed was going to pull into. A soft breeze ruffled her strawberry-blonde bob. "Why don't people realize how small their new homes are until they're standing in front of them with all of their belongings?"

Since Chloe had an insatiable thirst for understanding people, Emma had no doubt she was seriously searching for the answer.

"Some people have a difficult time visualizing space. They sort of understand it, on paper, anyway, but when it comes to fitting all of their belongings into five hundred square feet or less and still having room to move around, the concept is lost on them." At least, that had been Emma's observation over the past year she'd spent as a downsize specialist. Not all of her clients moved to tiny homes; some moved to smaller houses, others to condos and townhomes, but those who moved into tiny homes seemed most likely to misjudge.

When Emma had first moved into her tiny home—two shipping containers stacked one on top of the other, the top one smaller, creating a loft bedroom area inside and an often-used sundeck atop the bottom container outside, with a sliding glass door connecting the two—Emma had brought very little with her. She'd had the benefit of starting with a mostly empty area, then filling it as space and finances allowed. Most people didn't share Emma's circumstances.

"Here it comes." Jade gripped Emma's arm and shook it, binoculars blocking the excitement in her gray eyes as she kept them trained on the moving truck lumbering down the narrow dirt lane toward the house across the road.

Emma had become used to the privacy offered by the empty lot across the road and had been sorry to see it filled last week when the new tiny home had been towed in and placed. Mr. Tanner Reed's home, of all people. He'd been a difficult enough potential client, who hadn't even hired her after asking her to come to his home three times for free consultations. She couldn't imagine what kind of neighbor he'd make.

The truck pulled to the side of the road just before it reached the new house, hitting a tree branch, which broke and got hung up in the moss.

A black Lexus swung around the truck and into the driveway.

"Good thing the truck isn't blocking the view like it sometimes does." Jade kept the binoculars trained on Tanner Reed as he climbed out of his car, propped his hands on his hips, and stood staring at his new home.

He shoved his sunglasses onto the top of his head.

"That ain't gonna make it any bigger, honey." Jade laughed and set the binoculars aside in favor of her root beer. "Too bad I can't see his face. It's always great to see their expressions when they first pull up."

A small glimmer of hope trickled in. If Mr. Reed wasn't happy with his new surroundings, maybe they'd come haul the house away and restore Emma's view of the open field that led to the forest beyond Mini-Meadows.

Chloe felt around the side of her chair for her soda, not pulling her gaze from Mr. Reed. "You can almost always tell the people who are going to stick it out and those who are going to be gone within a few months by their initial reactions."

At least, Chloe could, since she had an amazing knack for reading people.

"Remember when Olivia and Nate first moved in? You guys didn't think she'd stick it out in such close quarters with a rambunctious little boy, but I knew she'd love it. I could see it on her face the instant she set eyes on her house; it was perfect, exactly what she'd needed."

Emma couldn't argue that. The two had moved in a month after she had, when she'd first met Chloe, and hadn't yet realized how adept she was at pegging temporary versus permanent newcomers.

Mr. Reed turned and looked at the moving truck, then scratched his head.

"Ta-da!" Jade grinned. "The moment of truth. Mr. Reed's residency is going to be short lived."

"Nope, and you know how I hate to disagree, but…" Chloe argued. "He's staying. You can see the determination in the set of his jaw and his stance. He's just trying to figure out how. Sorry, Emma."

"Yeah, me too." Who knew? Maybe this time, Chloe would be wrong.

Mr. Reed's gaze shifted to the three of them sitting there, and he swiped a hand over his mouth, then pulled his cardigan tighter around him. Since early autumn in Florida still brought heat and humidity, Emma could only imagine his chill came from something else, probably the realization he had a truck full of belongings that couldn't possibly fit in his new home.

"Excuse me," he called with a wave. "Might I have a word, Ms. Wells?"

"Sure thing, Mr. Reed." She set the popcorn bowl in Jade's lap and hurried through her home, which didn't take long, considering the entire two stories boasted only four hundred and eighty square feet. Even with a quick detour to her desk in the kitchen for her business card holder, she quickly made it across the street and extended a hand. "It's good to see you, Mr. Reed."

"Tanner, please." He took her hand in his ice cold one then released her, stepped back, and looked at the house. In their first three encounters, he hadn't bothered to correct her use of mister.

"Call me Emma." Which she'd told him three times already. Four, now.

"Emma, thank you. Um…" He hesitated, then gestured toward the moving truck. A red flush crept up his cheeks all the way to his salt-and-pepper hairline. "It seems you may have been right, after all."

While Emma thoroughly enjoyed watching people arrive at their new homes, those who loved them on sight and those who had sorely underes-timated the square footage, she never enjoyed seeing someone dismayed, which Tanner clearly was.

The truck driver, who was from a company Emma had never worked with, hopped down from the truck and strode toward them. "We're ready to start unloading."

"Of course you are," Tanner muttered.

"Excuse us a sec, please?" Emma took Tanner's arm and guided him out from beneath the shade of a huge moss-covered oak and into a patch of warm sunlight. "Mr. Reed—"

"Tanner, please." He stared at the house and massaged his temples.

"Tanner, then. Have you looked inside your new home yet?"

He shook his head. "I've seen the floor plans, of course, and the pictures, but I haven't walked through it since completion."

"Why don't we start there? I'll walk in with you if you want, and you can look around the space and see what you think before you unload, maybe get a better idea what you have room for."

"But..." He shivered, even in the sunlight. "What do I do with the rest?"

Emma hooked an arm through his and started toward the house. "Let's take one step at a time."

"Yes, thank you, Ms. Wells." He patted her hand. "Emma. I'll pay you for your time, of course, as I should have done in the first place."

"Don't worry about it. Believe it or not, most of the hard work is already done." She took the key from his shaking hand and unlocked the front door. "Let's just call it being neighborly."

He smiled for the first time since she'd met him. "Thank you, Emma."

"No problem." She led him into the front entrance, then gave him a moment to look around.

He hadn't bought the house from Tiny Cooper, who'd built Emma's house and always built in little additions that made tiny home living easier and more efficient, and Emma was curious to look around. She was always on the lookout for quality builders to recommend. Though Tanner's house had been built to look like a miniature version of a full-sized cottage on the outside—adorable with its shingled siding, flower boxes beneath the windows, and front stoop, complete with portico—the inside was one big open space, like a mini inline ranch.

The front door opened into the living room, followed by a kitchen area with a small refrigerator, stove, sink, and two top cabinets along one wall. The bedroom space took up the back wall. Emma assumed a door just before the bedroom area led to a bathroom. Not the ideal set-up in her mind, but functional, nonetheless. "What do you think?"

He stood in the center of the living room, turning a slow circle, and nodded. "It's exactly what I wanted."

"Good." Emma smiled. Looked like Chloe was right again. "Then we can go from there."

He stopped when he faced the closed front door. "Now what?"

Unless she was completely confident her clients had sufficiently downsized to be comfortable in their new space, Emma usually recommended they have their belongings dropped off in a storage container. That way, they could move in a little at a time and rent a storage space if need be to store the rest. Unfortunately, Tanner hadn't done so, and now the movers were standing outside, waiting to unload everything he owned in one fell swoop. I told you so's weren't going to help him, though. "Do you have all of your boxes sorted and labeled?"

"Sort of." He winced. "I didn't realize how much I still had left at the end and started tossing it all into boxes in order to be ready in time."

She nodded, often seeing the same situation. People didn't always anticipate how long it took to sort through years' worth of belongings and pack them all up. "You still have a couple of options, both of which involve renting a truck and a storage unit."

She shuffled through her business cards and handed him one for a nearby storage company and one for a local truck rental company. "The truck rental place also has people you can hire by the hour to help you move heavier items."

He took the cards, still clearly overwhelmed and looking a little dazed. "Thank you."

"The driver outside needs to unload the truck, though, so you can either call and get a storage unit set up quickly and see if he'll drop everything off there and move it in a little at a time, or you can have him drop all of it here and move out what you don't have room for."

He nodded. "Okay, I'll go talk to the driver. Thank you."

"You're very welcome." She shook his hand. "And welcome to the neighborhood."

Her cell phone rang, and she fished it out of her leggings pocket and frowned at Jade's number. "Hey, there. What's up?"

"Oh, honey, you'd better get out here. And take a deep breath first, because your day is headed downhill fast."

Chapter Two

Emma hurried outside with the phone still pressed against her ear. She skidded to a stop when she spotted what appeared to be a brand new, shiny red corvette parked in her driveway, standing out garishly against the pale pink color she'd chosen to paint her home. "What the...?"

"Wait for it..." Jade said in her ear, binoculars trained on the corvette from her new vantage point on the edge of Emma's sundeck, her elbows resting on the lower railing, feet dangling over the side, swinging slowly back and forth.

Emma turned her gaze from Jade back to the corvette, disconnected the call, and stuffed her phone back into her pocket. Her curly brown hair, turned to frizz compliments of the Florida humidity, clung to her neck. She pulled it all back into a ponytail and tied it with a scrunchie she kept on her wrist.

The driver's side door opened, and an elderly woman stepped out, looked around, and slammed the door shut behind her. She waved to Emma.

"Granny Rose?"

Though this woman shared the same sharp features and slim build as her paternal grandmother, the similarities ended there. Granny Rose's usual pencil skirt, silk blouse, stiletto heels, and pearl necklaces had been replaced with a pair of brand new-looking jeans—fold lines still creasing the legs across the thighs and shins, framing strategically placed frayed holes—a camisole blouse topped with three different length gold chains, matching hoop earrings, and gold high-top sneakers. In place of her traditional perfectly coiffed updo, her white hair hung in waves down her back.

Emma closed her eyes and shook her head, then slitted one eye open. It didn't work. Granny Rose still stood, hand propped on her cocked hip, in the middle of Emma's driveway.

Tanner must have followed Emma out because he stood at her side, his mouth hanging open in a wide O.

"What are you doing here, Granny Rose?" She strode across the street. "Actually, never mind that. Who are you, and what have you done with my grandmother?"

"Ha ha." Granny Rose looked past her and winked at Tanner, then returned her attention to Emma. "I'm done with this ridiculous feud between you and your father."

Feud? There was no feud. Her father had disinherited her, and she'd moved out. Period. End of story. They still spoke on the phone now and then and met for an occasional lunch date.

Granny Rose bopped around the car and opened the corvette's trunk, then reached for her monogrammed Louis Vuitton. "I told that son of mine if my granddaughter is disinherited, then so am I."

"Huh?" *Uh oh.*

Tanner beat Emma to the bag. "Allow me to help you with that, ma'am."

"Why thank you, good sir." Granny Rose fluttered her newly-extended lashes and strutted toward the front door with a brand-new pep in her step and Tanner in tow.

Emma glanced up again to find both Jade and Chloe now sitting on the edge of the sundeck, legs hanging over the side, staring wide-eyed and shoveling in popcorn at a frantic pace.

Emma followed Granny Rose into the house and ran smack into Tanner's back when he stopped short in the entryway. Didn't he have more important things to take care of?

Ginger peered out at them from beneath the cream fabric loveseat.

"You can leave my bag beside the door, thank you." Granny Rose offered Tanner her sweetest smile. "Emma will take it up to the bedroom later when the rest of my stuff comes."

Rest of…?

"In case you haven't noticed, Granny, there's not much room in here for a lot of stuff." How long was she planning on staying, anyway?

She clapped her hands together. "Well, now that I'm moving in…"

Wait, what? All coherent thought skidded to a stop. "You're what?"

"Moving in. Haven't you been paying attention?"

"Uhh…" Her mouth dropped open.

"Get with the program, honey." Jade nudged her side.

Emma hadn't even noticed her and Chloe come down the stairs.

"When your grandfather, the old fool, left everything to your father when he passed, he also left strict instructions for him to take care of the women." She gestured between them. "Meaning you and me. Disinheriting you is not taking care of you. So, I gave it most of a year, giving him time to correct his mistake, then I let him have a piece of my mind. I told him if you're out, so am I."

What had Emma done to deserve this? Oh, right. She'd refused to marry Bartholomew Prendergast. Apparently, arranging marriages went along with taking care of the women. Well, Emma could take care of herself just fine, thank you very much.

At least she could before this new teeny bopper version of Granny Rose showed up on her doorstep. What was she supposed to do now? She couldn't very well toss her out, but the house wasn't built for two of them, especially when one was her overbearing grandmother, or what was once her overbearing grandmother. Now she wasn't quite sure what was going on.

"Popcorn?" Chloe held out the bowl.

"I don't think popcorn's going to help."

"Probably not." Chloe shrugged. "But it certainly can't hurt."

One of the movers knocked on the doorjamb and poked his head into the open doorway. "Yo, Reed, you gonna tell me what to do with all this stuff, or what?"

"Oh, right. I'm sorry." He took Granny Rose's hand in his and brushed a kiss on her knuckles. "It's been a pleasure, ma'am. I hope we'll see more of each other now that we're neighbors."

Great, not only was she losing her bedroom and half her space to Granny Rose, but it appeared her perfect view wouldn't be coming back any time soon, either. And, to top it all off, Granny had managed to snag herself a man in a matter of seconds. Emma still had no luck in that department after a year out on her own. "You know what?"

"What?" Chloe asked.

"I have to go. I have a meeting with Mr. Aldridge at three, and I'm going to be late if I don't get out of here now." She kissed her Granny's cheek. "Make yourself at home while I'm gone, and I'll be back as soon as I can."

"Of course, dear, you go ahead and do whatever you would normally do." She winked. "I wouldn't want to cramp your style."

Emma reached beneath the loveseat and petted Ginger's head. Then, leaving the mess in her overcrowded living room to deal with later, she grabbed her purse and the keys to the older model Jeep Cherokee she'd been fortunate enough to acquire cheap at auction and rushed out the back door to the carport. If her phone dealings with Mr. Aldridge so far were any indication, he was cranky under the best of circumstances. She didn't dare be late.

Even after the forty-minute drive to Mr. Aldridge's, spent trying to clear her mind with a variety of radio stations that did nothing to help achieve the desired effect, Emma's muscles were taut as she pulled into the driveway. For the first time since moving into her tiny home, she regretted it had no room for a tub to soak in. The cramped shower stall just didn't cut it after a day like today.

She stood on the stone walkway surveying the house. Roughly four-thousand square feet to somehow condense into a four-hundred-square-foot space. Which…she flipped through a few pages on her clipboard. Yes! He'd purchased his home from Tiny's Homes, which meant the square footage would be accurate and there would be at least a few conveniently built-in storage nooks and crannies that would be helpful. Plus, Tiny would work with her at the last minute, making adjustments right up until Mr. Aldridge moved in.

She walked up three steps to the wide front porch and rang the bell, then waited…and waited. She checked the time on her phone and ran through her appointment calendar to be sure she had the right date and time. Yup. So, where was he? She didn't want to leave only to have to return again, driving close to another hour and a half round trip if he wanted her to come back.

She rang the bell again and tried to peek into the window beside the door. Curtains blocked any view of the interior. She debated ringing the bell again when the door swung open.

"I'm here, I'm here." A short, stocky man with graying hair and a killer grimace stood in the doorway. "Don't get your panties in a twist. What do you expect me to drop everything just because you can't wait a few minutes for me to get to the door?"

"Uh…" The urge to turn tail and flee was strong. She tamped it down. Living on her own, without the benefit of Daddy's help, meant sometimes dealing with clients she didn't care for. Although, those she enjoyed working with made up the majority of her clientele. She plastered on a smile. "Mr. Aldridge?"

"Yeah." He puffed up his bulky chest. "Who wants to know?"

She extended her hand—in for a dime and all that. "I'm Emma Wells, your downsize specialist. We have an appointment."

"Oh, right, you're the one who's gonna tell me what to do with all my stuff. I forgot you were coming." He stepped back from the door. "Come in, come in."

As she crossed the threshold, a growl brought her up short.

The biggest dog she'd ever seen, tan with a black face, stood in the archway between the foyer and living room, his ears perked straight up.

Her breath shot out, and she whispered, "Is that a dog?"

He stared at her as if she'd gone crazy. "Of course, it's a dog. What else would it be?"

A horse maybe? "What's his name?"

He patted the dog's head, which stood even with his chest. "This here's Butch. He's a Great Dane, sweet as they come. Say hello, Butch."

Butch nudged her hand.

She petted his silky fur. Seemed Butch really was a sweetheart, but Mr. Aldridge was going to need a bigger house if Butch was moving with him.

"So, Mr. Aldridge, since this is your first consultation, there's no fee for today, but if you'd like, I can leave you a contract to look over at your convenience," Emma said.

He held up a hand to stop her. "Let's walk through and see what you can do for me, then we'll sit down and sign the contract. If I hadn't already researched your work and decided to hire you, you wouldn't be here."

"Oh." Well, that was good to know. Emma had started her business a year ago, right after she'd moved out, and she was determined to build a good reputation.

"I want to be out of here by Saturday."

"This Saturday? That's less than a week away." She rapidly calculated his needs against his potential timeline. Not going to happen. Even getting a moving company would be difficult on such short notice.

"I'm well aware of when Saturday is, missy, and I'm not paying you to argue with me. If I want an argument, I can get one from my wife and son for free."

"I'm sorry. I didn't mean it as an argument, I was just surprised." A pang of sympathy for his wife and son drifted through her. "Will your wife and son be moving with you?"

"My wife and Butch will be moving with me." He ran a hand down Butch's back. "My son, Phillip, is a grown man. He can figure out how to make it on his own, like I did."

She started to jot the information into her notes. "What's your wife's name?"

"Mildred."

"Thank you." Best to keep it all business with Mr. Aldridge, since he clearly didn't engage well in small talk. So far, everything she'd said had ended in some sort of snippy comment from him. "If you'll show me around, I can offer some suggestions and figure out exactly what we'll need to get started."

He gestured toward the living room.

She entered, paused, and looked around at the beautifully furnished room. A large portrait of Mr. Aldridge and what she assumed was his wife and son held a position of prominence over an enormous stone fireplace.

"Don't bother stopping here. We're not taking any of this frivolous nonsense. You will have one week after we move out to get rid of everything we leave behind, then you'll hire a cleaner, and the house goes up for sale." He kept walking through the room without a glance at anything, then down a long hallway past several closed doors. When he reached a set of double doors at the end of the hall, he stopped and shoved them open. "This is all you need to be concerned with finding room for. My study."

A life-size tiger statue greeted her, a tray holding two sets of keys and a wallet gripped between its teeth. A three-sided leather sectional, with two ottomans taking up the center space, sat in the middle of the room, and a gorgeous mahogany desk stood sentinel before a wall of completely filled floor-to-ceiling bookshelves. Mr. Aldridge would be lucky to fit half of this in his new home.

And what about his wife's things?

It was going to be a long week.

Chapter Three

"Is that all you do is work?" Granny Rose nudged Emma's laptop aside and set a heaping plate of baked ziti and a side dish piled high with garlic bread on the breakfast bar in front of her. "It's Friday night. Don't you have somewhere to go?"

Emma sighed and leaned back on her stool. Truth be told, she could use a break. She'd been frantically trying to get Mr. Aldridge's essentials taken care of all week, and the movers would have finally loaded the last of them into the moving truck earlier this morning to be delivered first thing tomorrow morning. She was shot, and she still had to consign, sell, or donate a good portion of his belongings, which were still left in the house. A chore she wasn't completely comfortable with, since most everything left behind seemed to belong to Mrs. Aldridge, whom she'd only met once, briefly, when she'd signed the papers and told Emma to do whatever Broderick said.

"Earth to Emma." Granny Rose snapped her fingers in front of Emma's face.

She jerked back. "Oh, sorry."

The least she could do was set aside work long enough to enjoy the meal Granny Rose had prepared. "I really am sorry, Granny Rose. I've been consumed with getting this job done the whole time you've been here. It's not usually like this, though. I do work hard, but once I get this taken care of, we'll have more time to spend together. I promise."

"Good. Because I don't need a lot of attention, but I have to admit, I thought living with you would be more fun." Granny Rose smiled and dug into her ziti.

And Emma had to admit, living with Granny Rose, at least for the short term, wasn't turning out to be as bad as she'd expected, other than the fact she'd gained two pounds in less than a week. And the loss of her bedroom. While she thoroughly enjoyed curling up on her overstuffed living room loveseat to read a book, it was not meant for sleeping on every night. She missed her bed.

She took a bite of the ziti. "Mmm."

"Good?"

She swallowed. "Delicious, like everything you cook."

"Thank you." Granny Rose ate another bite then frowned.

"Is something wrong?" It couldn't be anything with the ziti; it really was perfect, tons of melted cheese, savory crumbles of beef, and tiny bits of carrot mixed with pasta and sauce. What wasn't to love?

"Don't take this the wrong way..."

Uh oh. Whenever Granny Rose started off that way, she was getting ready to take over your life and rearrange it to her satisfaction. "But?"

"I love you dearly, but this isn't exactly the bachelorette life I had imagined." She set her fork on her napkin and folded her hands on the table in front of her. "Quite honestly, you're boring."

Being called boring by your seventy-something-year-old grandmother. Did it get any more pathetic?

"I was figuring we'd have like a code or something, you know..." she waggled her thinning eyebrows up and down, "like hanging a bra on the doorknob in case one of us has company, the other will know to stay out."

Stay out where?

"And maybe we can double date sometimes."

Double date? Now that Granny mentioned it, Emma hadn't had a date in...well, too long.

"I was thinking I could go out with that nice man across the street, Tanner Reed, and you could... Well, dear." She winced. "That's when I realized you haven't brought a man around because you don't have one."

Emma shoveled in ziti to keep from having to answer. She was not having a conversation about her love life, or lack thereof, with Granny Rose.

16

"When you gave up your inheritance and moved out because you didn't want to marry Bartholomew, I assumed it was because you had another fella in the wings, if you know what I mean. But then, when you didn't bring him around, even after almost a year, I started to wonder. Living here just confirmed my suspicions."

Emma swallowed and started on the garlic bread. If she kept stress eating like this, her lack of a social life would be the least of her problems.

"But." Granny Rose held up both hands, a gesture that always meant she'd decided something and wouldn't be deterred. "Not to worry. I got to talking with Jade and Chloe, and we're going to fix that."

Emma choked. Wait until she got her hands on those traitors.

Granny jumped up and patted her on the back, hard, a few times, then handed her a glass of water and continued as if nothing had happened. "Anyway, don't you worry about a thing. I know you're busy, and you have to work hard, at least until you find a husband to support you properly, so I'm going to help you out. There has to be an eligible bachelor in this community somewhere, and we're going to find him for you. Jade, Chloe, and I are meeting up at Libby's Diner in the morning to start the search."

"Mr. Aldridge's truck is arriving in the morning, and I have to be there to help unload." Really? Granny just hijacked her life, and that was all she could come up with? No wonder it had taken her so long to reject Bartholomew's proposal.

Granny Rose stood and started clearing the dishes. "I know that, dear. That's why we're taking care of it for you, remember?"

Okay, she could deal with this. She pushed her plate aside, leaving one ziti noodle right in the center in protest. That was petty. She grabbed her fork and popped the noodle into her mouth. She'd find a different way to protest. After she dealt with Mr. Aldridge.

Since Granny Rose had insisted on taking care of the dishes, plus the fact Emma no longer knew where anything went because Granny had taken it on herself to rearrange the tiny kitchen to suit her needs more effectively, Emma fed Ginger. After checking to be sure the cat door to the small box she'd made for the litter box was open, she moved with her laptop to the desk at the far side of the kitchen. She'd given up the space that would have allowed for a small table in favor of her desk, since she usually ate alone at the breakfast bar or at Libby's with Chloe and Jade.

"Good night," Granny Rose called from across the kitchen.

"Good night, Granny Rose. Thank you for dinner." She stood and kissed Granny on the cheek. "I know I haven't been as attentive as I should be the past week, but I'll do better once this job is finished."

Granny Rose ran a hand up and down her arm. "Don't worry about me, dear. I appreciate you taking an old lady in when it can't be easy for you."

"Don't be silly. I love having you here." And it surprised her to realize that was true. Maybe she'd been a little lonelier than she'd realized. As much as it pained her to admit, Granny Rose was right. Maybe she did need to get out a little more, develop more of a social life than she'd had of late.

"And I love being here. Good night, dear."

"Night, Granny."

Once Granny Rose headed off to bed, Emma's first phone call was to Jade.

It rang four times—coward—before Jade finally picked up. "Before you say anything, I didn't actually agree. I just didn't disagree. Oh, I'm sorry. Granny Rose can be very convincing."

"Yeah, I know, but that's actually not why I'm calling." Business first, then she'd take care of the situation with Granny.

"Oh?"

"Mr. Aldridge is moving in tomorrow, and I have one week to get his house empty. Did you go over and talk to him or Mrs. Aldridge about what they wanted to consign to Little Bits?"

Jade's consignment and thrift shop, Little Bits, sat on the main road leading into Mini-Meadows, what the residents referred to as town.

"Uh…" she hesitated. "About that."

Uh oh. "What happened?"

"I did go out there and talk to them, but Mrs. Aldridge ran out of the room in tears after Mr. Nasty told her he was getting rid of everything. When I suggested maybe she'd like to put a few sentimental items in storage, he had a small episode."

"Small?"

"He threw me out."

Hmm…not surprising, really.

"I'm sorry. I know this is an important job for you, but that man is a monster."

She couldn't argue that. Besides, she might be able to use the situation to her advantage. "Okay. I'll tell you what, you nix every single man Granny Rose picks out for me, and I'll forgive you the Aldridge incident."

"Every man?" Jade gulped hard enough for Emma to hear.

A smile tugged at her. She had her now. "Every. Single. One."

Jade sighed.

Emma pumped her fist in the air. "Yes!"

"Hey, I didn't even agree yet."

"I know, but you sighed, so that's just as good." But now Emma was going to have to find a new consignment shop to refer Broderick to. Unless… "If I can convince Mr. Aldridge to give you a second chance, will you go back?"

"That depends."

"On?"

"If Granny Rose finds the perfect man, you have to agree to give him a try."

Emma bit back a retort. There was no perfect man. Which Jade knew full well, so Emma should be pretty safe agreeing to her terms. She really didn't have time to find a new consignment shop. "Fine. Gotta go."

"Don't forget our deal."

"Not likely." She shifted Ginger aside and sorted through the five million notes scattered across her desk for her latest to-do list. "If you find Mr. Perfect, I'm all in."

"Want to meet us at Libby's for breakfast?"

"Thanks, but I'm sure I'll be with Mr. Aldridge until way past breakfast. Nice try, but it's up to you to keep Granny Rose under control."

She said goodbye and hung up, then scrolled through her contacts and dialed Tiny's number.

He picked up on the first ring. "I figured I'd be hearin' from you tonight."

"Sorry, Tiny. I didn't get a chance to do the final walkthrough on Mr.

Aldridge's house yet. I figured I'd do it first thing in the morning, but is there anything I should know?" She stood and stretched her stiff back.

"Nah, hang on." The sound of papers rattling came through the line. "Okay, we got the built-in bench seating with storage underneath by the kitchen table. I went ahead and added the bookshelves you asked for in the bedroom, built the bed right into them, and it looks great, if I do say so myself."

Hopefully, Mr. Aldridge would agree. Emma didn't hold out much hope, since he'd yet to be agreeable about anything.

"So, you should be good to go. Have you spoken to Eric Hamilton yet?" Tiny asked.

"Not since this morning when he headed out to load Mr. Aldridge's full storage container onto the truck." Emma filled the tea kettle and set it on the stove to boil, then dropped two Sleepytime Tea bags into her oversized mug. Hopefully, it would help her relax enough to fall asleep.

"Do you know if he hired that girl to help out?"

"Arianna Jenkins?" She waited for the water to boil, poured it over the teabags, and left it to steep. "Was that her name?" Emma couldn't remember. "I know he was going to call her when this job came in at the last minute, said his regular guys were all booked."

"That's what he told me too, but I never spoke to him afterward."

Maybe she should check in with Eric and make sure everything was set for the delivery tomorrow. Not that Eric had ever missed a delivery, but she didn't want Mr. Aldridge to be the first.

"I'm sure he'll be there, one way or the other," Tiny said. "Anyway, you got a key for tomorrow?"

"Yes. Thank you. Mr. Aldridge gave me his. I'm supposed to get there before him and do the final walkthrough." Now she just had to hope she didn't oversleep in the morning. The way things were going, this would probably be her first good night's sleep since moving to the loveseat.

Once she was done getting everything in order for the morning, Emma curled up on the loveseat. She sipped her tea and read until her lids grew heavy and her eyes burned. After the third time she dropped the book and had to find her place again, she set the book aside, laid down in the cramped space, and closed her eyes.

Ginger jumped in behind Emma's legs and kneaded the thin blanket until she found a comfortable spot.

Within minutes, Emma's leg cramped, and she stretched it out, straightening it over the arm of the loveseat, knocking the lamp and her water glass off the side table.

Ginger screeched, dug her claws into Emma's leg on her way over her, and shot under the loveseat.

"Ouch!" Oh, well. At least Emma got to stretch her legs while she cleaned up the mess.

Then she cleared off the side table, put a pillow on it for her feet, and laid back down. No good; her back was killing her. Back to the kitchen for ibuprofen and another glass of water. Finally, she started to doze, drifting on that narrow ledge between wakefulness and sleep, just about to slip over the edge into oblivion.

She jerked awake. She probably shouldn't have drank the tea and the whole glass of water. She got up again and headed for the bathroom.

Giving up on sleep, she shuffled back through the paperwork to make sure she hadn't missed anything. Confident everything was in order, she once more headed to the loveseat, where Ginger peeked around warily before resuming her position beside Emma. Morning light had just begun to peek in around the edges of the curtains as she lay her head on the pillow. Her eyes finally drifted closed. She couldn't keep them open if she tried.

Ginger jumped onto the back of the loveseat, giving Emma a little more space.

The tiny house started to vibrate. Dishes rattled in the mini cupboard. The pen she'd left on her desk bounced off onto the floor. Emma launched herself from the loveseat and pulled the curtains aside just in time to see the moving truck rumbling past.

Great. Sleep was probably overrated, anyway, not that she would know lately.

She dressed quickly, careful not to wake Granny, fed Ginger, and grabbed the keys and paperwork. Since Mr. Aldridge's house was only four lots down, she didn't bother with the golf cart she usually used in the development. The walk helped her wake up a little anyway.

Though the Aldridge home now sat on a foundation, it had once been a train caboose. Mr. Aldridge had an obsession with trains, as evidenced by the massive train set Emma had finally convinced him wouldn't fit in his tiny home, though he didn't relent until they settled on a set of tracks around the top of the wall near the ceiling for his trains to circle.

Eric had already climbed out of the cab. "Hey, Emma."

"Hi, Eric." She met him by the back of the truck, her inventory sheet on top of her clipboard. "How's everything?"

"Eh, I guess it's all right now, but you almost didn't get this delivery." He patted the side of the truck.

"Why?" Eric was the most reliable driver she knew; that's why she always recommended him first for local moves. "What happened?"

"I got to Mr. Aldridge's house yesterday morning, spent half the day loading his belongings into the storage container. He wasn't there when I finished, so I went and did another job and returned later that evening for the check. And he refused to pay the next installment."

"Oh, no." That wasn't what she wanted to hear. Not only did she now have to worry about getting paid, she had to worry about Mr. Aldridge stiffing the people she'd begged to do this job at the last minute. "What ended up happening?"

He shrugged. "I locked up the container and told him I'd be back in the morning. If there was a check, I'd load the container onto the truck and make the delivery. If not, I'd unload everything he owned on his front lawn and leave."

Emma laughed, imagining Mr. Aldridge's indignation. "I take it there was a check?"

"Yup. In an envelope taped to the container. No note, no nothing." He grinned. "I'm a trusting person, but I'm no fool. I mobile deposited it before I even left the driveway."

"Good idea." Emma backed across the road to get out of the way.

Eric climbed into the truck, maneuvered it onto the small lot, then set the storage container in place on the front lawn. Once he parked the truck back on the road, he removed the padlock from the container.

Emma returned to his side. "Didn't you hire that new girl to help this morning?"

"Yup. She helped me load up yesterday, then didn't show up this morning." He set the lock aside.

"Ah, man, didn't you just hire her for this job?"

He nodded. "I think maybe the job turned out to be too much for her. Anyway, now I have to unload most of this myself. My brother said he'd come by later to help me with the bigger items. Thankfully, with tiny homes, there aren't too many."

"I'm sure I'll be around all day if you need a hand with something."

"Thanks." He rolled up the back of the container.

Emma stepped inside. Might as well grab something on her way in for the walkthrough. When she set her clipboard on top of a box, her gaze landed on the rocking chair she'd spent half an hour talking Mr. Aldridge into putting on his front porch rather than in the house.

Something that looked like a full-sized mummy sat in the chair, fully wrapped in plastic sheeting.

"What is this?" She poked the plastic.

"What's what?"

"This mummy thing." She didn't have to check her inventory sheet to know she hadn't seen it before. She leaned closer, squinting to see through the clear plastic sheeting. Whatever it was had been wrapped multiple times.

Eric moved a box to get a better look and pointed to a label affixed to the mummy-thing's chest. "Can you see what the label says?"

Though the sun had already started to rise, shadows still bathed the truck's interior. Emma pulled out her phone and shined the light on the label with the name Broderick Aldridge scrawled in permanent marker. She gasped and jerked back, knocking the box and her clipboard to the ground. She'd have tumbled out of the container if Eric hadn't caught her.

"Hey, watch where you're going." He held on for a second longer to make sure she had her footing. "Can you tell what it is?"

She fumbled the phone, shining the light onto the mummy's upper body. A familiar face stared back at her, still recognizable through the thick plastic. "It's Broderick Aldridge."

Chapter Four

A buzz of excitement sizzled through the crowd of lookie loos that had begun to form across the road from where Broderick Aldridge met his unfortunate demise, despite the early morning hour. The police officers and a detective had already questioned both Emma and Eric… multiple times…and had asked them to wait around in case they had any more questions. Emma's head spun, and she searched the growing crowd for a familiar face to help ground her. The one she settled on first did nothing to quell her nerves.

Granny Rose stood between Chloe and Jade, her silk robe loosely belted over her matching hot pink negligee, her feet encased in marabou and spiked heels that made Emma's insteps cramp just looking at them, and her hair done up in the old-fashioned rollers she'd been sleeping in for as long as Emma could remember. Well, at least some things never changed.

While most of the crowd gawked at the police activity surrounding the storage container on Mr. Aldridge's postage stamp lawn, Tanner Reed stood ogling Granny Rose, his eyes practically popping out of his head.

With a sigh, Emma started toward her friends and Granny but paused when a dark sedan nudged its way through the crowd and came to a stop behind a police cruiser. She pulled the mass of frizz the Florida humidity, and probably stress, had sticking to her neck into a sloppy knot and tied it with a scrunchie as she watched a man and a woman emerge from the car.

The woman, Mrs. Mildred Aldridge, older, sophisticated, well put together, reminded Emma of Granny Rose in her pre-late-life crisis days.

When Mrs. Aldridge stopped short in the middle of the road and looked around, the man, whom Emma recognized from the painting in their living room as her son, Phillip, gripped her elbow and spoke quietly in her ear, then led her toward the nearest police officer.

Emma's focus was diverted by Jade waving frantically to get her attention, then pointing toward the woman's retreating back and mouthing Mrs. Aldridge. Torn between escaping to watch the unfolding drama with her friends and offering her condolences to Mrs. Aldridge and her son, Emma hesitated just long enough to avoid getting caught smack in the middle of the shout-fest.

"What are you talking about?" Mrs. Aldridge folded her arms across her chest. A scowl carved deep lines in her features. "He was fine, his usual pleasant self before going to bed last night."

While Emma could certainly understand the sentiment, the sarcasm dripping from her tone seemed inappropriate, all things considered.

The officer's voice was too low for Emma to hear, so she inched closer and angled herself to better see Mrs. Aldridge's expression. If she was expecting to find grief etched in the lines of the newly widowed woman's face, or even disbelief, she'd be sorely disappointed. At best, her pinched expression, punctuated by a dramatic eye roll, held minor annoyance.

Detective Montgomery, the same detective who'd questioned Emma, strolled over, pushed his glasses up his nose, and gave Mrs. Aldridge the once over with his all-seeing dark eyes. "Ma'am, if you'd come with me, please."

She turned her growing fury on him. "Look, I don't know what's going on here, but I've had just about enough. Now, I insist on seeing Broderick. Immediately."

"Mother, why don't we step back and let the police do their work?" Her son gripped her elbow and tried to steer her away. Sweat beaded on his forehead and dripped down the sides of his face. The growing heat of the day, or had nerves gotten the better of him?

Detective Montgomery took her other elbow in what looked like a tug-of-war between the two. "I'm sorry, sir, but I'm afraid I'm going to need to speak with your mother. And you. Come with me, please."

Phillip looked around, seemed to be searching for some way out, then slumped and followed the detective toward the small caboose and up the three steps to the covered porch—what used to be the front of the train car but now sat at the side of the house since it was set across the property.

Since there was no way she could follow discreetly, Emma joined Jade, Chloe, and Granny Rose.

Jade pounced the instant she joined them. "Rumor has it it's Aldridge that's dead. Is that true?"

Neither the police officers nor the detective who'd questioned her had told her not to say anything, so she figured it was okay to confirm. "Yes."

"And you found him?" Granny Rose shivered.

Emma nodded, her attention focused on the tiger statue that had just been unloaded and set aside. "Can you believe they even asked me where I was last night?"

"See…" Granny lifted a finger to make a point. "That's why you need a husband."

Chloe turned away to hide a grin.

Jade simply lifted a brow.

Emma knew full well she shouldn't ask, should just let the matter drop without even acknowledging it. "What does me finding Mr. Aldridge have to do with not having a husband?"

Dang. Would she never learn to keep her mouth shut?

Granny Rose patted her shoulder in a gesture of comfort. "Well, dear, if you had a husband to take care of you, you wouldn't have to be up at the crack of dawn working. Therefore, you wouldn't have stumbled upon a dead body. Plus, you'd have had company in the sack and, thereby, an alibi."

Emma's right eye twitched. She started to disagree, but Chloe gave her one sharp head shake, and Emma clenched her teeth to cage whatever argument might have popped out.

It didn't matter, anyway, because Granny's attention had already been diverted by Tanner Reed's approach. "Good morning, ladies."

Thankful to have that conversation cut short, Emma smiled. "Good morning, Tanner. How's everything?"

"Great. At least the house is great. Exactly what I wanted." He kissed Granny Rose's hand when she offered it, both of them seemingly oblivious to the rollers in her hair as she peered flirtatiously from beneath her fake eyelashes, one of which sat just a little cockeyed. Tanner's gaze was only half on Emma as he spoke. The other half stayed riveted on Granny Rose, and twin patches of pink tinged his cheeks. "Thank you again for your help, by the way, Emma."

"Of course." Though he'd already thanked her nearly every day since he'd shipped most of his things to storage and moved in.

As Tanner watched the unfolding drama, one hand fluttered to his cheek. "Oh, my. Can you even believe it? A murder in Mini-Meadows? I have to admit, I'm somewhat surprised. I did a tremendous amount of research before I bought a house here, and I was under the impression it was a safe neighborhood."

"I assure you it's a very safe neighborhood." Though the beehive of police activity probably made that hard to believe.

"Yeah," Chloe leaned past Emma to chime in. "It's usually boring as all get out 'round here. Just the way I like it."

"Besides," Emma added, "Mr. Aldridge wasn't killed here. He was already dead in the storage container when it was dropped off this morning."

"Really?" Granny's eyes lit. "How was he killed?"

"I don't know." And it hadn't occurred to her to ask.

She frowned. "But you did find the body, didn't you?"

"Yes, but I couldn't tell how he was killed." And she didn't want to know. At least, she hadn't before Granny Rose mentioned it. Now, she had to admit to some level of curiosity.

"I bet he was stabbed." With pursed lips, Granny Rose eyeballed the container as if it would shout the answer. "Stabbing is personal, and that man was so unlikeable, I bet someone just couldn't take it anymore and stabbed him with whatever they found handy."

"You could be right, Granny Rose." Jade chewed her lower lip, still staring at the container. "It wouldn't surprise me one bit. He really was an obnoxious jerk."

"Jade!" Emma admonished in a harsh whisper. The last thing she needed was someone overhearing a statement like that. At the scene of the crime, no less.

"What?" She shrugged, but emotion stormed in her eyes, emotions Emma couldn't quite place. "Just because he's dead doesn't make it any less true."

Detective Montgomery descended the steps from the porch, looked around until his gaze fell on Emma, and started toward her.

"Uh, oh." Granny Rose elbowed Jade in the ribs. "You think he heard us talking?"

"From all the way over there?" Emma shifted her gaze from the detective. If she didn't make eye contact, hopefully, he'd keep on walking.

"Hmm...a detective would make a great husband." Granny seemed to consider him for a moment, then fluttered her lashes and grinned at Emma. "Maybe he'll frisk you and take you in. Wouldn't that be a story to tell the grandchildren."

In her hurry to escape the thought, Emma stumbled forward and almost plowed into the detective. "Oh, sorry. I must have tripped."

"No problem, ma'am." He held out a hand for a moment to be sure she was steady. "Mrs. Aldridge said you have the key to the house?"

"Uh, yes." She patted her pockets. Where had she left that key? Her clipboard was still in the storage pod, but—she found it in her back pocket and fished it out. "Here you go."

"Is that the way you usually handle things, giving the key to the owner on moving day?"

"Well, uh...I umm..."

He smiled, an easy, crooked smile that danced in his eyes and instantly lowered her tension level.

But who knew? For all she knew, he practiced that easygoing demeanor, possibly designed to put suspects at ease long enough for him to move in for the kill, in the mirror each morning. Then again, Emma wasn't a suspect. As far as she knew. Technically, she wasn't even a witness, since she hadn't actually seen anything happen.

"It's not a trick question, Ms. Wells. Just curious about anything out of the ordinary."

"I'm sorry. I've never been questioned by the police before this morning." She tried for a smile and managed a shaky one. "I guess I'm a little nervous."

"No problem." He slid his sunglasses on against the rising sun, and the rays glinted off the gold band on his left hand.

Oh, well, at least Granny Rose wouldn't be trying to play matchmaker between him and Emma. Probably.

"Mr. Aldridge was..." How to best phrase what Broderick Aldridge was? "Difficult, I guess. Most of my customers walk through their new homes before they show up to move in, but he asked me to do the final walkthrough and gave me his key. It's not totally unheard of, but not exactly the norm."

He nodded, pulled a notebook and pen from his shirt pocket, and jotted something down. "And was everything okay when you arrived?"

"I don't know. I never made it into the house. Eric and I opened the storage container first. I figured I'd take a few things in with me, but then we found Mr. Aldridge, and I didn't want to mess anything up, so I never went into the house." Okay, now, if she could just stop rambling. Not her fault; nerves did that to her. And it was either talk or eat, and since there was no food around...Gah, now she was even rambling in her head.

"You mentioned Mr. Aldridge was difficult. Did you and he have a disagreement?"

"No, not exactly." Since she'd learned early on to just do as he said, and the client was always right, and all that.

"So, in what way was he difficult?"

She thought back to their first meeting, his manner, the easy way he dismissed her concerns about his wife and son and all of their belongings. "He was rude, abrasive, and he only seemed to care about himself."

"Can you be more specific?"

"Not really." She could probably try to describe the vibe between him and his wife, the way Broderick commanded and Mildred meekly obeyed. Emma had lived in that same atmosphere for most of her life. But it was just a gut feeling, and wouldn't do anything to prove or disprove any involvement in Broderick's murder.

She glanced at Jade, hoping she'd offer some input about her run-in with Broderick, but she'd stepped back behind Chloe and Granny, making herself all but invisible to the detective. Hmm...come to think of it, except for that one kind of callous comment, Jade was unusually subdued.

Detective Montgomery frowned and scratched his head as if unsure where to lead her. "Did you have any occasion to speak with his wife?"

"Only briefly when she signed the papers and told me to do whatever Broderick said." For a moment, Emma was dragged back to the argument with her father over her refusal to marry Bartholomew. What would her life be like now if she'd simply surrendered and done as he ordered, like Mildred did with Broderick? Would resentment have built in her, eaten away at her, pushed her toward something drastic? Well, moving out and leaving everything behind was pretty drastic, but could she have been pushed to murder? She doubted it, but that didn't mean Broderick's wife hadn't been.

Detective Montgomery closed his notepad and stuffed it back into his pocket, then pulled out his card and handed it to Emma. "Thank you, Ms. Wells. If you think of anything else, just give me a call."

"Will do." She tucked the card into her pocket and turned back toward her friends.

Granny Rose was looking past Emma when her eyes went wide an instant before she whirled back toward Emma and shot her a wide, toothy grin, then started winking repeatedly and nodding her head in the direction she'd been looking. Either Granny wanted Emma to look to her left, or she'd developed some sort of nervous tic.

Emma tried to ignore her as she made her way slowly back to her friends. Her curiosity got the best of her, though, and she discreetly—she hoped—turned her head.

A man stood at the back edge of the crowd, his hands stuffed into the pockets of his casual linen pants. Subtle reddish-blond highlights streaked sandy brown hair brushed back off his face and worn past his collar. That and his dark tan spoke of a man who enjoyed his share of time soaking up the Florida sunshine. He studied the crime scene, his eyes hard, jaw clenched, then ran a hand over his goatee, turned, and walked away.

Emma couldn't help watching him go, intrigued despite herself. A cop? Maybe. The rigid posture, harsh expression, the way his gaze jumped from one spot to the next as he surveyed the activity, missing nothing, certainly pointed that way. And yet, he'd turned and left the scene, sauntered back down the dirt road that led deeper into the development.

Hmm…While Emma didn't know everyone who lived in Mini-Meadows, it wasn't a large community, and she'd seen most everyone at one point or another on Main Street or in one of the shops if nothing else. But she'd never seen him. That much she was sure of.

When he turned the corner, she returned her gaze to Chloe, Jade, and Granny Rose.

Granny's grin had spread across her entire face and was now accompanied by a very satisfied gleam in her eyes.

Emma heaved a sigh and started toward them, her mind scrambling to figure out what else she could insist she'd been watching as the handsome stranger had wandered off and coming up empty.

Thankfully, she was saved the trouble when Phillip Aldridge yelled, "What are you doing, Mom? Mom?"

Emma spun toward the sound.

Mildred Aldridge descended the steps to the front lawn, her son hurrying after her. "I'll tell you exactly what I'm doing; I'm getting rid of all this junk."

"But, Mom…" he whined as he stumbled along at her side. "We could sell it all and make a small fortune."

But Mildred wouldn't be deterred as she strode straight across the lawn without even slowing. "I don't want a small fortune. I want this stuff gone."

"But—"

"But nothing. None of this garbage is coming back into that house. My house." She stopped in the shadow of a large, moss-draped oak, then raised her voice to be heard over the crowd of onlookers. "If I could have your attention, please."

A soft hum rippled through the crowd, then all conversation dropped off.

Emma nudged her way between Chloe and Jade to watch.

"Is anyone interested in purchasing this heap?" She gestured to the caboose home at her back. "Cheap?"

"Sorry, sweetie," Granny Rose whispered. "I love living with you and all, but it's kind of cramping my style."

Huh?

She stepped forward and raised a finger. "I might be interested. How much?"

Seriously?

Mildred spread her hands wide. "Make me an offer."

Granny did, a ridiculously low one, to Emma's thinking, way less than Broderick had paid for the house.

Phillip, who looked like he might either throw up or pass out if the green pallor he'd taken on was any indication, stood beside his mother and kept a firm grip on her arm.

"I'll take it. But..." Mildred hurried to the car she and her son had arrived in.

Phillip stumbled along at her side. "Mom, you can't be serious about this. You could get twice that for the house. Easily."

"This comes with the house." Ignoring her son, she swung the back door of the car open and hooked Butch's leash to his collar as he bounded out of the back seat, then approached Granny and held the leash out to her. "Do we have a deal? You get the house for practically nothing, and Butch gets a new home."

Emma lunged forward and grabbed Granny Rose's arm. "Granny, I don't think—"

"You've got yourself a deal, lady." She took the leash from Mildred and reached up to pat Butch's giant head. "Well, aren't you a cutie, Butch."

His head stood just about even with Granny's shoulders, and he outweighed her by a good fifty pounds or more. When he gave one loud bark, he practically knocked her over. No way could this be a good idea.

"I don't know about this, Granny Rose."

"It'll be fine, dear. You can get back to your boring bachelorette life, and I'll have some space to do my own thing."

Not with Butch in the house, she wouldn't.

"Of course, I'm pretty sure I won't be allowed to move in right away, what with this being a crime scene and all, but I'm sure we can manage until it's cleared and the paperwork gets done." She turned toward Emma's tiny home with Butch in tow. "Come on, Butch, let's get you settled in."

Emma stared after her, mouth agape.

Jade nudged her ribs with an elbow in perfect Granny Rose style and lifted her chin in the direction the intriguing stranger had gone. "Look on the bright side. At least now Granny Rose might be too busy with moving and Butch to continue her search for your Mr. Right. Unless, that is, you've already got your sights set on Mr. Tall, Dark, and Broody."

Chapter Five

By the time everyone cleared out of the Aldridge property, breakfast time had come and gone. Not yet ready to face whatever calamity might await her at home, where Granny was no doubt introducing Ginger to her new housemate, Emma took the coward's way out and talked Jade and Chloe into a quick lunch at Libby's Diner before work. They couldn't take long, though. With gossip running rampant, people would flock to the businesses along Main Street for news. Since Pocket Books and Little Bits were gossip hot spots, Chloe and Jade would have to open up soon.

For the moment, though, Libby's Diner seemed the place to be. The chrome and glass building looked like a miniature version of a diner straight out of the 1950s, complete with a black and white checkered floor, red vinyl booths, and a stool lined counter. Emma, Jade, and Chloe were seated at a booth near the front door. Not Emma's favorite place to sit, she much preferred the back corner where there was less traffic, but it was the only available seating when they'd arrived and they didn't have time to wait. Seemed most of Mini-Meadows had the sudden urge for lunch at Libby's.

Emma left her menu closed on the table. No need to open it. Finding her client dead, Butch moving in, and Granny Rose on the loose playing matchmaker—yup, most definitely a cheeseburger and fries kind of day.

Apparently, Jade agreed, since she ordered the same, though without much enthusiasm. She folded her napkin into some kind of origami-looking triangle that might be a sailboat. "So, did the detective tell you how Mr. Aldridge was killed?"

"No, he didn't say, and I didn't ask." Maybe she should have, but at the time, she'd just wanted to get out of there. Being questioned by the police was more anxiety-inducing than she'd have thought, even if she was innocent of any wrongdoing.

Chloe ordered her usual salad, since she was on a perpetual diet that she insisted never netted any meaningful results. She looked fine to Emma, curvy, sure, but in all the right places.

Jade sat back, closed her eyes, and massaged the bridge of her nose. As Emma had noticed at the crime scene, she was still uncharacteristically quiet. Of the three of them, Jade was the most outgoing, always up for something fun or adventurous, always smiling and chatty—maybe not in a bubbly way, like Chloe, but boisterous just the same.

"Are you okay, Jade?"

"Huh?" She looked up quickly and set her sailboat-looking thing on the table, where it promptly fell over.

"You seem like something's bothering you today."

"I'm fine." She waved off the concern with a smile. "Just a little tired."

Though Emma could tell there was something more on her friend's mind, she let it drop. She couldn't blame Jade for not wanting to talk in the middle of gossip central, especially with the low buzz vibrating through the crowd indicating the rumor mill was already up and churning. She'd offer to lend an ear later when they were alone.

The front door opened, and Eric Hamilton strode through, his jaw clenched tight. When he spotted Emma, his features relaxed. He waited for Libby to hurry past, her arms loaded with trays, then approached their table. "Hey, Emma. I was going to call you right after lunch."

"How are you doing?" Emma had been looking forward to lunch with her friends, maybe finding a discreet way to pick their brains about the handsome stranger at the Aldridges's, but there wasn't another seat in the place. "You're welcome to join us if you'd like."

"Thanks. I can only stay for a minute, though." He nodded to Jade and Chloe as he perched on the edge of the bench next to Jade, across the table from Emma and Chloe, then glanced at his watch. "I already ordered take-out and have an estimate scheduled in an hour."

While she was friendly with Eric, and might occasionally hang out with him in a group of friends, he never called her unless it was work-related. "What's up?"

Eric looked around, then leaned across the table closer to Emma and lowered his voice. "I just wanted to let you know Aldridge's check bounced."

"Are you kidding me?" The words blurted out, squeaky and high-pitched, before she could contain them.

A few people glanced in their direction, and she reminded herself to keep her voice down.

"Mr. Aldridge didn't pay the final installment in our contract yet either, and I doubt Mildred will be all that quick to pay it when she didn't want to downsize in the first place." Plus, now she'd have to worry he'd stiffed all the other people she'd put him in contact with. Jade was right to walk away from him. A trickle of guilt that she'd tried to talk Jade into taking him back on snaked through her. Then another thought brought everything else to an abrupt halt. "You didn't happen to talk to Tiny and see if his check cleared, did you?"

He frowned. "No. I haven't spoken to anyone else."

"Great. Okay." She knew one thing for sure, if Tiny's check bounced, and Mildred wasn't able to sell the tiny house to Granny Rose, Butch was going back. "I'll give him a call after lunch and find out."

"You'll let me know?"

"Yeah." She felt awful. She'd asked him to take the job at the last minute, and now, not only was he out the money, but one of his containers was held up at the crime scene. "I'm really sorry, Eric."

"Don't worry about it, not your fault. At least it was a small job." He bounced a knee up and down for a minute without saying anything, then frowned. "The only thing I'm really out is the one day's pay for Arianna, if I can even find her to pay her, that is."

Maybe Emma should offer to reimburse him for that? Not that it was her fault Aldridge had stiffed him, but she had begged him to take the job for her, had wanted to be sure the move would go smoothly, and he did hire

Arianna for the job. Even if it wasn't Emma's fault, she couldn't help but feel responsible. "You never heard from Arianna?"

"Nope, not a word. I tried to call her a little while ago, and there was no answer."

"Hey, guys…" Libby hurried past again, her sneakers squeaking against the tile. "Don't worry, I haven't forgotten y'all, just busier'n popcorn on a skillet in here."

"No problem," Emma called after her. It wasn't like Libby could have anticipated Aldridge's death and the flow of customers that would descend afterward and called in another waitress. Besides, the thought of going home to work amid the chaos that was Granny Rose didn't exactly appeal. Better to just sit where she was and contemplate who could have killed Broderick Aldridge.

Jade checked her watch. Unfortunately, it seemed she wasn't as willing to linger. Not that Emma could blame her. Once she opened Little Bits, the customers would no doubt shop as they flocked in to gossip.

Since Emma couldn't do anything to rush their order, she returned her attention to Eric, who seemed to have more on his mind than what he'd already said. Something about Arianna obviously had him concerned. Hmm… "Were you trying to get in touch with Arianna for something else or just to see why she didn't show up this morning and pay her for yesterday?"

He rested his forearms on the table, scooted closer to the edge of his seat. Jade and Chloe leaned in with him.

He lowered his voice even further. "Listen, I didn't say anything about it earlier, because I didn't think it mattered, and, well, a person's personal business should be personal, you know? Especially in a town this size, where gossip is the biggest pastime. She seems like a nice kid, and I didn't want to say something that might mess her up down the line."

Emma only nodded, not sure where he was going or why he seemed so distressed.

"Yesterday, when we were loading up Aldridge's things, I found her standing outside the open window eavesdropping on an argument. I reamed her about it a little, you know? Saying how it was unprofessional and all."

"Do you think that's why she didn't come back?"

"Heck, I don't know." He threw up his hands and flopped against the seat back. "It's not like I yelled at her or anything, but I let her know her behavior was inappropriate. She seemed to take it all in stride, apologized, then acted fine the rest of the time we were loading up, but who knows?"

"Do you think Aldridge knew she was listening?" Not that Aldridge seemed to care who was listening whenever Emma had witnessed him on a rant.

Eric folded his arms and shook his head. "No idea. If he did, it didn't stop him from carryin' on, but I really don't know."

She shouldn't ask what Aldridge was yelling about, especially after Eric had just accused Arianna of being unprofessional for listening, but it's not like Emma was eavesdropping or anything, just curious, so what could it hurt?

Chloe saved her from her internal debate. "Could you tell who was arguing or what they were arguing about?"

"Yeah… well, sort of…" He blew out a breath. "Not exactly. I didn't see who he was arguing with, but it was hard not to overhear when Arianna was so focused on what was going on inside that I had to walk over to her, right next to the open window, to get her attention."

Libby approached again and set a stand and tray beside the table. "Sorry about the wait, guys."

Emma smiled at her. "No problem. It's pretty packed in here."

"No kidding." She doled out the food at warp speed, then stood and pushed her sagging pink updo into place with the back of her wrist. "Getcha anything else?"

Chloe and Jade thanked her and shook their heads.

"We're good, thanks." Emma's mind was still on the conversation with Eric. Not surprising Aldridge argued with someone, since it seemed he argued with everyone, but she couldn't help wondering who'd stirred the hornets' nest that time.

"I'll be back in a sec with your to-go order." Libby pointed at Eric as if just realizing he wasn't eating with them, then disappeared into the back.

"Anyway…" Eric continued, "Mildred was there when I got there, and I saw Phillip go in not long after, but I don't know if anyone else was in the house besides the three of them. When I walked up to Arianna, Aldridge was yelling. Loudly. Something about another woman, and he said he wasn't going to answer any more questions about her."

"About whom?" Emma sipped her sweet tea—fresh brewed, ice cold with plenty of sugar. No one made sweet tea like Libby.

He shook his head, spread his arms wide, and shrugged. "I don't know. He never said a name, just that he was done answering questions about her. Then I tuned him out and spoke to Arianna, like I said, and waited for her to walk away. As I was leaving, I did hear him mention a name, but I'm not sure if it had anything to do with the part about the woman. Seemed to me it was a separate issue."

"Whose name?" Chloe frowned at her salad, then eyed the fries overflowing from Emma's plate.

He hesitated, then glanced apologetically at Jade. "Jade's."

"Huh?" She froze, a French fry halfway to her mouth. "Me?"

"I didn't hear anything else, because I couldn't stand there and listen after I'd just given Arianna a hard time about it, but, yeah, I definitely heard your name. Sorry."

Jade lowered the fry to her plate and waved off the apology. "No need to apologize. I appreciate you letting me know."

"Sure thing."

Though Jade's face paled, and she appeared more terrified than appreciative, Emma kept her mouth shut.

"Here you go, Eric." Libby handed Eric his to-go bag. "Do you want me to go through the order with you?"

"Don't worry about it, Libby. Thanks." He stood and handed her a folded bill, then turned back to Emma. "Anyway, I just wanted to let you know about the check, but I've got to run. If I hear anything else, I'll get in touch."

"Thanks, Eric, I appreciate it. Can you let me know if you hear from Arianna too?"

"Sure thing." He rapped his knuckles against the tabletop twice, then left.

"So, what do you think?" She kept a careful eye on Jade as she spoke, searching for some clue as to what was going on with the other woman.

Chloe poured ketchup onto a side plate, snatched one of Emma's fries, and dunked it. "If Jade's name was mentioned, maybe they were arguing about consigning stuff. I can't imagine Mildred was happy about all of her things getting dumped while he kept everything of his."

"No, me neither, but I never saw any indication she would argue with him even if she wasn't." Emma dipped a fry of her own, took a bite. Hot salt and grease—yup, just what she needed.

Chloe shrugged, pushed her salad around for a minute, then set her fork down and grabbed another fry.

Jade looked up from her plate without eating anything. "Eric didn't say someone was arguing back, just that Aldridge was yelling."

Huh...that was true. "So, you think it was Mildred he was talking to?"

"Maybe he was yelling at both of them. We considered Mildred wasn't happy about all of her stuff getting sold, but what about the son?" Chloe frowned. "Phillip, was it?"

Emma nodded, her thoughts following along with Chloe's.

"Maybe he was unhappy he was being forced to move out."

"Could be." Earlier, Mildred had referred to the house they were supposed to be moving out of as hers, so Emma figured she planned to stay now that her husband was gone, but what about Phillip? Would he stay too? Mr. Aldridge had made it clear everyone was to have their belongings out as of today, so surely Phillip had already made plans for somewhere to live. Unless he never planned on leaving in the first place. "I didn't give it much thought before just now. I guess I just assumed Phillip was taking care of moving himself, but I never saw any of his things packed, and no one asked me to arrange for Eric to move anything other than what Aldridge chose to take with him."

What she had given thought to was his wife's belongings. Mildred had packed only what Broderick had approved, had left everything else exactly where it was for Jade, or whoever, to dispose of. At the time, Emma had felt bad for her, figured she couldn't take the thought of selling, consigning, or donating all of her possessions, but what if she was wrong? What if Mildred hadn't ever planned on moving at all?

"Here you go, Chloe." Jade tossed her napkin on the table and stood, leaving her food untouched. "Why don't you take that salad to-go for dinner and have my cheeseburger and fries for lunch?"

Chloe's eyes narrowed at the plate. "I thought you were hungry?"

"Me too, but I guess not, and I hate to see it go to waste, but it's starting to empty out in here, and Main Street is getting more crowded, so I want to get the shop open." She pulled cash from the back pocket of her jeans and counted out bills for her lunch.

"Don't worry about that," Chloe said, "I'll get it."

"Nah, it's my treat. Enjoy. Sorry I have to run out." And with that, she dropped the cash on the table, turned, and fled.

Emma got up to let Chloe switch to the other side of the table. "Does Jade seem unusually quiet to you?"

Chloe frowned after her before sliding into the booth. "I'm glad you noticed too. I thought it was just my imagination. When she first showed up at the crime scene, her hands were shaking. I thought maybe she was just upset about a murder in Mini-Meadows, but it seems like something more than that."

Since Jade was an unusually content person, completely happy with her life and prone to act impulsively to do whatever struck her, her moodiness was way out of character. Maybe she knew more than she was saying about whatever Broderick was yelling about. "I think I'll stop by Little Bits after we eat and see if she'll tell me what's going on."

Chapter Six

Emma walked the block down Main Street, the only paved road in Mini-Meadows, to Little Bits, enjoying the more crowded than usual town as the sun beat down on her. It wasn't often—or ever—that a murder happened in Mini-Meadows, and like the diner, all of the businesses were packed with residents searching for news. Not that there were a ton of people, but like the homes in Mini-Meadows, the businesses were all tiny.

Golf carts lined the road, all parked at angles in their mini parking spots beneath the row of palm trees that stood guard along both sides of the road from the entrance walls to the end of Main Street—though she'd have preferred moss-covered oaks, which were not only beautiful but would also offer a good amount of shade along the sidewalk and covering the parked carts. Not that the roads weren't wide enough for full-size vehicles, they were, but most people preferred the small carts for getting around the neighborhood. Emma had left her cart under the carport in favor of walking into town. Come to think of it, she'd have to take Granny Rose to get a cart if she really was going to move in, couldn't have her racing around the dirt roads in her shiny red corvette.

Emma waited at the corner, which boasted Mini-Meadows' only traffic light, while golf carts buzzed up and down like busy bees around their hive, then crossed as soon as the first break in traffic allowed. When she opened the door to Little Bits, despite the closed sign still hanging in the window, the clang of the cowbell on the door had Jade jumping and whirling toward her.

Emma stopped short. "You okay, Jade?"

She laughed off the question with a wave of her hand and returned to the pile of clothes she was sorting through at a table beside the register. "I'm fine. You just startled me is all."

Emma didn't bother mentioning the fact that Jade had left the door unlocked, despite the sign in the window, and the cowbell clanged every time a customer opened the door. It usually didn't even phase her. "You were uncharacteristically quiet at lunch."

She shrugged and lifted a shirt, then poked a shaky finger through a large burn hole in its back. "Can you believe the junk people leave here? Who would wear this?"

Emma leaned back against a table and folded her arms to watch Jade work.

She tossed the shirt in the garbage with more force than necessary, lifted another, then slammed it back onto the pile.

Emma studied her, searching for a clue to her current mood—surely something more than the death of a stranger, even if he had fired her. Despite getting out of bed early with all the excitement, Jade was as well put together as always. In a vintage style that worked well for her, she'd paired a black, ankle-length skirt, buttoned down the front, with a lightweight pink sweater and killer lace-up boots with a heel only Jade would find comfortable being on her feet all day.

She hadn't had any recent breakups, and finances shouldn't be an issue. The small consignment and thrift shop usually did a fairly steady business. People who were downsizing needed to get rid of their things, and a good number of Mini-Meadows' residents were professional bargain hunters. "You said you were in a hurry to get here and open, but you left the closed sign up. Do you want me to turn it to open?"

Tears glistened in her eyes as she plopped onto a tattered armchair nearby.

Emma hurried to the door and turned the key Jade kept in the deadbolt, then grabbed a bottle of water from the mini fridge in the back room and brought it to Jade.

The tears rolled down Jade's cheeks as she accepted it and took a sip.

Giving her a minute to collect herself, Emma grabbed a rusted kitchen chair with what might once have been a yellow faux leather seat but had since turned a mustardy brownish yellow, dragged it to Jade, then sat facing her and waited for her to look up.

When she finally did, it was with a weary sigh. "I think I might have been the last person to see Broderick Aldridge alive."

Emma gasped before she could stop herself. Whatever she'd expected Jade to say, it hadn't been that. "What are you talking about, Jade?"

"Except for his killer, of course," she hurried to add.

"Jade, what are you talking about? Where did you see Aldridge? And when?" Emma's mind raced. She's spoken to Jade after dinner the evening before and had found Aldridge early this morning. When could Jade possibly have seen him?

Jade capped the cold water bottle and rolled it back and forth over her forehead. "Last night, after I spoke to you, an old friend of mine called, the kind you talk to now and again but not every day, so when you do talk, there's a lot to catch up on?"

Emma nodded, trying to follow what one event had to do with the other.

"I guess I mentioned a client who was downsizing and gave me a hard time, then fired me. When she asked his name, and I told her, she went really quiet."

"Did she know him?"

"Yeah. She didn't say how, but she did say she knew him, and he'd been really kind to her. I had a hard time reconciling that crotchety old geezer with the man Whitney described, but I figured, what the heck?" She looked up at Emma. "You know?"

"Sure," Emma agreed, since Jade seemed to be waiting for an answer. "So, you went over there? Last night?"

She clasped her hands around the water bottle, let it dangle between her knees, and lowered her gaze to the floor. "Whitney said she was in town for a few days and planned to go line dancing at this place we used to hang out at, asked if I wanted to meet up with her. I haven't seen Whitney in a while, and it seemed like fun, so I agreed to go."

When she paused for another gulp of water, Emma waited quietly, giving her the space she clearly needed to sort through whatever had happened. And knowing Aldridge, if Jade had stopped there in the late evening, he wouldn't have greeted her with open arms, despite anything her friend Whitney might have said.

"At first, I just drove past the Aldridge house, told myself if he happened to be outside loading the storage container, I'd stop and say hi, see if I could talk to him, apologize for whatever I might have done to offend him." She paused, tilted her head back and forth, rubbed her neck for a moment, then sighed.

"And was he out there?"

"He was standing outside, looking at the open, mostly full storage container, hands on his hips." She winced. "I actually felt kind of bad for him, because he looked kind of lost, you know?"

Emma nodded. She'd seen that stance and expression many times; it usually went along with thoughts of *what was I thinking trying to downsize however many thousand square feet into one storage container?*

"So, I turned around and went back. Whitney didn't offer any details of their encounter, but she insisted he'd been kind and had a good heart, just a prickly personality. Plus, I figured I owed you because of the whole Granny Rose matchmaking debacle."

"I'm sorry I gave you a hard time about that. I was really just teasing."

Jade lifted a brow.

Heat flared in Emma's cheeks. "Well, mostly, anyway."

"Don't worry about it." She offered a half smile. "It's not like you were wrong. We did get roped in by Granny Rose, but she's tough to say no to."

"Tell me about it." As evidenced by the fact that Granny and Butch were both currently taking up residence in her suddenly-way-too-tiny home. "Anyway, so what happened when you stopped?"

Slumping against the seat back with a sigh, Jade shifted her gaze to the window. "Let's just say the conversation was short and not so sweet. I apologized for getting off on the wrong foot, asked him if he'd reconsider consigning or selling any of their items to Little Bits...."

"And, what did he say?" Emma prodded.

"He snapped at me, asked me if pigs had suddenly sprouted wings, and suggested not-so-nicely that I leave the premises, among other things."

What a jerk! The thought brought an instant rush of guilt at thinking badly about someone who'd just been killed, and she cringed. "Did you leave?"

"After I told him quite loudly, certainly loud enough for neighbors to have overheard and mention it to the detectives, that I didn't want to work for him and that I only stopped by because I felt bad for his wife being married to such a monster...or words to that effect." With one arm wrapped tightly around herself, Jade chewed the thumbnail of her other hand. "Emma, what if the police think I had something to do with him getting killed?"

"Did the police contact you?"

"No. Not yet, anyway."

"So maybe no one overheard."

"Could be, I guess, but it wasn't late enough for people to be in bed yet, and it was loud, Emma. Really loud. You know Broderick, not like he could let it go after that. He yelled at me all the way to my car and stood in the middle of the road, shaking his fist at me as I drove away."

"Okay, that's good."

Jade's mouth dropped open, and she lowered her hand to her lap. "That's good? Honey, we need to work on your definition of good."

"No, I'm serious." She tried to envision the scene, spectacle really. "If the yelling drew the attention of neighbors, as it would in most neighborhoods, they'd have gone to their windows and peeked out. And what would they have seen?"

Jade spread her hands wide and shrugged. "Me yelling at an old man and him screaming back?"

"No, you driving away. They'd have seen you leaving and the very much alive Mr. Aldridge yelling after you."

"Hmm..." She sat up straighter. "I hadn't thought of that."

"And once you got to the club to meet Whitney, you'd have an alibi for the rest of the evening."

"Yeah, um...." She lifted a finger in the air. "About that. Turns out Whitney never showed up. I got there, went inside, and couldn't find her, so I went back out to the parking lot and tried to call. When she didn't answer, I sent her a text. When she didn't get back to me, I gave up and went home. I didn't see anyone I knew in the club, and to be perfectly honest, I no longer felt like partying, so I went home, took a hot bath, and crawled into bed to watch an action movie with tons of explosions to suit my mood."

"Someone had to have seen you at the club?"

"I guess, but since I didn't recognize anyone, I doubt anyone would even remember me."

Emma doubted that. Jade had an exotic beauty and a comfort in her own skin that turned heads and made her memorable under any circumstances. The fact that she didn't realize it only added to her charm. "Okay, but they have to have traffic cameras that caught you pulling into the parking lot."

"Yeah, and pulling right back out again a few minutes later."

"Maybe there are cameras inside."

Jade gave a non-committal shrug. "I guess. Maybe."

"Why didn't you just tell the police what happened?"

"Because they didn't ask." Even as she said it, she looked away. "And because I was scared. Besides, he was alive and his usual nasty self when I left him."

"Jade, we need to go to the police. If you go in and talk to the detective, tell him what happened, it will show you have nothing to hide."

"But what if he doesn't believe me?"

They'd have to cross that bridge when they came to it—if they came to it. "If you make them question all the neighbors to come up with the information and make them hunt you down to question you, they're going to find it suspicious."

"You think?"

"I would. If you just come clean, tell them what happened, I think it would look better."

She nodded slowly. "I guess you're probably right."

Emma blew out a sigh of relief. She'd about run out of arguments, but keeping what happened to herself couldn't possibly be the right thing to do. She hoped. "Did you see anyone else while you were there?"

"Huh?" Jade stood, set the water bottle aside, and returned to the clothing pile. Her hands shook as she started to sort through items for damage.

"At Aldridge's." Emma joined her, lifted a blouse, and checked it over. "Did you see anybody else out there? His wife? Son? Anyone lurking around?"

"Nah, it was quiet." She set aside a vintage paisley-print dress trimmed in lace that would no doubt make it into Jade's personal wardrobe once she'd freshened it up and repaired a hole in the seam. "He was out there all by himself, staring at the open container. There were lights on in the house, and shadows flickering, but more like someone had left a TV going than people moving around inside."

"Okay. Detective Montgomery left me his card, and he seemed really nice when I talked to him." She'd leave out how intimidated she'd felt. It wouldn't do Jade any good, only increase her already through-the-roof anxiety. "He said to call him if I thought of anything else. Do you want me to reach out and talk to him?"

"Would you mind?"

"Not at all." She hung the blouse on a rack beside Jade. "I'll give him a call and see if we can go down to the police station after you close tonight. Would that work?"

"Yes." Jade rounded the table to throw her arms around Emma. "Thanks, Emma."

"Any time."

Using the palms of her hands to wipe her cheeks, Jade laughed. "I can't tell you how relieved I am. When Chloe called this morning and said Broderick Aldridge had supposedly been found dead, I was terrified."

Come to think of it… "How did Chloe find out anyway? It was ridiculously early this morning, barely sunrise."

"Granny Rose called her."

Of course, she did. Granny Rose made a habit of knowing things. Hmm… Mini-Meadows might just be the perfect place for her, after all. "I'll call Detective Montgomery as soon as I leave, then I'll come back and pick you up and bring you to the police station around six-thirty, if that works."

"It's perfect, thank you."

"Sure thing." Emma's phone rang, and she pulled it out and checked the caller ID. Tiny Cooper. While she liked Tiny, like Eric, he only called for business. She only hoped he was calling about a new job and not about anything related to Broderick Aldridge, though she had a sneaking suspicion she was wrong.

Chapter Seven

After promising to call Detective Montgomery and return after closing to pick Jade up, Emma walked out onto Main Street. They'd walked to Libby's together, but with Jade and Chloe back at work, she'd make the fairly short walk home alone. She thought about stopping in to Pocket Books to say hi to Chloe and see if she'd heard anything new, but recognized the idea for what it was—procrastination. She'd just left Chloe after lunch. Even Mini-Meadows' rumor mill didn't move at warp speed, mostly.

Besides, much as she dreaded whatever Tiny might have to say, she did have to call him back, as well as call Detective Montgomery. The walk would not only clear her head but give her a few minutes of peace to make the phone calls, since she had no idea what kind of chaos she'd be walking into when she got home. Maybe Butch and Ginger would hit it off and be best of friends. She sighed. One could hope.

She dialed Tiny first, pretty sure that would be a quick call.

He answered on the first ring. "Hey there."

"Hey, yourself."

"'fraid I got bad news for ya."

Of course, he did. She massaged her temples. "Aldridge's check bounced."

There was a moment's hesitation while the open line hummed, and she held her breath.

"Yup. Sorry. How'd you know?"

"Eric's bounced too." Emma stopped in a small patch of shade offered by a palm tree and tried to think. "So, what happens now?"

"Well, I assume the police will eventually release the crime scene, and since the final payment wasn't made, I'll give Mrs. Broderick the opportunity—"

A laugh blurted out before Emma could contain it.

"Exactly. So, then I'll list it for sale."

"Okay. All right." She had to think. "Mr. Aldridge made the first two payments, right?"

"Yup. Just the final check was returned."

That being the case, maybe he'd be willing to sell Granny Rose the tiny home at a discounted rate. "Once you speak to Mildred and get the go-ahead from the police, will you get in touch with me? I may have a buyer."

"Will do. Thanks."

Emma disconnected the call, looked both ways, and hurried across the street with new determination. Granny Rose might still get the house, but Butch was going back to Mildred. If nothing else, on principle alone. She had to have known Broderick's check was going to bounce before she'd made the deal with Granny Rose, and no way was she going to get away with deceiving her like that.

Plus, Emma really wanted to get a peek inside the Aldridge house, see if Mildred had settled back in, and maybe find out if Phillip had ever packed and moved out or if he planned on staying put. Returning Butch would give her the perfect opportunity. Not that it really mattered. It's not like she was trying to solve the mystery of his murder or anything, but her curiosity had the better of her. Okay, if she couldn't admit the truth to herself, who could she admit it to? At the end of the day, she was just plain nosy.

She strode down Main Street and turned onto the narrow dirt road that would lead to home and was nearly there before she remembered to call the detective. When he answered in his clipped, no-nonsense manner, she almost hung up. What was it about him she found so intimidating? It's not like she had anything to hide. And he did have that cute crooked smile.

"Hello?" Impatience sharpened his tone.

"Yes, Detective Montgomery, hi. This is Emma Wells. I'm sorry to bother you, but I have some information for you, and I'd like to know if I could come in to talk to you later this evening?"

"What time?"

She quickly calculated how long it would take Jade to close up and drive to the station. "Around seven?"

"I'll tell you what, since I'll be in the field most of the day, why don't you let me know where you'll be, and I'll come to you?"

Her cheeks heated. Of course, he wouldn't just sit at the police station all day waiting for someone like her to come in and drop a clue in his lap. Seemed she had a lot to learn about murder investigation. "Sure. That'll be fine. I'll be at Little Bits, the consignment shop on Main Street, when you first turn into the development on your left."

"See ya then." He disconnected without anything more.

Emma tucked the phone back into her pocket, lifted her hair off her neck, and enjoyed the slightest bit of a breeze on her skin. This far back into the development, large oaks, and moss swaying in the gentle wind offered at least some relief from the sun's intensity. When she turned onto her driveway, she paused a moment, listened intently for any sounds of chaos coming from inside, then held her breath as she opened the door and peeked inside.

Granny Rose sat on the love seat, her feet tucked up beneath her, reading a steamy romance novel. Butch sat at her side, head cocked, a line of drool hanging from his sagging jowls, and Ginger stared daggers at Emma from beneath the loveseat.

When he spotted her, Butch jumped up, trotted the two steps it took to reach her, and licked her arm.

"Yes, hello, Butch." She patted his head, hardening her resolve to return him to his rightful owner. He really did seem like a good dog, despite Ginger's obvious annoyance, but she couldn't let Mildred get away with scamming her Granny.

With a sigh, she flopped down on the loveseat next to Granny Rose. It was barely past noon, and it had already been an endless day. And it was only going to get worse. "Granny Rose, we need to talk."

She set her novel on the side table and turned to face Emma, then frowned. "Is everything okay, dear?"

"Can I ask you something?"

"Of course." She patted Emma's knee. "You know you've always been able to talk to me about anything."

Tension eased out of Emma's muscles, and she relaxed into the soft cushions. Granny was right. She'd always been there when Emma needed someone to talk to, had always listened intently, even if her advice was sometimes not what Emma would do and often involved some form or another of the same theme—getting a husband—as if that would solve all the problems in the world. Who knew? Maybe for Granny, it had. "Do you really want your own home here in Mini-Meadows, or was it just a spur-of-the-moment reaction?"

Granny tilted her head and studied Emma. "You know, when I first came to stay with you, I don't know what I expected, really. You've seemed happy this past year, peaceful in a way you hadn't while living at home, but I couldn't understand how you could be happier here, living alone in a shipping container, than you were in your father's beautiful home."

Emma started to bristle at the question everyone had hammered her with for the past year since she'd moved in. Then she realized how Granny had phrased it, her father's home. It didn't matter that Granny had lived there most of her adult life with Grandfather before he'd passed away, she still hadn't referred to the house as hers.

"But since I've been here, I've found a certain...." She shook her head, as if unsure how to capture exactly what she was trying to say, and looked around the cozy space. "Serenity, if that makes sense."

Emma nodded; it was the same feeling she'd experienced her first few nights in her new home. "It makes perfect sense."

"I lived in that house most of my life, and it never felt like mine. It was always your grandfather's. Not that I didn't love our life, love everything about living with him. I miss him to this day, you know, would give anything to have him back, to have my son back to the little boy I held in my arms and adored." A single tear rolled down her cheek, and she wiped it away.

Emma took her hand and squeezed. She thought of Mildred, wondered if she'd felt the same way, like she'd always lived in her husband's home.

But she hadn't sensed any of the love she'd always felt between Granny and Grandfather between the Aldridges. Without the love, that feeling could probably turn suffocating. But could it push someone to murder?

Granny Rose sucked in a deep, shaky breath and blew it out slowly. "But that was the past, and we can't go back. And if I could, I wouldn't change a single thing. But my husband is gone now, and my son is grown, and once you left, the house just didn't feel like home anymore."

"Oh, Granny Rose, I'm so sorry." Guilt swamped her. When she'd made the impulsive decision to move out, she'd never even considered Granny's feelings, hadn't realized the toll it would take on her. Even though they'd kept in touch, it wasn't the same as being involved in the day-to-day of someone's life.

"No, dear, don't be." She patted their clasped hands. "The way I see it, home isn't about the house you're living in but the people you surround yourself with. And, while you might not have found Mr. Right yet, which we'll remedy shortly...."

Emma bit back a sigh.

"You have surrounded yourself with wonderful friends, found a nice place here, a peaceful place all your own. And I got to thinking, I've never had a place of my own. I got married young and went from living in my father's house to living in my husband's house, which then became my son's house, and I never had a chance to have something that was just mine. And when I saw that little caboose, something spoke to me. I know I can't stay with you forever, and I really want a place of my own. That house is perfect, my own space, but still close by. A safe place where I can finally find out who I am."

"I understand exactly how you feel, Granny." And whatever it took, Granny Rose was going to have that house. "And what about Butch? Do you want him, or did you just take him to get the house?"

At the sound of his name, Butch, who'd lain back down at Granny Rose's feet, perked his head up and sat.

"I've never had a pet either." When she reached out to pat his head, Butch propped his chin in her lap and looked adoringly up at her. "Butch spoke to me just like the house did, and with Mr. Aldridge gone, he has no one else to love him. He's part of home."

She blew out a breath. Okay, so Butch wasn't going back. Now what?

"Besides, that Tanner Reed across the street sure is a looker." Granny winked and had Emma rethinking her determination to make sure she got the house, but only for a moment.

Granny Rose was right where she was supposed to be, giant teddy bear dog and all. Now it was up to Emma to make sure it stayed that way.

"So, now that I've answered all your questions...." She released Emma's hand and sat back. "Why don't you tell me what's going on?"

She should have known Granny Rose would see right through her; she always had. Emma gave her a quick rundown of the events that had transpired since that morning, ending with her request that Tiny contact her before selling the little caboose home.

"Hmm..."

"That's it? Hmm?"

"Well, what were you expecting, dear?"

Hmm...what was she expecting? Nothing, actually. She'd just needed to talk through it out loud. "I'm going to go out to the Aldridge's. I should have just enough time before I have to meet up with Jade and Detective Montgomery."

"Good idea." Granny Rose stood and brushed the dog hair off her fuchsia velour pants. "And I'm going with you."

"You're...what?"

"I'm going with you. I'm the one she made the deal with, after all. Besides..." She kissed Butch's head. "You be good now, and don't harass Ginger anymore."

Maybe Emma shouldn't go. Maybe she should just stay home and mind her own business. She should probably stay put and referee whatever went on between Butch and Ginger. What reason did she really have to go out to the Aldridges' and bother Mildred when her husband had just passed away? "Besides what, Granny?"

She frowned for a moment, seeming to have lost her train of thought, then perked up. "Oh, right, besides, maybe I can get a look around while you're questioning Mrs. Aldridge and figuring out how I'm going to keep the house and Butch."

Emma's stomach rolled. "Look around?"

"Yeah, you know, like they do in those spy pictures." She grinned and waggled her eyebrows. "Just call me Granny Bond."

Oh, boy. What had she gotten herself into?

Chapter Eight

Emma knocked tentatively on Mildred Aldridge's door.

Granny Rose fidgeted at her side, rocking from one foot to the other.

With any luck, Mildred wouldn't answer, and they could just go home and try to purchase the house from Tiny.

The door eased open a crack—so much for luck—and an eye peered out at them. "I am not taking that dog back."

"Actually, we're not here about Butch." Emma tried to peek past Mildred into the house but couldn't see anything.

"Besides, I wouldn't give that sweetie back if you paid me," Granny said.

The eye narrowed, but a moment later, the door opened a little farther. "What are you doing here then?"

"First, let me say how sorry I am for your loss," Emma started.

She snorted.

Okay, best to just get on with it, then. "I'm here about the returned checks, Mrs. Aldridge."

"Speak to my attorney." The door started to swing shut, but Granny stuck her foot inside.

Emma hurried on before Granny ended up with a bruise. "Actually, I wanted to speak with you about the house too. Granny Rose would still like to buy it, and we want to see if we can work something out with you."

"Really?"

"You don't think I'm standin' here getting my foot crushed in your door for nothing, do ya?" Granny gave the door a shove inward.

"Oh." Mildred swung the door wide. "I'm sorry. I hope you're all right."

"Fine, fine." Granny waved her off as she strode through the door, despite the lack of an invitation. She stopped in the foyer and looked around. "I could use a restroom, though. These days I need to…powder my nose a lot more often than I used to."

Mildred frowned but gestured down the hallway. "It's down there."

"Thanks." Granny bopped in the direction she'd indicated, waited until Mildred had turned back around, then shot Emma a wink over her shoulder.

Great, Granny Rose was probably going to get them both in trouble. Of course, if she was busy poking around the Aldridge house, she couldn't very well play matchmaker. This might actually work out to Emma's advantage. "Umm…could we maybe go sit down and talk?"

"I suppose." Thankfully, Mildred turned in the opposite direction from where she'd sent Granny, who was probably pawing through the dresser drawers or engaging in some equally inappropriate and no doubt illegal behavior.

Emma followed Mildred into the living room and sat on the sofa she indicated. She wasn't sure what she'd expected, but the house looked exactly as she'd left it. All of the furniture still sat in place; no boxes or any other sign of packing littered the room. She guessed that was normal, considering everything they were supposed to take with them had already been shipped to Mini-Meadows, but it seemed there should have been at least a few last-minute items. The kind of things people are still using, then toss into a box or two just before moving out and stuff in their trunks or on their back seats to take with them, things forgotten or overlooked in the mad rush of moving day. But the only thing noticeably absent was the family portrait that had hung over the mantle.

Mildred perched at the edge of an armchair across from her. "So, what is it you want to speak to me about?"

"I have to be honest, I was disappointed today to hear that the check Mr. Aldridge wrote to the moving company I recommended, the man I begged to take your job on as a favor at the last minute…." Her anger started to rise, coloring her tone a bit harsher than she'd intended. She took a deep breath, let it out slowly. She'd have to work to curb the temper if she was going to get anywhere with Mildred. "The check was returned, Mrs. Aldridge. As was Tiny Cooper's for the final installment on the caboose home."

Mildred schooled her expression, but not quick enough to conceal the momentary shock before she recovered her cool demeanor. She slid back into the seat, crossed one leg over the other, and smoothed her skirt. "It wasn't my job, it was Broderick's, and he's gone."

"But you still have a responsibility to pay the people who worked for you." Though any hopes of getting her own money had fizzled since this morning, she'd at least like to get Eric and Tiny paid.

"Like I said, those people didn't work for me, they worked for Mr. Aldridge, so speak to my attorney." She shrugged a slim shoulder and started to stand.

"I don't think there's any need for attorneys." This conversation was not going well. The last thing she wanted was the need to hire an attorney of her own to combat whatever Mildred tried to do. "As far as Eric goes, he did complete the job of moving Broderick's things out, which you would have to deal with now that he's gone anyway."

"Huh..." She pursed her lips in thought.

Sensing an opening, Emma rushed on before Mildred could decide she was wrong. "And as for Tiny, you're selling the house to Granny anyway, so maybe you could get him paid so the whole thing doesn't get held up in court for the next however long."

Not that she would wait until it was all resolved to get Granny Rose situated in her own home. If this fell through, she'd find another caboose and have Tiny custom build it to Granny's specifications, but this one was only four lots down from Emma's, and Granny had never lived alone before, so being close was an added bonus. "Actually, that's all I really wanted to say. If you don't pay Tiny for the house, Granny can't buy it from you because you won't be free to sell it. At the end of the day, we can just wait and buy it from Tiny when you default."

Emma bit back the threat of returning Butch. Even if it might push Mildred to honor Broderick's obligations, he belonged to Granny now, so that made him family. Speaking of Granny... Emma stood as if to leave, a bluff really, but more of an excuse to try to look down the hallway for any sign of Granny Rose.

"Wait." Mildred jumped to her feet and hurried toward a small antique desk on the other side of the room. "You're right, of course. I don't know what I was thinking. There must have been some sort of mistake. I'm sure I can straighten it out with the bank, and in the meantime, I'll make sure there are funds to cover both checks, and you can go ahead and tell Mr. Hamilton and Mr. Cooper to redeposit."

Emma nodded. That was easier than she thought. Maybe she should submit her own bill as well while Mildred was feeling generous.

A door slammed open from the other side of the room, and Phillip Aldridge strode in, his face burning nearly purple as he pinned his mother with a murderous glare. "What do you think you're doing?"

To Mildred's credit, she set her feet and lifted her chin. She'd probably have stiffened if her posture wasn't already perfect. "This doesn't concern you, Phillip."

"Of course, it concerns me. You're giving away my inheritance."

Emma had a feeling Phillip must have been standing in the hallway with his ear pressed against the door longer than she or his mother realized.

Mildred glowered right back at him. "Unless you want to go live in that shack your father purchased, I suggest you change your tone, mister."

Her steel surprised Emma. Apparently, Mildred wasn't the soft-spoken pushover Emma had imagined her to be.

Phillip clenched his teeth tight, worked his jaw back and forth, then stormed from the room.

"I'm sorry. I hope I didn't cause any problems between you and your son." True enough. Emma hadn't meant to cause trouble, but at the same time, she needed to do right by those she'd asked to help and worked with on a regular basis. As far as her own bill, she'd wait and submit it after everything else got sorted out.

"Don't worry about it." But for the first time, Mildred looked strained, as if the weight of responsibility might be too much for her to handle. She opened a laptop, pulled up a bank website, and her eyes went wide. Her gaze shot to Emma an instant before she shifted the screen so Emma could no longer see it. If her deep scowl was any indication, something was wrong. Instead of commenting on whatever it was, she tapped a number of keys and continued their conversation as if nothing had happened. "Everyone deals with grief in their own way. Phillip is just having a difficult time parting with his father's belongings. Sentimental value, I suppose."

Even as she said it, the sentiment didn't ring true. But Emma wasn't about to argue. She'd already accomplished what she'd set out to, and it was past time she found Granny Rose and got out of there. She stood and offered a hand. "Thank you, Mildred, I appreciate you taking care of this."

Giving her hand a quick shake, Mildred started toward the front door. "Yes, of course. Now, if you'll excuse me, I have more pressing matters to attend to."

And Emma would bet those pressing matters involved whatever she'd seen in the bank account that had caused such obvious concern. Curiosity got the better of her. Maybe, if she angled herself just the right way, she might be able to get a glimpse of the screen on her way out.

"You let go of me right now, young man," Granny's outraged voice echoed through the room an instant before she appeared in the entryway.

Phillip had her by the arm and not so gently tugged her along after him. "Look what I found snooping through my room."

Emma hurried toward him. "You let go of my grandmother right now."

He released her with a quick shove and whirled on Emma.

"I don't know what you're talking about." Granny turned on him and smoothed her short sleeve, which had bunched up in Phillip's grip. "I just got lost on my way back from the powder room. It's a big house when you're used to living in the close quarters at Mini-Meadows."

Except that the mansion she'd spent most her life living in was easily twice as large as the Aldridge's. Thankfully, they didn't know that.

Anger surged through Emma. "I can certainly understand why you'd get upset finding someone in your room, but that's no reason to manhandle an old woman."

"Hey!" Granny huffed, indignant.

Phillip scowled. "I barely touched her, just guided her out of my room."

"Well, if you touch her again, barely or any other way, I'm calling the police." Emma shot a quick glance toward Granny. She seemed okay, not even a red mark on her arm, but still.

"And if I find her on my property again, I'll call the police myself." He pointed a finger in Emma's face. "And press charges."

Okay, she definitely didn't want to be the one to explain to her father how Granny Rose was arrested mere weeks after moving in with her. She buried some of the anger, had to if she was going to protect Granny. Especially since he seemed more than angry enough to follow through on his threat. "I'm sure she didn't mean to intrude. Granny tends to get confused now and then."

Granny puffed up. "Now, see here—"

Emma shot her a warning glare, and she huffed and firmed her lips into a tight line.

"Thank you for helping her find her way back." The words stuck in Emma's throat, and she had to choke them out. Better that than having Granny go through being arrested, though.

He propped his hands on his hips and took a step back. "We've already had stuff go missing, thanks to that other woman you sent over here."

Alarm bells clanged in Emma's head. "Other woman?"

"The one from the consignment shop. So, how am I supposed to know this one didn't steal anything?" He flung a hand toward Granny.

"First of all, young man, what would I want with any of your tacky belongings? And secondly..." Granny held her hands high and turned in a circle. Besides her velour pants and T-shirt, she only had a small fanny pack strapped around her waist. "Where would I put it?"

"Phillip." Mildred's voice held a note of warning that did nothing to stop her son's rant. "Your father already assured us Jade doesn't have anything belonging to us."

"And you believed him?" His eyes nearly popped out of his head.

Apparently used to his tantrums, she simply shrugged. "Why not? Your father told Emma to take care of getting rid of everything after we left because he didn't want to deal with any of it. Jade was never alone in the house to have had the opportunity to steal anything. And why would your father have consigned anything with Jade, whom he dismissed?"

"Because it was worth a fortune, and it was supposed to be mine." Phillip seemed to think everything now belonged to him. What about his mother? Didn't she deserve to inherit anything? Or, like her own grandfather, had Broderick Aldridge left everything to the man—and she used the term loosely, since he was more of a spoiled overgrown child—of the house?

"For the record, if your father had consigned anything with Jade, it wouldn't be stealing." No way would Emma let him sully Jade's reputation, especially after Broderick had treated her so poorly when she'd tried to make amends as a favor to Emma. "Besides, when Jade came out here the first time, your father threw her out. Then when she came again last night, tried to apologize and offer her services, he asked her to leave again, and not very nicely, I might add."

"Last night?" Mildred's eyes narrowed in suspicion. "When was she here last night?"

Uh oh. In her hurry to defend Jade, she hadn't thought about what she was saying, nor had she realized they didn't know Jade had stopped by. If they had been home, and if the argument was as attention getting as Jade suspected it was, how could they not have noticed? "She saw Mr. Aldridge outside and stopped to apologize, offered to let bygones be bygones and continue with the job. And he asked her to leave again."

"See…" Phillip pointed toward Emma as if she'd agreed with him. "I told you Jade probably stole the stuff."

"Phillip!" The cold hard anger in her voice finally cut through Phillip's tantrum. "This discussion is over."

"But—"

"Not. Another. Word." She stared him down until he finally relented and stormed out of the house. "I apologize for my son's behavior. He's not himself since his father's death."

Emma had a feeling he was exactly himself, spoiled, nasty, and entitled.

"Are you okay, ma'am?" Mildred asked Granny Rose.

"Oh, I'm fine. The little brat didn't hurt me."

"Fine. Now…" She walked to the front door, opened it, and practically booted them out. "If you'll excuse me."

Emma followed Granny Rose out and didn't say anything until they got into the car. Rage boiled at the thought of anyone touching her grandmother. "Are you really all right, Granny? Are you sure you're not hurt?"

"Oh, please." She waved a hand. "I'm not that frail, dear."

"You're sure? Because I could call Detective Montgomery…."

"Is that the hottie who interrogated you this morning?" She grinned, and her eyes lit with mischief. "Come to think of it, that boy should be punished for manhandling an old lady. Shame on him."

"True, but if you're okay, we're going to let it go, because how am I supposed to explain what you were doing in his room?" She shouldn't even ask, but… if Emma did everything she was supposed to do, she'd currently be Mrs. Bartholomew Prendergast. "Did you find anything in there?"

"Well, I can tell you one thing, if that boy had any intention of moving out, he wasn't taking anything with him. Unless he unpacked it all the minute he walked back in the door a couple hours ago. There were clothes all over the floor, but it looked more like he was just a slob than a rushed unpacking job. I didn't see any empty boxes or suitcases lying around."

"No, neither did I." With one last look at the house, Emma shifted into gear and backed up.

"The little monster probably tosses his stuff wherever he takes it off and expects the housekeeper to come along and clean up after him."

"True." Granny's assessment didn't seem far off. "Then again, very little of Mildred's stuff was supposed to be coming, and what was had already been shipped."

"So, what do you think? That the two of them killed Mr. Aldridge off?"

"I don't know what to think." But she was beginning to wonder if that was a possibility.

"Well, whatever happened to the old geezer, his son sure is in a hurry to get his hands on that inheritance."

"He is, isn't he?" It probably wouldn't hurt to mention the Granny Rose incident to Detective Montgomery. Was it really such a far stretch to think a man with as short a fuse as Phillip Aldridge had could be pushed to commit murder? Especially when the man doing the pushing was as miserable, nasty, and stingy as Broderick Aldridge.

Emma glanced in the rearview mirror and caught herself just in time to keep from slamming on the brakes.

An older man dressed in a suit hurried across the Aldridge lawn away from the house, then smoothed his jacket, tucked his hands into his pants pockets, and strolled across the street as if he had a perfectly valid excuse to be there. So why did Emma have a sneaking suspicion he didn't?

With one backward glance toward the house, he climbed into the driver's seat of a dark-colored sedan.

As she rounded a curve, Emma lost sight of him. She hit the brakes and pulled to the side of the road, then tapped her hand against the wheel impatiently while she waited for two cars to pass. The instant they did, she whipped around in a quick U-turn.

"Hey!" Granny braced against the dashboard. "What gives?"

"Did you see that man?"

"What man?" She squinted at Emma, then looked around.

"Someone was on the Aldridge property. I saw him walk to a car parked across the street." She scanned the road where the sedan had been, but it was gone. Where could he have gone so quickly?

"You sure it wasn't Phillip?"

Could it have been? She didn't get a good look at his face. More of an impression, really, but he seemed older to her. "I don't think so."

With no idea where he'd gone, she turned around, accelerated and headed toward home, but her mind lingered. Who was he? A detective, maybe? A reporter? Broderick's killer? And why was he sneaking around the house? Did Mildred and Phillip know he was there?

She briefly entertained the thought of returning and telling Mildred about him, but something stopped her. Really, it was none of her business, and the last thing she needed was another confrontation with Phillip. Besides, unless he'd turned invisible, or she'd imagined the whole thing, the only place he could have disappeared to so quickly was the Aldridge garage. Which meant at least one of them knew he was there. Still, she couldn't rid herself of the sneaking suspicion he wasn't nearly as innocent as he'd tried to appear.

Chapter Nine

After dropping Granny Rose off at home, with numerous reassurances from her that she was fine, Emma left her Jeep in the driveway and headed to Little Bits in her golf cart. She'd have walked, if not for the fact it might well be dark by the time she headed home. One thing Mini-Meadows didn't boast was street lights, and the development could get pretty dark on a cloudy night, especially the outer edges that were surrounded by a forest of towering trees. Not to mention, if the gathering clouds were any indication, they were in for storms.

But for now, Main Street was still bustling—as much as Mini-Meadows bustled—and Emma had to park a few spots down from Little Bits. She pulled into a mini parking spot, angled toward the curb, climbed out, and stretched. Too many nights cramped on the loveseat, not sleeping, were starting to catch up with her. And yet...the thought of Granny leaving jarred her, left her a little sad. She and her parents had always lived in the Wells mansion with Granny Rose, and after Emma's mother had taken a job in Italy and moved out when she was a teenager, Emma and Granny had become very close.

Not that her mother hadn't asked Emma to go with her, she had, but leaving high school and everything else she knew to move to another country hadn't appealed at the time. It still didn't. Emma didn't share her mother's restless, adventurous nature. The small, cozy, hometown feel of Mini-Meadows suited her so much better.

"Hey, Emma." Chloe waved from the doorway of Pocket Books.

"Hey." With one last shoulder roll to ease some of the stiffness and tension from the day, Emma strolled toward her. "What's going on?"

"I've been swamped since I opened." Chloe held the door open for her to enter. Where Jade's style ran toward vintage, Chloe opted for a more casual look in jeans and a lightweight powder blue sweater, since she spent most of her day in the air conditioning.

"Thanks." The cold air slapped Emma in the face, just the wake-up call she needed. Chloe might have been busy all day, but the shop appeared empty at the moment, and while Emma couldn't see past the rows and rows of bookshelves packed into the small, two-story space, Chloe wouldn't be standing around dawdling if she had customers.

Emma paused just inside the doorway and inhaled deeply. She always loved walking into Pocket Books, the aroma of books and coffee, the hushed tones, and the immersion in fantasy brought an immediate sense of peace. She indulged in one moment to enjoy it before reality intruded, and she sighed and turned to Chloe. "Have you heard anything new?"

"Lots and lots of wondering what happened mingling with rumors about Broderick Aldridge's confrontational nature."

"Broderick Aldridge didn't even live in Mini-Meadows yet and, as far as I know, he didn't know anyone here. How are rumors already flying about his confrontational nature?"

Chloe shrugged and weaved between tables containing stacks of books with Emma on her heels. The back corner of the shop held a row of coffee pots and hot water for tea or cocoa as well as a refrigerator filled with cold water bottles and a case that boasted a variety of cookies, pastries, cupcakes, and Danishes thanks to Delia Sanderson who owned Tantalizing Temptations, the bakery next door.

"Do you want something to eat?" Chloe took a plate from the pile on a nearby table set up for customers to help themselves.

As much as she wanted to say yes, she needed to save her allotted daily calories for Granny Rose's cooking. Apparently, lasagna was on the menu tonight. "No, thanks. Just coffee would be great."

Chloe opened the case and took out an apple Danish, then turned to pour two cups of coffee. She handed Emma's cup across the counter, then took her own plate and cup to one of the several reading areas scattered throughout the shop and settled into an armchair. "Anyway, I haven't heard from anyone who knew Aldridge directly, it's all a friend of a friend had this to say, and my uncle's brother's mother had that to say. You know how it is."

Emma nodded as she set her coffee on a side table and sank into the chair across from her. "According to Jade, her friend Whitney said he was a nice guy."

Chloe practically choked her bite of Danish down. "Seriously? Well, if so, she's the only one I've heard of with that particular opinion. How does she know him?"

"Jade didn't elaborate, just that she said he was a nice guy, so Jade went back out to apologize to Mr. Aldridge and offer her services."

Chloe's eyes bugged out. "She did what?"

Emma had forgotten Chloe hadn't been privy to the earlier conversation between her and Jade and brought her up to speed on Jade's failed attempt, her worries about being the last to have seen him alive, and Emma's trip out to the Aldridge house to pay Mildred a visit. She ended with the confrontation with Phillip.

Setting her half-eaten Danish aside, her jaw clenched. "He laid hands on Granny Rose?"

"She says she's okay, and I think she is. There wasn't even a red mark, but still...."

"Yeah, still, what kind of man does that?"

She was right. What kind of man grabbed an elderly woman out of anger? The kind who'd kill his own father? "He seems awfully worried about his inheritance."

"You think he killed his father for the money?"

With a quick glance around the tiny shop, Emma lowered her voice. The last thing she needed was to be overheard spouting something like that. She'd need that attorney for sure when Phillip Aldridge slammed her with a defamation suit. Hmm...an attorney. Could the man in the suit have been Mildred's attorney? Or Phillip's? "I'm not saying that."

Not exactly, anyway, though she couldn't deny the thought had crossed her mind.

"Then what are you saying?" Chloe pushed.

She shrugged. No point in not being completely honest with Chloe, as long as no one else was listening. She had great deductive reasoning skills in addition to being a master at reading people, so her input could prove valuable. "He's spoiled, used to getting his way, completely consumed with his quest to gain his inheritance as quickly as possible, and doesn't seem to even see his mother. It's like she doesn't exist, like she's not entitled to anything."

"You don't like him."

"Not at all." She thought of mentioning Mildred's odd behavior when she'd looked at the banking page on her computer, but Emma couldn't be sure anything was off. That was just an impression and wouldn't be fair to discuss, especially when she'd made good on the checks. Supposedly.

Chloe contemplated her for a moment as she sipped her coffee. "Are you sure your opinion isn't being colored by the similarities between the Aldridges' financial situation and your own grandfather's will?"

Was it? She didn't think so, and yet, certainly her own sourness at how her grandfather had left things, with her father in charge of his estate, ultimately having complete control over not only her but Granny Rose as well, could be factoring in. Emma didn't care for herself—she was a grown woman and could take care of her own needs—but Granny deserved peace at her age.

Anyway, that train of thought would accomplish exactly nothing. Besides, at least her father had tried to do what he thought was in their best interest, hadn't tried to cheat them out of anything or steal everything out from under them, which was the impression she had of Phillip. "I don't know. Maybe, I guess I might be comparing the two, letting my own situation and my intense dislike of Phillip color my opinion."

"As long as you recognize that. Anyway, that's neither here nor there, the latest gossip trickling in has to do with Arianna Jenkins." Chloe looked past Emma toward the big display window and frowned.

"The girl Eric hired to help move the Aldridges?"

Leaving her Danish on the table, Chloe stood and moved toward the front of the shop.

Figuring she spotted a customer coming in, Emma set her coffee aside and walked with her. "Chloe?"

"Huh?"

Emma followed Chloe's line of sight out the picture window but didn't see anyone headed toward the shop. With dinner time approaching, the crowd on Main Street had thinned considerably in the few minutes Emma had spent with Chloe. "Arianna Jenkins?"

"Oh, right." Chloe shook off whatever had gripped her. "Supposedly, no one's seen or heard from her since the day she was out at the Aldridge's."

"Eric mentioned that this morning too. Did anyone file a missing person's report?"

She shook her head absently and frowned again.

Emma turned and scanned the street. "Is something wrong?"

Leaning over the display of fall-themed cozy mysteries in the window, Chloe looked down the road. "I thought I saw Phillip Aldridge walk past, but I didn't see where he went."

Emma opened the door and stepped out with Chloe right behind her. "Which way was he going?"

She gestured down the road toward Little Bits.

Jade. "I have to run, Chloe. I want to make sure Phillip isn't going in to bother Jade."

"Sure. Go. I'm closing up now anyway, so I'll meet up with you in a few minutes. Maybe we can grab something to eat."

"Granny Rose is making lasagna. You're welcome to come; she makes enough to feed a small army." Maybe it would save Emma from eating leftovers for lunch tomorrow.

"Sounds good. I'll see you in a few...."

But Emma was already hurrying down the sidewalk. She skirted the wrought iron tables and chairs scattered in front of the bakery, returned Mr. Henderson's wave, and felt a little bad for not stopping to help him pull his big sign into Teacup Grooming, but she had a sinking feeling in her gut that Phillip had beat her to Jade. Chloe wouldn't have said anything if she hadn't been pretty sure she'd seen him.

At least Detective Montgomery would be there soon. Not that it would matter—if Phillip put a hand on Jade, he'd need more than a detective. Jade was no elderly woman.

Even as she pulled the door open, Phillip's raised voice reached her. "…and I demand a list of everything you took from the house and insist you return it all immediately."

Jade stood in front of the counter, hands planted on her hips, chin jutted in defiance. "And I already told you, I didn't take anything from the house, nor did your father give me anything except a snotty attitude and a headache. Apparently, the apple doesn't fall far."

"Well, there's stuff missing," Phillip whined. A grown man. Whining. What was the world coming to? "Valuable stuff, including a priceless antique vase."

"And you know what?" Jade's expression twisted in disgust. "I find it deplorable that you've already taken inventory when your father hasn't even been gone for twenty-four hours. You oughta be ashamed of yourself, boy."

A smile tugged at Emma. Jade sounded an awful lot like Granny Rose.

Phillip pointed a finger an inch from Jade's face. "Now, you listen here—"

No way would she tolerate that. Jade stiffened. "Honey, if you want to walk out of here with that finger, I suggest you remove it from my face and do so immediately."

Rage colored Phillip's face a deep crimson. "I don't care what you suggest."

"Last chance."

"Okay, enough." Emma stepped between them and faced Phillip. "Jade asked you to leave. You have no business in here, and Detective Montgomery is on his way."

No need to tell him the appointment had already been scheduled. Let him sweat.

"Fine, but I'm going out to that shack he bought to see if I can go through the stuff that's in the storage container, and if I don't find what I'm looking for there, I'll be back." He turned with a huff just as the cowbell clanked, indicating a customer.

Maxwell Merlin, a friend who did computer work from his own tiny home and had a major crush on Jade, sauntered in, hands stuffed into two of a multitude of voluminous pockets dotting his neon green pants.

After a quick double take—Max had that effect on people—Phillip shoved past him on his way out the door.

Max tugged at the collar of his bright yellow spandex shirt and stared after him. "Was it something I said?"

"Oh, it's not you." Jade waved it off and started folding a pile of linens on a nearby table. "He's like that to everyone, it seems."

"Takes after his father, I guess." Emma picked up a fitted sheet and started to fold, though she couldn't get it nearly as exact as Jade did. "Don't worry about it, Jade."

She just shook her head. "So, Merlin, what's going on?"

"Uh…" Twin red patches flared in his cheeks, almost blinding in combination with the outfit. "Nothing. I was across the street at Libby's when I saw Emma come in. I figured I'd stop in and say hello."

"Hello," Jade said straight-faced.

He grinned. "Hey there."

Emma couldn't help but smile. Max, long and lanky, with dark blond hair and a flamboyant personality that perfectly matched his garish sense of style, and Jade, adventurous and bold, with her long dark hair and exotic beauty, her style leaning more toward vintage sophistication; they'd make such a cute couple, if Jade ever got around to giving him a chance.

"So." He gestured over his shoulder in the direction Phillip had gone. "What's his deal?"

"He thinks his father consigned something with me that I decided to keep." She slammed the sheet she'd just folded onto the table.

"What makes him think that?"

"I have no idea. Actually, the old geezer wouldn't say more than two words to me, and both of them went something like *get* and *lost*."

"Huh…."

"Yeah, that about sums it up." Giving up on the folding, Jade massaged her temples. "Does anyone happen to have any aspirin?"

Max patted his pockets, shrugged, and propped a hip against the table. He shot a quick glance toward Emma, but when no information about Jade's current attitude was forthcoming, he returned his gaze to Jade and frowned.

Moodiness wasn't Jade's thing, and it seemed Max didn't know what to make of it or how to proceed, so he remained wisely silent.

"Sorry, I don't have any, but Chloe'll be here any minute, and she always seems to have everything you could ever hope to need in that bottomless bag of hers." Emma pointed toward a chair. "Why don't you sit down a few minutes. It's probably just a tension headache."

"Ain't that the truth." After she flopped into the armchair, Jade swiped tears from beneath her eyes. "I just don't understand. I did nothing wrong, yet every time I turn around, I seem to be cast straight to the center of this mess."

"Calm down, Jade." Emma sat on a stool next to her and patted her hand. "Detective Montgomery will be here any minute."

"Detective?" Max lurched upright and pointed toward the doorway. "Did that guy do something to you?"

"No, no. He's coming to talk to me about the murder."

Max's big brown eyes went wide. "Murder! What murder?"

Jade just stared at him a moment. "How could you possibly not have heard about that, Merlin? Emma found Broderick Aldridge, the new guy who was supposed to be moving into the caboose house, dead in his storage container this morning when Eric dropped it off."

"Whoa." Running a hand through his permanently disheveled, dirty blond hair, he gaped at Emma. "Really?"

"Merlin." Jade studied him. "How could you not have heard about this if you just came from Libby's?"

"Uhh...um...it's like..." The more he stammered, the redder his face turned. "I hadn't actually gone inside yet. I was working all day, and I realized I hadn't eaten anything and I was starving, so I was on my way to grab some dinner."

Jade lifted a brow.

And Max offered his most disarming smile, which seemed to have no effect on her at all. "Anyway, if you want, I can do a run on that guy, see if there's any skeletons in his closet you could use to get him to leave you alone."

Hmm, that wasn't a bad idea. "Could you really do that?"

"Sure. I'm pretty much a wizard when it comes to computers and accessing data, aka hacking." He shrugged and shot her a cocky grin. "Why do you think they call me Merlin?"

"Because it's your last name?" Jade deadpanned.

"Oh, right, well, that too." His sheepish grin only added to his charm.

If he wasn't so hung up on Jade, Emma might just snatch him up for herself... Whoa! Yikes. Her thoughts slammed to a stop like they'd hit a brick wall. What had Granny Rose's constant matchmaking comments done to her? Okay, enough of that. Best to keep her mind on the matter at hand. Murder—a much safer topic than her love life, or lack thereof.

"If you could find anything out about him, that would be great, thanks." Then, if Phillip decided to bother Jade or Granny again, they might have something to use to get him to back off.

"No problem." He backed up, tripped over his own feet, and regained his balance. "Then I'll just maybe stop back in and let you know what I find."

Jade finally relented and smiled at him. "Thanks, Max, that would be great."

Detective Montgomery walked in, nodded toward them, and stepped to the side.

"Oh, well, I guess I should be going then. I'll let you know if I find anything." Max hurried out.

Emma leaned close to Jade. "He's like half in love with you, ya know."

A genuine smile softened her expression. "Yeah, I know."

"You're always on me about finding Mr. Right; why don't you give him a chance?"

"We'll see." She shrugged it off and held a hand out to Detective Montgomery. "Thank you for coming, Detective."

He shook her hand, nodded toward Emma. "Ms. Wells said you had some information regarding Mr. Aldridge's death."

She blew out a breath. "I think I may have been the last person to see him alive."

"Besides the killer, that is," Emma hurried to add.

He glanced back and forth between the two of them. "Of course."

Chapter Ten

While Emma invited Detective Montgomery to sit, Jade offered coffee or something else to drink. He looked beat, his shirt wrinkled, sleeves pushed up, tie loosened. Seemed the investigation into Broderick's murder was taking its toll on everyone involved.

"I wouldn't mind a cold water." He pulled out his notebook and pen, then settled into an armchair as if expecting a long chat.

"So…" Not quite sure if she was supposed to be included in the conversation or not, Emma leaned against the counter and waited for Jade to return from the back room. "Do you have any idea who killed Mr. Aldridge yet?"

He studied her, tilted his head. "Do you?"

Phillip's name almost blurted out, but she caught herself just in time. Not liking someone was no reason to accuse them of murder, even if he had put his hands on Granny Rose and intimidated, or, at least tried to intimidate, Jade. "How would I know?"

Thankfully, Jade returned and handed out water bottles before their conversation went any further, and Emma lost her battle to keep from implicating Phillip Aldridge.

Jade perched on the edge of a seat across from the detective, sucked down half the bottle of water, then capped it and set it aside. She blew out a breath, fluttering her bangs, a sure sign she was nervous. "Where do you want me to start?"

"Well, since you called me here, why don't you just start at the beginning and go through what happened." His warm smile loosened some of the knots in Emma's gut. "If I have any questions, I can stop you and ask you to clarify."

Jade nodded and took a deep, shaky breath in. "Okay, so, last night I was talking to my friend, Whitney, who I haven't spoken with in a while. We got to talking about Mr. Aldridge, which, well, who isn't, right? At least now. But last night, he was only a conversation starter for those of us unfortunate enough to have had the displeasure of working with him."

When she paused, wrapped her arms around herself, he nodded for her to continue.

"Anyway, we started talking about him, and I told her how I went out to his house as a favor to a friend…." She shot Emma an apologetic look. "And how he wanted to get rid of all of his wife's things, and then he was nasty to me and threw me out. That was when Whitney told me she knew him, and that he was a nice guy."

Detective Montgomery frowned. Maybe it was the first he'd heard that sentiment, as well, and found it just as shocking as Emma had. Still did, actually. "Did she say how she knew him?"

"No, just that she did." Jade picked the water bottle back up but didn't drink. Instead, she began to peel the corner of the label without saying anything.

Watching her, his pen hovering above his pad, the detective prodded. "What's Whitney's last name?"

"Jameson."

He jotted a note in his book and returned his gaze to Jade, giving her his full focus.

"Like I said, I haven't seen Whitney in a while, so we agreed to meet up and go dancing. Since the club was out by Aldridge's, I drove past his house on my way there. He was standing outside by the storage unit, so I figured I'd just stop and try to make amends, see if I could salvage the job, which I did. Stopped, I mean. The job was a wash. He didn't accept my apology and asked me, not so nicely, to leave."

Guilt tugged at Emma. She knew full well Jade only returned to Aldridge's for her, so she wouldn't have to deal with trying to find someone else, someone he'd approve of. Especially since there was probably no one he'd have approved of.

When she stopped, the detective waited, his pen poised. "What happened then?"

"That's it. I left and went to meet up with Whitney. When she didn't show, and I couldn't reach her, I just went home."

Tapping the back of the pen against the pad, he pushed his glasses up his nose and studied his notes. "Have you spoken to Ms. Jameson since?"

"No."

"Is that unusual for her to make plans and then not show up?"

Jade considered for a moment. "Not really. Whitney's kind of scatter-brained. She's not married, not seriously seeing anyone, has no kids, bounces from job to job, so she just goes with the flow wherever the moment takes her, ya know?"

"Do you have her address?"

"Sure." Jade pulled out her phone and scrolled.

Nerves sizzled through Emma. "Do you think something happened to Whitney?"

Jade paused her scrolling and looked up as if the thought had never occurred to her.

"Not necessarily, just being thorough."

But Emma didn't quite believe him. Something in his eyes betrayed his calm demeanor. "But you've heard her name before, right?"

He studied Emma with renewed interest that almost made her squirm.

She held his gaze and ordered herself not to fidget.

After considering her for another moment, he shifted his gaze to Jade and then back to Emma. "At Phillip Aldridge's insistence, Broderick's attorney, who is the executor of his will as well as a close family friend, shared the details of his father's final wishes. Her name came up in connection with the will."

His lips firmed, and she doubted she'd get any more from him, but she tried anyway. "Did he leave her something?"

"Aren't wills a matter of public record?" Jade asked. "So, it's not like we can't find out anyway."

"Mrs. Aldridge inherited the family home. Phillip inherited nothing—"

Emma barely caught the smirk that tried to surface. Seemed karma had paid young Aldridge a visit and given him a good swift kick in his spoiled little—

"And Whitney Jameson inherited the rest of the estate."

"What?" Her thoughts faltered. That didn't make any sense. She briefly thought about sharing the conversation Eric overheard between Mr. Aldridge and some unknown person regarding *another woman*, but that would be hearsay, nothing more than gossip really. Plus, the only other woman's name mentioned had been Jade's, and hadn't Phillip referred to her as *that other woman* that very morning? Of course, if she brought up that conversation, she'd also have to bring attention to the fact that Granny Rose had been snooping through the guy's bedroom. Which brought her to the guy she saw sneaking out. But, again, if she mentioned him, it might also lead to the Granny Rose debacle. Nope, better to keep her mouth shut. Besides, it seemed more and more likely to her the guy was probably Phillip's attorney. And, speaking of Granny Rose…"Do you know who inherited the tiny home he was moving into?"

"I didn't read through all of the details, but if it's part of the estate, it now belongs to Whitney Jameson. At least, it does if Phillip Aldridge doesn't win when he contests the will, as he's promised to do."

No surprise there. "Were you aware that the check to the moving company and the final installment of the tiny home payment were both returned?"

"I hadn't heard."

"I went out to speak to Mrs. Aldridge about it earlier, and she transferred funds and told me to have the contractors redeposit."

He flipped through his notebook, went several pages back before he paused. "That would be Tiny Cooper and the man who found the body with you, Eric Hamilton?"

Emma nodded.

"How well do you know Mr. Hamilton?"

Now Emma did squirm. No way could he think Eric had anything to do with Broderick's death. "We're friendly, sometimes end up out with friends in the same place at the same time. You know how it is in such a small community."

He nodded. "I do, yes. One of the biggest perks and drawbacks."

She smiled. There was no arguing that. "Mostly, our relationship is professional. Eric is very conscientious, he always shows up when he says he will, calls if there's a problem, and is very careful and respectful of people's belongings, so I often recommend him."

"Have you ever seen him lose his temper?"

"Eric?" Emma straightened. "I've never even seen him raise his voice."

"How did he react to the check being returned?"

She thought back to their conversation. If anything, she'd been more upset about it than he was. "He was annoyed, but didn't seem particularly surprised. He'd been concerned enough about the possibility in the first place to mobile deposit the check before loading the container onto the truck."

Lips pursed, Detective Montgomery scribbled something on his pad Emma couldn't quite make out, not for lack of trying, then turned to Jade. "Do you know Mr. Hamilton?"

She shrugged. "Sure."

"Did you see him at Mr. Aldridge's on the night you were there?"

"No, I didn't see anyone but Mr. Aldridge."

"Thank you." He stood and tucked his notepad into his pocket, then held out a hand to Jade, which she shook. "I appreciate you coming forward. If you think of anything else, you know how to reach me."

That's it? Emma didn't know what she'd expected, but she'd thought it would take longer than it had and involve a lot more questions. Maybe even a torture device or two—figuratively, at least.

Jade nodded and glanced at Emma.

She just shrugged. Something was up with Eric, but she couldn't figure out what, and Montgomery wasn't being very forthcoming. "Um…Detective, do you mind if I ask…Do you know how Broderick Aldridge was killed?"

"Blunt force trauma to the head."

So, someone had beaten him to death! Surely, they couldn't think Eric had done something like that, even if he was angry. The image of Phillip ranting, anger coloring his face, his grip around Granny Rose's arm, popped into her head. While she didn't want to start hurling accusations, she didn't feel right letting his actions go either. "Not that I'm accusing anyone of anything, but I've seen Phillip Aldridge lose his temper on more than one occasion. I can't imagine he took the news about the will very well."

A small smile played at one corner of his mouth, but he simply firmed it into a line. Still, he couldn't keep the humor from dancing in his eyes. "You could say that."

"Do you think he knew about it beforehand?"

"No, I'd say he was most definitely caught off-guard." Finally, the smile did form, both cocky and endearing. "Now, if you're done with your interrogation, I have a few matters to attend to."

Heat crept up her face. "Sure. Sorry."

"Don't worry about it." He laughed and held out a business card to Jade. "And if you think of anything else, please don't hesitate to call."

"Thanks." Jade tucked the card into her skirt pocket as he turned and left.

Following Jade as she headed to the back room to throw the water bottles into the recycle bin and begin her closing routine, Emma tried to make sense of the information Detective Montgomery had given them. "Why do you think Aldridge would have left everything to Whitney?"

"I have no idea." She dropped the bottles in the recycle bin, turned, and pulled out her phone. A moment later, after a quick check for text messages, she tucked it back into her pocket. "But I'm a little concerned that I haven't heard from her now that I know she inherited everything."

"Yeah. I don't blame you. Have you tried to call or text her?" Emma asked anyway, even though she assumed that's what Jade had been checking for on her phone.

Catching her bottom lip between her teeth, Jade looked around the room, then sighed and headed out front. "Numerous times."

"Do you want to run past her house?" While Jade started counting out the register, Emma moved to tidy the racks and tables. Since she liked to sleep in whenever possible, Jade always tried to leave the shop ready to open in the morning.

"Can't. She moved up to Jacksonville after we graduated."

"Do you know where she was staying while she was in town?"

Jade opened the safe beneath the register and, tucked the envelope inside, then locked it back up. "She didn't say."

If she moved up to Jacksonville years ago, what was she doing back in town? And could the fact that she'd shown up and happened to inherit the bulk of his estate the same day Broderick Aldridge was murdered be a coincidence? "What about family? Does she still have family in town?"

"Not that I know of. She doesn't have siblings, and her mom left town not long after Whitney did. I'm not that friendly with her to know who else she might have kept up with here, but we might be able to look into it." Leaving the garbage bag she was tying up in the pail, she went to the computer on her desk.

"What are you doing?"

"I figured I'd check her social media, see who she's friends with or follows, see if she posted anything after we spoke."

"Good idea." Emma yanked the bag out of the pail to throw in the dumpster on their way out. "But would you mind doing it from the computer at my house?"

She shrugged. "Doesn't matter. Why?"

"Granny Rose is making lasagna, and I don't want to disappoint her by being late." It was bad enough she was going to have to break the news that the little caboose house wasn't Mildred's to sell. Buying it from Tiny would have been one thing, since she already knew he would have had no intention of moving into it, but Whitney was an unknown. "Besides, I guess I have to eventually go home and see how Ginger and Butch are getting along."

"That's probably a good idea."

The cowbell rang, and Chloe walked in and spotted them next to the computer, Emma holding the bag of garbage. "What'd I miss?"

"Oh, not much," Emma said. "But it seems Mr. Aldridge was beaten to death."

"Hmm…" she considered. "Not surprising, really. I guess he managed to

84

push someone too far."

"Yeah, and he left almost everything he owned to a woman named Whitney Jameson."

Chloe frowned. "Jade's friend?"

It didn't surprise Emma that Chloe knew who the woman was. Her interest in people allowed her to remember names with ridiculous accuracy. Plus, she and Jade had grown up together. "One and the same."

"So, now what?"

"Now we have to find Whitney, make sure she's okay, and pray she's looking to sell that tiny home." Because if she wasn't, Butch was apparently Emma's newest housemate.

Chapter Eleven

The first thing to hit Emma when she opened her front door was the overwhelming aroma of oregano and garlic. Her mouth began to water. "Hey, Granny Rose, I'm home."

"Just in time. I'm just about to put dinner on the table." She eyed the breakfast bar that served as Emma's dining room table. "So to speak."

Since Granny had a perfect view of the front door from the kitchen area, there was no need to let her know she'd brought company.

"Hey, Chloe. Hey, Jade." Granny Rose set four places on the breakfast bar. "Hope you're both hungry."

Butch took up three-quarters of the kitchen, and if his sitting at attention, his gaze riveted on Granny Rose, was any indication, he'd already been privy to a sample of Granny Rose's cooking.

Emma looked around, then peeked under the loveseat. "Where's Ginger?"

"She's upstairs having an attitude." Granny gestured with a thumb toward the stairway. "Apparently, she's not too fond of her new houseguest."

"She'll warm up." Emma hoped so, since it looked like Butch might be a more permanent fixture than originally intended.

With a non-committal grunt, Granny Rose set a pitcher of ice water on the kitchen counter in easy reach of the breakfast bar.

"Trust me, as soon as I start cleaning up dinner, she'll come down to be fed." Since only three stools fit comfortably at the bar on a regular basis, Emma kept one folded against one wall in the small pantry cabinet on the off chance she had more than Chloe and Jade over. She grabbed it and set it at the far end of the breakfast bar.

Granny pulled two trays of lasagna—looked like leftovers were an inevitable part of Emma's future—out of the oven and set them on the stovetop beside the potful of extra meat sauce. A plate of garlic bread sat on the counter beside an antipasto salad.

"I think you've outdone yourself this time, Granny Rose." Emma kissed her cheek. "Thank you."

"Of course, dear. It's the least I can do after you let me stay with you and before I move out."

"About that…" Emma didn't have the heart to dash her hopes, but at the same time, she had to be honest with her. "It seems Mrs. Aldridge didn't actually inherit the tiny home."

Granny paused. "What are you talking about?"

"Well, Jade and I met with Detective Montgomery, and it seems the will was already read. Mildred inherited the house they were living in. Phillip got nothing."

"Huh."

"And a woman named Whitney Jameson inherited everything else."

"Including my house?" She stood still, oven mitts swallowing up her hands, looking lost.

"It seems so. I'm sorry, Granny."

"Don't be, dear. We'll figure it out." She looked over the dinner she'd laid out. "Whoever this Whitney woman is, what are the chances she'd want to move to Mini-Meadows?"

That was true, especially if she had a job in Jacksonville, where she was currently living.

With a shrug, Granny Rose removed the mitts and set them aside. "So, we'll just find her and ask her if she's willing to sell."

"I'm on it." Jade hurried to the desk and was already banging away on the keyboard as she sat. "I was planning to try to find her anyway."

"Is there anything I can do?" Chloe asked.

"You just sit right down. You too, Emma. Everything's already done." Granny Rose took a plate from the bar and filled it with antipasto salad, added a couple pieces of garlic bread, and sat down at the breakfast bar.

Butch trotted behind her and plopped right back down at her side.

"He seems to be really well-behaved." At least Mr. Aldridge had done something right.

"Oh, he is." Granny nodded and gestured toward him with a piece of bread in her hand.

Butch took that as an invitation and snatched it. It disappeared in one bite.

"Hey," Granny scolded, waving a finger at him. "What did I tell you about that?"

Butch sulked, or at least seemed to, then peered up at her with those big brown eyes.

She huffed. "Down."

Butch lay down grudgingly, still eyeballing Granny's empty hand.

Thunder rumbled, low and deep, and rain spattered against the metal roof. When Emma had first moved in, the intensity of the storms against the tiny home frightened her. Now, she found a certain comfort in cozying up in her own space while the weather raged outside, especially while the scent of home cooking filled the house and friends and family surrounded her. She filled a bowl with salad and used every ounce of her willpower to resist the garlic bread. "Why don't you come eat and leave that for after, Jade?"

She tapped a few more keys, then relented and went to fill her plate.

Keeping an eye on Butch from the corner of her eye, Granny Rose sipped her water. "So, why would Mr. Aldridge have left the bulk of his estate to this Whitney woman?"

The scent of garlic teased Emma, begged her to sample just a taste. No. Not happening. She was standing firm on that. "I don't know, but my friend Eric, who was moving Aldridge's things, said he overheard Broderick yelling at someone, saying he wouldn't answer any more questions about another woman, whatever he meant by that."

Granny's brows shot up. "You think he was having an affair and left everything to his mistress?"

She had no clue, but Jade might. "Do you think Whitney would have fooled around with a married man?"

Jade took the stool at the end of the breakfast bar and set her plate, loaded with salad and bread, down in front of her. Some people were just blessed with a great metabolism; Jade was one of them. "I don't really know her well enough to say, but I can't see her dating someone twice her age. Whitney has a ton of energy, is adventurous, likes to live on the edge."

"Well, an affair with a married man would certainly qualify as living on the edge." Chloe took a bite of lasagna and practically moaned. "Granny Rose, this is amazing."

Maybe Emma should have gone the same route as Chloe, skipped the salad, and gone straight for the pasta. If the rumbling in her stomach was any indication, the salad was not going to fill her enough that she'd forego the lasagna. Ah, well, one could always hope.

"Thank you." Granny smiled. One of her favorite things was cooking for people who enjoyed and appreciated it.

"True, I guess." Jade frowned. "But Broderick Aldridge just strikes me as too fussy, too set in his ways, too, I don't know…."

"Nasty. Mean." Feeling guilty for admitting it didn't make it any less true. "Controlling."

"Yeah," Jade agreed. "Exactly. Whitney always struck me as too independent to get involved with someone like that."

"So, if not an affair, then what?" Blackmail, maybe? Could Whitney have had something on Broderick that he didn't want anyone else to know? But even if she did, and even if he was paying her to keep her mouth shut while he was alive, why leave her everything in his will? What would he care what anyone thought after he was gone? Emma dismissed the thought. Broderick Aldridge did not strike her as a man who gave two hoots about anyone else's opinion of him.

Jade just shook her head. "I have no idea."

"Well, at the end of the day, it doesn't really matter, as long as she doesn't want to move in here." Granny got up and put her salad plate in the sink, then filled her dish with lasagna. How she managed to stay so thin, Emma couldn't even imagine. Of course, with Emma gone from the house, she probably hadn't cooked much the past year. Especially since her father tended to work late and eat out a lot.

The thought brought a sudden wave of understanding. Granny Rose was here because she was lonely. She'd gone from having a houseful of family, to basically being alone. Emma got up and went to her, wrapped her arms around her, and kissed the top of her head. "Don't worry about it, Granny Rose. If you want to live in Mini-Meadows, you will. You and Butch are more than welcome to stay with me until we find you the perfect house."

Granny patted Emma's hand. "Thank you, dear."

"Of course." Giving in, as she knew she would, Emma put her salad plate in the sink and took a piece of lasagna. She inhaled deeply as she walked back to her seat, and her mouth watered. She could start her diet in earnest as soon as Granny Rose settled in her new home. "First things first, though. For now, we'll try and find Whitney and see if she wants to sell, since I know you fell in love with the caboose house."

"I'll see if I can find her right after we're done eating, and we'll go ask," Jade said.

"Who knows? Maybe she'll even tell us what her connection to Broderick is." Because the curiosity was getting to her. Not that it was any of her business. Hmm... How unfair was that? While it seemed she'd inherited a heaping dose of Granny Rose's nosiness, her good metabolism had eluded her. Too bad.

The next rumble of thunder brought Ginger out of hiding and tentatively down the stairs. She stopped a few steps up, eyed the lasagna on the stove, and crouched to pounce the short distance. One sideways glance from the corner of her eye found Emma watching her, and she stretched out on the step, shot a leg in the air, and began to clean herself as if she'd intended to do so all along. Maybe she had. Maybe she hadn't been enticed out of hiding by the scent of the food but rousted out by the growing storm, but Emma doubted it.

As she grated fresh parmesan onto her plate, Emma's thoughts returned to the conversation with Detective Montgomery. "Hey, Jade, did you find anything weird about Detective Montgomery's questions about Eric having a temper?"

She shrugged. "It kind of came out of left field, but I guess it's his job to think of everything."

"I guess." But why would he be leaning toward Eric? "You think Broderick was killed because he angered the wrong person? A crime of passion, so to speak?"

"To be honest," Granny Rose said. "The way Phillip was carryin' on about his inheritance, I kind of figured he offed his old man for the money."

"I thought so too, and it could be, but Broderick did have a way about him. Maybe he just pushed the wrong person too far." The first bite had her taste buds springing to attention. "This is amazing, Granny."

"Thank you, dear."

With that, conversation shifted to more mundane topics; Emma's schedule for the week, routine Mini-Meadows gossip, Ginger's pointed way of ignoring Butch. When they finished eating, Emma and Chloe started to clear the dishes while Granny Rose fed Butch and Ginger, and Jade returned to her seat at the desk.

Since she'd already started the search before dinner, it wasn't long before Jade called to Emma. One perk of the house being so small, it was easy enough to hear her even over the running water and clatter of dishes being washed. One downside of her tiny home, she'd given up a dishwasher in exchange for cabinet space.

"Whitney posted a picture of herself in front of the bed and breakfast she's staying at when she arrived in town." She popped a mint from a bowl on Emma's desk into her mouth and scrolled.

"Well?"

"Huh?" She glanced up, then returned to her scrolling.

"Is the bed and breakfast nearby?"

"Yup, about ten minutes from here." She glanced at Granny Rose. "Good news, it's pretty exclusive, and my guess is if that's the kind of luxury she enjoys, she'll have no interest in making a home in Mini-Meadows."

"Whew." Granny pretended—at least Emma thought she was faking—to wipe sweat from her brow, then hooked Butch's leash to his collar. "That's good to know."

"All right, I'll take a ride to the B and B tomorrow morning and see if she'll talk to me." Emma handed Chloe the next plate to dry.

"I'll take a ride with you," Jade offered. "She's more likely to speak to you and be agreeable if she knows we're friends."

"Thanks, Jade. Do you think eight's too early? I figure that'll be enough time for me to get you back before Little Bits has to open and still make my appointment at eleven with a new client." She started on the silverware, spreading it across a towel on the counter beside the sink for Chloe to dry once she'd finished putting away the leftovers.

"Yeah, that'll work." She returned her attention to the screen.

"Is there anything else on Whitney's Facebook?"

"Nah, nothing after the post when she first arrived in town, but I did find something a few weeks back I can't explain, a cryptic message about a life-changing experience."

"That's all it says?"

"Pretty much." She shrugged and read. "Isn't it funny how your life can take an unexpected turn in an instant, how everything you thought you knew could turn out to be a deception, how your life could completely and irrevocably change in the blink of an eye, and there's nothing you can do about it? Unless there is...."

"Did anyone comment on it? Maybe elaborate a little?"

She chewed on her bottom lip. "There are a lot of comments agreeing, lots of there, there's, a few that happened to me's, but...wait. Here, there's a comment from a woman who says 'I'm here for you if you need me. You don't need to go alone.'"

"That's it?"

"That's it. Whitney 'liked' the comment but didn't respond. Still, I get the impression the woman knows what she's referring to."

"What's her name?"

"Rachel Cummings."

Chloe shook her head. "Never heard of her."

"Me neither." Jade shifted through the stuff on Emma's desk and pulled out a notepad and pen. "I'll jot down the name, and if we can't find Whitney, maybe we can find Rachel and ask her what that meant and if it has anything to do with why she's in town."

"I'm going to take Butch out." Granny stood by the door holding Butch's leash while he danced back and forth, eager to go out. Probably because he didn't know a storm was raging outside.

"It's raining pretty hard, Granny Rose. Why don't you finish up the dishes with Chloe, and I'll walk Butch?" It might give her a few quiet minutes to think.

"You're sure you don't mind, dear?"

"Not at all." Granny Rose didn't need to be out in a thunderstorm. Emma grabbed her raincoat from a very narrow closet space with an accordion door beside the front door, her umbrella from the top shelf, and braced herself for the wind-whipped rain.

Jade's low whistle stopped her just short of opening the door. "Something else on Whitney's Facebook?"

"No." She held up her phone. "Actually, I just got a text from Max Merlin. Apparently, Eric Hamilton was just picked up in town and taken in for questioning in the death of Broderick Aldridge."

Chapter Twelve

The minute Jade slid into the Jeep's passenger seat the next morning, Emma pounced. "Did you hear anything else about Eric?"

Jade raised a brow at her, closed her door, and slid her sunglasses on. "No. Not really. I called Merlin this morning, and he said he went into Libby's for dinner after he left Little Bits last night, and it was pretty empty, so he decided to linger over dessert with some friends he ran into and wait out the storm. He was still there when he texted me to say Eric had been picked up for questioning."

Emma checked her rearview mirror and pulled out as Jade buckled her belt. The sooner they made it out to the bed and breakfast where Whitney was staying, the sooner she'd have an answer for Granny Rose. "So, how'd he find out about Eric?"

"One of the waiters was talking about it, said he went out back to dump the garbage and saw the police cars on the next road over with their lights flashing." Jade flipped the sun visor down and opened the mirror, then took her make-up bag out of her purse. It always amazed Emma that she could do her eye makeup in a moving car. Sure, blush and lipstick were easy enough, but if Emma tried to apply eyeliner or mascara in a moving vehicle, she'd more than likely put out an eye. "He walked over to see what was going on, and two officers were leading Eric out to one of the patrol cars."

"Was he arrested?" Stopping at the traffic light, she watched Jade expertly apply a smoky gray shadow and blend it while barely paying attention. Maybe Emma should ask her for some tips, although finding time to add anything else to her morning routine would probably be just short of torture.

Especially with only one bathroom, Granny Rose having taken over her bedroom, and Butch now in residence seemingly indefinitely.

"I don't know if they actually arrested him. Merlin didn't say he was handcuffed, but he didn't say he wasn't either, just that he was taken in for questioning." She moved to the next eye and repeated the process. "He's supposed to stop by later and let me know if he finds out anything about that or Phillip."

When the light changed, Emma returned her focus to the road and drove out of the development, lost in her own thoughts. No way could Eric have killed Broderick. He'd been with her when she'd found him, and he'd seemed just as shocked as she was. Hadn't he?

Besides, what reason would he have to kill him? Just because he'd refused to pay the next installment in his contract? Small claims court would be a whole lot less complicated than murder. She tried to think back to the argument he'd told her about. Nothing seemed out of the ordinary, really. Especially considering Broderick Aldridge argued with just about everyone. Besides, Arianna had been there with Eric at the time. How could he have killed Broderick with a witness?

A witness who was now, by all accounts, missing. "Have you heard anything about Arianna Jenkins?"

Jade finished off her lips and dropped the tube of lipstick back into her bag. "Nothing. As far as I know, she hasn't been found, but you know how it is, the fact that she's seemingly disappeared warrants gossip. Once she's found, unless it's scandalous in some way, not so much."

True enough.

When she made one last turn, the bed, and breakfast came into sight. An old plantation-style home with a massive amount of land surrounding it.

Jade gestured to a wide cobblestone driveway. "There. Make a right."

Emma pulled around the oleander-lined circular driveway. While the pink flowers were certainly beautiful, they were also deadly. If Broderick had been poisoned instead of beaten, Whitney undoubtedly would have had access to the murder weapon. Emma stopped herself before she could continue the train of thought. What? Was everyone going to be a suspect in her mind now? When had she become so cynical? Of course, Whitney did inherit the bulk of Aldridge's estate.

Besides, it couldn't have been Whitney. Phillip Aldridge sat smack at the top of Emma's suspect list. And Mildred was a close second. Maybe they'd done it together? Or one killed him, and the other helped cover it up. Especially since it seemed at least Phillip hadn't known about the changed will. It was reasonable to expect if Mildred had known, Phillip would have too. Especially if they were plotting the old man's demise. Surely, she would have told him. Of course, they could have killed him for some other reason. Money wasn't the only possible motive. Whether or not they expected to inherit his fortune, the two of them seemed happier with him gone, if nothing else. Maybe they'd hired the man in the suit to do the job.

And what if it wasn't Mildred and-or Phillip? Who stood to gain the most from Broderick's death? Financially, Whitney, who'd made plans with Jade and hadn't shown up. Could she have been trying to use Jade as an alibi? If so, why would she not have made an appearance, even if only for a few minutes?

Emma shook her head, trying to clear the random sequence of thoughts ricocheting around, and climbed out of the car. The beautiful old plantation home boasted large pillars and an elegant front porch, complete with a wide swing and several seating arrangements. Paddle fans on the ceiling stirred the already hot, humid air. "Do we knock or just go in?"

Jade shrugged and twisted the handle on the double front doors. "It's open, so I guess we can go in."

An older woman wearing a smart black suit and a professional smile stood behind a reception desk across the lobby. She looked up from her computer and smiled. "Welcome. Come on in. Do you have a reservation?"

Jade closed the door behind her and crossed the marble floor to the desk. "No, actually, we were hoping to speak with one of your guests. She's an old friend, and I was eager to catch her before she left for the day."

"Sure thing. What's your friend's name?"

"Whitney Jameson."

The receptionist, with a nametag that read "Donna," scrolled through the registry and frowned. "Hmm…that's weird. We don't have a Whitney Jameson listed. Are you sure she's staying here?"

Disappointment surged, and Emma turned her attention to her surroundings.

While Jade talked to the receptionist, Emma wandered the lobby. An ornate curved staircase wrapped around the reception area on either side. Thick runners ran up the center of each set of stairs. What appeared to be antiques dotted the lobby; chairs, settees, even a couple of roll-top desks. Jade was right about one thing, if these were the surroundings Whitney enjoyed, Mini-Meadows wasn't for her. Of course, if they'd been wrong about her staying here, then Mini-Meadows might just be perfect.

"Come on, Emma." Jade hooked Emma's elbow and led her toward one of the staircases.

"Whitney's here?"

"Yeah, but registered under another name." Her jaw clenched and unclenched. "The receptionist called up to let her know we're on our way."

Emma started to ask if she said anything about where she was the night she stood Jade up but thought better of it. If the receptionist had called ahead, Jade obviously hadn't spoken to her. But she could tell something was wrong by the length of Jade's purposeful stride. "Are you annoyed she didn't show up the other night?"

Jade shrugged it off. "Not really. That's typical Whitney, but I did get a little worried when I didn't hear from her the next day."

They started down the second-floor hallway, but before they could reach Whitney's door, it opened, and Whitney stepped out. She wore faded jeans and a pink t-shirt, her hair tied in a sloppy knot at the top of her head, and no makeup. Tear tracks marked her cheeks beneath puffy, red-rimmed eyes. She scrubbed her hands over her face, her pink, rhinestone-studded nails the only hint of a woman who liked to indulge herself. "Jade, I am so sorry. I got sidetracked the other night and forgot we were supposed to meet up, then things got out of control. Come in, please."

She hugged Jade hard, then stepped aside for her to enter the suite.

"Don't worry about it. I'm just glad you're okay." She studied her intently.

"You are okay, right?"

"Sure." Her gaze dipped to her feet. "Why wouldn't I be?"

"I don't know. Maybe because you made plans to meet me then didn't show up, and you're registered here under an assumed name."

For just an instant, fear flickered in Whitney's eyes. Then they shuttered over, and she smiled. "I'm fine, just a bit overextended. Now, please, come in."

Taking her at her word, and not mentioning the fact that the other woman had obviously been crying, at least for the moment, Jade introduced Emma, and the three walked in together.

"Hey, would you guys like breakfast? I can have something sent up."

Not only would breakfast give them reason to prolong their stay, it might give things a more casual chat with friends feel that would put Whitney at ease. Emma offered a smile. "Sure, we'd love to stay for breakfast, thank you."

While Whitney ordered up room service, Emma took a good look around the majestic space at the lap of luxury, and her mood improved. This was about as far from tiny home living as you could get.

They settled at a massive round table with a view of the gardens that must have cost a pretty penny. For a moment, Emma had to wonder how Whitney could afford all of this. At least, before she inherited Broderick's money. Had Jade mentioned what Whitney did for a living? She couldn't remember, but she didn't think so.

Jade looked Whitney in the eye. "Look, Whitney, I'm not upset you didn't show up the other night, but I got worried when I didn't hear from you, so I looked at your social media to see if you'd posted anything recently."

Whitney laughed. "So, that's how you found me?"

"Yup." Jade sat back, her gaze still intent on Whitney. She didn't crack the slightest hint of a smile. What was going on with her? While she was much more outspoken than either Emma or Chloe, it wasn't like her to be so confrontational. "And I noticed a post from a few weeks ago, something about a life-changing event."

Emma held her breath. The way she figured it, this was the moment

Whitney would either talk to them or throw them out. Probably without breakfast, which might be just as well, considering she was still battling the lasagna calories.

"Yes, well." She paused, studying Jade, perhaps trying to gauge what she knew, which was obviously more than she'd let Emma in on.

Jade folded her arms across her chest. "Would that life-changing event have anything to do with the fact that you're registered here under the name Whitney Aldridge?"

Shock stemmed the flow of questions that threatened to burst from Emma.

Whitney slumped back in the chair as tears flowed over, and she simply nodded.

"So? What then? You couldn't have married him, he's already married. Were you having an affair with Broderick Aldridge?"

Her watery eyes went wide. "Oh, man, no way. Absolutely not."

"Then?" Jade paused, waited for Whitney to collect herself.

When she finally did, a knock on the door interrupted, and Emma went to answer. She opened the door to the same woman who'd been at the reception desk, fished some cash out of her pocket for a tip, then thanked her and pushed the cart into the room. The scent of bacon made her mouth water as she set the serving bowls filled with food out on the table and passed everyone plates, cups, and mugs. She filled a cup for each of them from the pitcher of orange juice.

Ignoring the food, Whitney poured herself a cup of tea, blew on it, then set the cup on the table without drinking. "Eat something, please. It will make me feel more comfortable talking."

Jade filled a plate with scrambled eggs and bacon.

Emma did the same and added two pieces of rye toast. She forked up some scrambled eggs.

"Broderick Aldridge was my father."

Emma's hand stopped halfway to her mouth. Thankfully. If she'd had a mouthful when Whitney shared that nugget, she'd surely have choked. Her gaze shot to Jade, but she seemed equally surprised.

"What are you talking about?" Jade asked.

"I found out by accident, did one of those DNA things with some friends, just something fun to pass the time, and I joined the website. Next thing you know, I'm finding out my real father isn't who I thought he was. When I confronted my mother, she told me the truth. She'd had an affair with Broderick Aldridge, had gotten pregnant. She says my father knew, but he forgave her, and they just moved on with him raising me as his own."

"Did Broderick know?"

She blew out a breath and shook her head. With the worst of the telling behind her, she scooped eggs onto her plate. "Not then, he didn't, no. But when I arrived in town a couple of weeks ago, I went to see him, told him the truth about my paternity."

Emma winced, trying to imagine Broderick's reaction to some woman showing up on his doorstep and announcing she was his daughter. He did not strike her as a man who was fond of surprises. "How'd he take it?"

"He was shocked, as I'm sure you can imagine, but he wasn't unhappy. He was actually quite kind. I told him I didn't want anything from him, didn't want to disrupt his life or his marriage or anything, that I only wanted to see him and let him know."

"And what did he say?" Emma leaned forward, all but forgetting her breakfast.

"He said he'd like some time to sort things out. He was in the middle of preparing to move to Mini-Meadows, but he asked me to come by again the following week."

"And did you?"

She nodded, finished chewing, and washed down the bite with some orange juice. "Then he called the other night, asked me to stop by. That's why I got in touch with you, Jade, I figured I was headed out there anyway, so we could maybe meet up and have some fun, alleviate some of the, I don't know, tension at the whole situation, I suppose."

Jade shook her head. "So, why didn't you show up?"

"I went to see him, have dinner with him and his wife as he'd invited me to do. But when I got there, Mildred was not exactly happy to see me."

Emma didn't imagine she would be. "Was he married to her at the time of the affair?"

She pushed her food around the plate without taking another bite. "Yes. Phillip Aldridge, that weasel, is apparently my older half-brother."

"Does he know?"

She shook her head. "Not that I know of. The supposed dinner, which we never did get to eat, didn't go well. Broderick basically told Mildred I was his daughter, the result of an affair he'd had while married to her, and that he had changed his will to include me instead of Phillip since I had clearly made my own way in life and Phillip had hung around mooching off Broderick, or words to that effect."

Would that, combined with the fact he was moving them out of the family home and leaving all of Mildred's things behind be enough to push her over the edge? If so, it wasn't really too far of a stretch to think she'd clobbered him with something. Heck, he deserved a good knock on the head really. But not death. No one deserved that. Maybe it had been an accident. She'd just been so irate she'd hit him with something and hadn't expected to kill him. "How did Mildred take it?"

"About as well as you'd expect." She shoved her plate back. "She blew up. If you ask me, the stuff that came spewing out of her mouth had been building up for a long time."

Emma's heart ached for Mildred. She didn't particularly like the woman, but no one deserved to be treated the way her husband, the man who should have cherished her above all else, had treated her. "I'm sorry."

She shrugged it off. "Yeah, me too. Especially when he was so accepting, but like I said, I have no interest in being a home wrecker."

If her current state was any indication, she was telling the truth about that. "What did you do?"

"I left. What else could I do? I'm sorry I didn't meet up with you afterward, Jade, I was just too upset to go out and enjoy myself. I should have called you."

"Don't worry about it, Whitney." She reached across the table and squeezed her hand. "Like I said, it's not a big deal."

"Listen, I don't mean to be rude, but if there's nothing else, I'd like to go take a shower and maybe have a good cry. You guys can finish up eating and let yourselves out." She shifted her chair back and stood.

"Actually, there is one more thing," Emma said.

"What's that?"

"I was wondering what you plan to do with the tiny home in Mini-Meadows."

"Tiny home?" She shook her head. "I don't have a home, tiny or otherwise, in Mini-Meadows."

Uh oh. Alarm bells clanged in Emma's head, drowning out all the other questions. Her gaze shot to Jade. "Uh…"

Jade stood and rounded the table. "Whitney, I could tell you'd been crying before we got here. What had you so upset?"

"Just the whole situation." She threw up her hands, let them drop. "Why?"

"Ah, man." Jade slid a hand through her hair, shifted the loose strands over her shoulder. "Okay. I'm sorry to be the one to tell you, Whitney, but Broderick Aldridge was killed sometime early yesterday or late the night before."

"Killed?" She flopped back onto her chair. Her hand flew to her neck, and she fished a charm hanging from a chain out from beneath her shirt, clasped it tightly in both hands. "I don't understand. Was there an accident?"

"No, he was murdered."

"Mur…no, that can't be." She shook her head, the adamant denial very convincing. "Who would want to hurt Broderick?"

Probably best not to tell her the list was a long one, starting with anyone who'd ever met him. "Did you see anyone else when you were out there that night?"

"Just the movers. They were in and out, packing things into the storage container." Propping her elbows on the table, still gripping the necklace, she cradled her face in her hands. "I can't believe this is happening."

Jade rubbed her back, offering what comfort she could.

"I'm so sorry for your loss, Whitney," Emma said, not sure what she could do to comfort the woman.

"Thank you." She sniffed and pulled a tissue from a box on the table. She lifted the chain over her head, opened her hand to reveal a chunky, gold man's ring, a lion's head with two ruby eyes. "He gave me this, said it held great sentimental value, had once belonged to his father, and he wanted me to have it. The vase on the table too. It was his mother's."

The vase was beautiful, hand painted if Emma had to guess, and definitely an antique. Though, she didn't know how much sentimental value it could have held since he hadn't packed it to move to Mini-Meadows. Unless maybe he'd planned to bring it there himself. Either way, at least now she had a good idea where the items Phillip accused Jade of taking had gone.

"He accepted me, wanted to get to know me, and now he's gone, and I'll never even know who he was." Closing her hand over the ring, she folded her arms on the table and lowered her head to rest there. Soft sobs shook her.

Emma's heart ached for Whitney, despite the fact she probably wouldn't have liked Broderick if she'd gotten to know him. Seemed most people didn't, even his own wife and son. But who knew? Maybe Whitney would have changed him. Maybe having someone to care for and love, someone who loved him back, would have brought him joy other aspects of his life apparently hadn't. Whitney was right, they'd never know because someone had cut his life short.

Though they stayed with Whitney another few minutes, they finally left, at her insistence, with a promise to get in touch if they heard any news. Emma was glad Jade hadn't mentioned Eric being picked up for questioning in Broderick's murder. No sense spreading rumors before they knew for sure what was going on.

"So, what do you think?" Emma asked as soon as they were back in the Jeep.

"I don't know what to think." Jade slid her sunglasses on and looked back up at the old plantation as if she could see what Whitney was up to through the walls.

"No, me neither." Emma shifted into drive and started down the driveway, keeping an eye on the bed and breakfast in her rearview mirror. She didn't know what she expected, maybe for Whitney to leave, but where would she go? Home? Not to see Mildred, for sure. "How well do you really know Whitney?"

"I told you, we're not real close, more like casual friends. Why?" Jade stared out the window, distracted probably by her own thoughts rather than the beautiful scenery.

"Do you know her well enough to be sure she didn't have anything to do with Broderick's death?"

"What do you mean?" She turned her attention to Emma and frowned. "Why would Whitney kill him?"

"I'm not saying she would have done it on purpose, though as far as motives go, she did probably inherit a pretty hefty sum, but she could have killed him by accident after things got out of control."

Jade shrugged and returned to staring out the window. "I guess it could have happened that way. When he was so rude to me the first time I spoke with him, I was pretty irate, but the second time, I could have slapped him for sure. But pick up something heavy enough to kill him and hit him over the head with it? I don't think I was mad enough to have lost control like that."

"But you're not that quick-tempered. Others are." Emma pulled up her mental list. She could now put Mildred, Whitney, Eric, Arianna, and Jade, all with Broderick Aldridge on the day he was killed. Everyone except Phillip. Did that mean Phillip didn't kill him or that Phillip was the only one smart enough not to have been seen with him on the day he died?

"I guess. I don't know Whitney well enough to know if she's got that short a fuse."

"No, but we know Phillip does." And Emma always came back to him. What could have pushed him to lose his temper and kill his father? The list was probably long, but she'd place a pretty hefty bet losing his inheritance to some long-lost sister topped it.

Jade tore her gaze from the passing woods to look at Emma. "Be honest, Emma, do you actually believe Phillip could have killed his own father, or do you just dislike him that much?"

Emma squirmed in her seat. How could she answer that honestly when she wasn't even sure herself? He did have a short temper. Plus, according to Whitney, he hadn't known about her, which meant he didn't know he'd been cut out of the will, so he had every reason to believe he'd inherit.

"It's okay, you don't have to answer, but think about it."

She nodded, grateful to be able to avoid the subject, but she would have to give it some thought. It wasn't fair to accuse someone of murder just because she disliked him. Immensely. With good reason.

Chapter Thirteen

Emma dropped Jade off at Little Bits half an hour later than expected. She backed out of her parking spot and shifted into gear, then paused when she spotted Granny Rose walking down the sidewalk with Butch in tow. Walking might not quite be the right word for the steady bop Granny was doing down Main Street, headphones plugged into her ears, leash hung over her wrist, hand resting on Butch's back.

Watching her brought a smile to Emma's face and a feeling of joy to her heart. Granny Rose had been afforded all the luxury of having a wealthy father followed by a wealthy husband, and yet, Emma had never seen her as happy as she looked in that moment, bopping along to a beat only she could hear, her new best friend prancing beside her.

"Dang!" With everything else going on, she'd never gotten an answer about whether or not Whitney wanted to sell the tiny home in Mini-Meadows. Now she was going to have to see if she could get back in touch with her. She added asking Jade about it to her mental to-do list. She'd have called while she was driving, but it would probably be better to let Whitney have a little space to deal with everything. Selling the little caboose house was probably not at the top of her list of priorities.

Emma made the forty-minute drive to the Orlando suburb to meet with her new client in peace, trying to use the time to empty her mind of everything weighing on her of late. No easy task when a friend and business associate had been taken in for questioning in the murder investigation of a client. Then again, hadn't Emma herself been questioned? It wasn't like Eric had been arrested, probably, just taken down to the station. Who knew? That might be the normal way of questioning a witness. Perhaps Detective Montgomery had only agreed to see Jade in the shop because he was out in the field but would have brought her to the station otherwise. No matter how she envisioned it, Emma just couldn't see Eric as a killer.

She flipped on the radio but turned it off again just as quickly. She wasn't in the mood for music. She just wanted quiet, needed to revel in the silence enveloping her, with nothing more than the hum of the tires against the pavement to soothe her nerves. Her eyelids grew heavy, and she started to swerve, then jerked upright an instant later. Okay, that might be a little too relaxed. Somehow, she needed to get some sleep in the very near future.

She reached the two-story colonial sooner than she'd have liked and parked in the driveway behind a pickup truck. Gathering her things, she took a deep breath and smiled. This was the part of her job she enjoyed most, meeting new people, finding creative ways to help them.

Hooking her purse over her shoulder, she shifted her clipboard, and locked the car, then dropped the keys into her purse. As she climbed the two steps to the front porch and knocked, her phone rang. She'd just started to reach into her pocket for it when the door opened.

A very pregnant woman smiled out at her. "Hi there. You must be Emma Wells."

Emma held out a hand. "Ms. Moreno?"

She shook Emma's hand. "That's me. But, please, call me Gabriella."

"Gabriella, thank you. It's a pleasure to meet you."

She swiped the back of her wrist across her brow and tucked a few strands of long brown hair that had come free of her bun behind her ear. "Believe me when I tell you, the pleasure is all mine. Come in, come in."

"Thank you." Emma followed her through a living room filled with enough knick-knacks and tchotchkes to keep Jade in business for the next year.

"Come on back to the kitchen. I've been packing, so don't mind the mess." She gestured around at the stacks of boxes, full, empty, and every stage in between.

"No worries. Um." She always felt the vaguest sense of discomfort on meeting a potential client and having to tell them most of what they owned would probably not be coming with them.

When Gabriella reached the kitchen, she shifted a stack of dishes from one of the chairs and a blender off another, then gestured for Emma to sit. "Can I get you something to drink? Sweet tea?"

"Sure. Tea would be great." Better to break the ice a little first. She looked around the cozy kitchen. Even in its current state of disarray, she could tell Gabriella kept the kind of home people felt welcome in. "So, what made you decide to downsize?"

It had been Emma's experience that most women who were expecting were looking for a larger house with a yard, the exact kind of house Gabriella already lived in.

She rubbed her very swollen belly. "I'm due any day now."

A niggle of panic shot through Emma. It must have shown on her face, because Gabriella laughed, a musical sound that put Emma instantly at ease. "Don't worry. I won't go into labor on you."

"That would be much appreciated." But the way her life was going lately, she didn't hold out much hope.

"Sit, let me get our tea, and we'll chat. I like to get to know the people I'm working with, especially those who are going to be responsible for all of my most prized possessions."

"Of course. I don't blame you at all." She'd taken an instant liking to Gabriella Moreno.

Emma's phone rang again, and she took a discreet peek at the number. Granny Rose, Great. She hoped nothing was wrong, but she didn't want to take a personal call while in a business meeting with a potential new client, so she tucked the phone back into her pocket. She'd call Granny back as soon as she was done. Granny had both Jade and Chloe's numbers in case of an emergency, and both of them were in their shops at Mini-Meadows, literally minutes away if Granny needed them.

"Here you go." Gabriella set Emma's tea on the table along with a plateful of what looked like homemade cookies, then sat across from her with a sigh. "Please, have some cookies. I was in the mood for something sweet and went way overboard. If you don't eat some, I might well finish them all."

"Thank you." Emma helped herself to a frosted oatmeal cookie.

"Now, to answer your question. When I found out I was pregnant, I was surprised, but excited. Having kids wasn't even on my radar yet, but I was still thrilled, no matter how unexpected. My husband, on the other hand, well, not so much. He didn't want kids. Oddly, we'd never discussed that before we got married. I guess I just assumed we'd get married and start a family. Anyway, he suggested putting the baby up for adoption. Which was not happening. Then he gave me a choice. Him or the baby." Her eyes narrowed in anger, then she rested her hand on her belly, and her expression softened. "I guess you can see what I decided."

"I'm sorry."

"Don't be. Better to find out now that I married a jerk—not because he didn't want children, some people don't, but because of the way he acted when I told him, like a spoiled child determined to have his way—than to find out ten years down the road." She waved it off.

While that was probably true, Emma still admired Gabriella. The path she'd chosen wouldn't be an easy one. Assuming she no longer wanted to discuss it, since she'd dismissed the subject, Emma bit into her cookie. "Oh, wow. This is delicious."

"Thank you." She grinned. "My Granny's recipe. I'll give you some to take home."

"That would be great, thank you."

"No, thank *you*. Really." She bit into a chocolate chip cookie, then brushed crumbs from her fingers onto a napkin. "So, anyway, now it's going to be just me and my little one, so I want something smaller. I don't want to spend my baby's childhood cleaning a huge house and tending a yard when I'm not working. Maybe when he or she is a little older, that will be back on the table, but for now, I just want the pretty little condo I picked out for us to spend our time getting to know each other."

A quick moment of regret the woman wasn't moving into Mini-Meadows surprised Emma, and she almost suggested it. It wasn't often she met someone with Gabriella's vitality, the kind of person you just wanted to be friends with.

Emma's phone rang again, and her cheeks heated. She checked the screen. Granny again. "I'm sorry."

"No problem. You can go ahead and answer it."

"That's all right. I can return the call when we're done." But a small niggle of fear began to creep up her spine.

"Okay, but if you need to take it, feel free. I'm just happy to be off my feet for a few minutes."

"Thank you." While she'd have enjoyed relaxing with Gabriella for a while longer, she needed to get this done and find out what was going on with Granny. "So, when would you like to move?"

"As soon as possible. I already closed on the condo and started packing, but I don't know what to do with all of this." She gestured vaguely around the kitchen.

The moment of truth. "You understand you won't be able to take all of it with you?"

"Of course." She took another cookie, completely relaxed, obviously not surprised by the fact all of her belongings wouldn't fit in her new surroundings. "It's not a problem. I just want to take what I need for myself, and the baby and the rest can go."

Emma barely resisted the sigh of relief that begged to escape. After the Aldridge fiasco, she needed a nice, smooth job to remind her how much she loved what she did. "Would you like me to send someone out to give you a price to buy everything? Or perhaps you'd be interested in consigning some of it?"

"Honestly, if someone would be willing to pay a set price for everything and just take it out of here, I'd be thrilled. Then I could set that money aside for stuff I need for the baby."

"Great." She pulled Jade's business card out of her holder and handed it to Gabriella. "Give Jade a call, and she'll set up an appointment to come out and talk to you."

"Perfect, thank you." She frowned at the card.

"Is something wrong?" Emma braced to run if Gabriella was having any kind of contractions.

"Not at all, just a little overwhelmed now that this is all actually happening."

Whew! Okay, that was a problem she could deal with. "Don't worry. I'll help you take care of everything."

"Thanks, you're a real lifesaver." She shot Emma an infectious smile.

Once they'd signed the contract and Gabriella had written a check for the first installment of Emma's fee, Emma went over a list of everything she'd need. A mover, for sure, and she'd definitely tag Eric for that, as long as he wasn't in prison. Emma choked.

Gabriella jolted and leaned forward. "You okay?"

"Fine, sorry, just a tickle in my throat." She waved Gabriella off and sipped her tea. Couldn't she go even five minutes without the events surrounding Broderick Aldridge rearing their ugly heads? She tried to pull herself back together. Now, if she could just remember what they'd been discussing. "We can also talk about some built-in storage options that will be helpful if you'd like?"

"That would be amazing." She sat up straighter, squirmed with excitement as her eyes lit up. "I was hoping for some bookshelves. I don't mind parting with the other stuff, but I'd love to keep my books and add children's books to my collection."

"You bet. I know someone who builds tiny homes and occasionally takes side jobs doing just that sort of thing. He's amazing." Plus, calling Tiny would give her a chance to find out if he'd heard anything from or about Eric. So much for clearing her mind of anything to do with the investigation.

Her phone rang again. She looked at the caller ID, and fear jerked through her at the sight of Chloe's number. No way she'd interrupt a meeting with a potential client for no reason. It was time to wrap things up. "Thank you so much for the tea and cookies."

"It's the least I can do with all the work you're saving me." Gabriella stood and stretched her back. After a brief search through a couple of piles she came up with a Ziploc bag and filled it with cookies. "I hope you enjoy them."

"Thank you again. I'm sure I will." *Probably all on the way home once I find out what's going on.* "I'll be in touch after I speak to Tiny and Eric, and I'll touch base with Jade and make sure she knows to expect your call."

"Perfect, thank you." She walked Emma to the door and saw her out.

Unable to wait another minute, Emma dialed on the way to her Jeep, then climbed in and cranked up the air conditioning, even though she was pretty sure the overheated feeling she was currently experiencing was caused by anxiety.

Granny picked up on the first ring. "Well, it's about time."

"I'm sorry, Granny Rose, I was working. Are you okay?"

"I am now."

"Oh, no." Her gut cramped. "What happened? Are you hurt?"

"Well, no, but I could have been."

Emma sucked in a deep breath and counted to ten while she blew it out. "What happened?"

"Someone was following me while I was walking with Butch. I didn't notice anything wrong at first, but then Butch started acting weird, making this growlish noise low in his throat and looking over his shoulder. I mean, I guess it's his shoulder. Right? Well, anyway, that's neither here nor there."

Emma offered a small prayer for patience as she started the Jeep and backed out of the driveway. "So, what happened, Granny Rose?"

"Oh, right. So, we're walking along, mindin' our own business, when Butch starts acting strange. So I look over my shoulder, figuring maybe there's a squirrel or something behind us. But there wasn't."

Emma stopped at the stop sign on the corner and massaged the bridge of her nose between her thumb and forefinger. No sense prodding her any further. Whatever was going on, Granny would get to it in her own time. For now, Emma would have to content herself with the knowledge that both Granny and Butch were safe and unhurt.

"...following us and taking pictures."

"Whoa. Wait. What?"

"Aren't you listening to a word I'm saying?"

"I'm sorry, Granny, I'm driving, and I just got sidetracked for a minute. What happened? Who was taking pictures?"

"I said, someone was following us. I couldn't see who was driving, but there was a woman on the passenger side with the window rolled down, and she was taking pictures of me and Butch. Then the driver slowed down by your house, and the woman snapped at least one picture of that before taking off."

It wouldn't be the first time someone had snapped pictures of houses in Mini-Meadows. When people decided to buy a tiny home, they often drove around and took pictures of some that might suit their needs, but why in the world would someone be taking pictures of Granny and Butch? An image popped into her head, her petite Granny bopping along in her velour sweatsuit and gold high-tops, earbuds in, with a giant of a dog walking beside her. They did make quite a picture. Could it be something that innocent, someone who was simply entertained by the odd pairing? Maybe. But either way, Emma didn't like the idea of someone possibly stalking Granny Rose. "Where are you now?"

"I'm at Pocket Books with Chloe."

"All right, stay there. I'm already on my way, and I'll be there as fast as I can." She stepped a little harder on the gas. "Did you get a good look at the woman? Could you describe her?"

"Not really. She had a scarf or hood pulled over her hair and was wearing sunglasses. Oakley's. But I think I'd recognize her if I saw her again."

"Okay, what about the car?"

"It was just a car. A blue one."

Okay, so she could tell what brand of sunglasses the woman was wearing but had no clue about the make or model of the car. Just that it was blue.

"Or it might have been gray."

Emma sighed.

"Now that I think more on it, it was probably a bluish-gray."

Emma glanced in her rearview mirror and merged with traffic on the turnpike. Barely noon, and it had already been a long day. And she still had to get in touch with Tiny to see if he'd take Gabriella's job, call Jade and make sure she knew to expect Gabriella's call, and contact Eric about her move—if he wasn't in jail for Broderick's murder, all while worrying why someone had been following Granny Rose. She opened the bag of cookies and dug in.

Chapter Fourteen

Confident Granny Rose was safe at Pocket Books with Chloe for the moment, Emma finished off three cookies, called Eric and arranged to meet up with him, left a message for Tiny to call her back, and got in touch with Jade about Gabriella, all while driving back to Mini-Meadows. After a quick check-in with Granny to assure herself she was really okay, Emma left her car parked in front of Pocket Books, crossed the road, and walked the block over to Eric's house.

Despite Granny Rose's assurances that she was fine and the flush of excitement when she retold the story of the woman taking pictures, anxiety still churned in Emma's gut. First Phillip Aldridge had put his hands on her, and now someone was possibly stalking her. Granted, it might have nothing to do with Broderick's murder, but still, Emma didn't like Granny on anyone's radar.

Come to think of it; what could Granny possibly have to do with Aldridge's murder? Nothing that Emma could see. But hadn't Jade said Granny was the one who told Chloe Broderick's body had been found? How could she have heard that so early in the morning that her hair was still in rollers? As soon as Emma finished speaking to Eric, she'd have to remember to ask.

Because the sooner Broderick Aldridge's killer was found and put away, the safer Emma would feel.

She walked up the gravel walkway to the front door of Eric's small, dark blue home and knocked, hoping she wasn't about to come face-to-face with a killer. She dismissed the thought almost as quickly as it came into her head. She'd known Eric for a little over a year, and he was a nice guy. Then again, did that mean he didn't have a temper she'd yet to witness? Did it really mean he wasn't a killer?

Eric opened the door looking tired and worn out, his dark eyes bloodshot and sunken in black circles. "Hey, Emma, come on in."

As he stepped back to allow her entry, his size suddenly struck her, making her feel claustrophobic in the tiny space. She'd never realized how big he was, easily a bulky six-two. And moving boxes and furniture all day would probably make him strong, definitely strong enough to have killed Broderick. She edged cautiously past him and headed toward the slightly cluttered kitchen space he'd indicated.

Like hers, Eric's home was made from shipping containers, though his were set together as an L with only one floor rather than stacked atop one another. His furnishings were sparse, as was to be expected, with a big screen TV taking up a good portion of one living room wall and a row of gaming systems on a low coffee table in front of a comfortably worn recliner. He offered her a seat at a small round table covered with papers. Apparently, Eric had opted for the table instead of a desk. File cabinets, some of the drawers overstuffed and open, lined one wall in the kitchen.

"So…" She sat, wondering how best to bring up the fact that he'd been picked up and questioned in Broderick's death. Leading with have you killed anyone lately was probably not the best approach. "How's everything?"

He laughed, though it held no humor, and slumped into the other chair, rubbed his hands over his face. "I guess you've already heard I was arrested and questioned last night."

"Arrested?" And he was sitting between her and the front door. Her heart rate kicked up. "Why would they arrest you?"

Propping his elbows on the table, he shoved his hands into his hair and squeezed the short strands.

She waited him out.

After a moment, he lifted his gaze to hers, slouched back, and dropped his hands into his lap. "Because my fingerprints were found on the murder weapon."

"Uh…" She tried to form words, to say something, anything. Nope. Not happening. With her brain stalled and no witty response forthcoming, uh was the best she could do.

He held his hands out in a gesture of surrender. "I didn't do it, Emma. I didn't kill him. All right, I'll admit our conversation over the check might have been a little more heated than I said earlier, but I did not kill anyone."

"How did your fingerprints end up on the murder weapon?" While she had to say something, that probably wasn't the best response. Unfortunately, it was the best she could do under the circumstances.

He blew out a breath, tilted his head back and forth, and sank back into his seat. "When I was out at Broderick's the other day, Arianna got a flat tire. I changed it for her and put everything back into her trunk, the jack, the lug wrench, the spare tire."

"You didn't mention that earlier."

He shrugged. "I didn't think it mattered. It was such a stupid thing. Something that happens all the time. I never thought a thing of it, just changed the tire, put everything away, and moved on."

"Okay, so then what?"

"The police found the lug wrench I used in the overgrown weeds in the lot next door, nearby where the storage container we found Aldridge in was positioned at the time."

"He wasn't killed in the container, though?" He couldn't have been. At least, there was no evidence of any kind of struggle or beating that she'd noticed.

"No, he was killed about thirty or forty feet away in the empty lot next door, then wrapped and stuffed into the container." He looked at her, straight into her eyes. "And it wasn't me who did it."

She nodded. Despite the evidence, she believed him. He was either innocent or a killer who deserved an Academy Award. "What do you think happened?"

"I have no idea. The lug wrench somehow got out of Arianna's trunk after I changed her tire, hit Aldridge over the head, and landed in the lot next door. All without getting any prints on it other than mine."

"Which means that someone probably wiped it off and just missed one of your prints."

"Or intentionally left mine to frame me."

Huh. Would that even be possible? If someone picked up the lug wrench and beat Broderick with it in a moment of anger, a crime of passion, would they be able to think enough to place their hand where Eric wouldn't have put his? Probably not. Unless it was premeditated. Then someone could have been careful. Or, perhaps the killer had worn gloves. But who would wear gloves in ninety-degree weather?

Movers. Didn't they sometimes wear gloves? She'd never seen Eric wearing them, but others did. "Did anyone ever find Arianna?"

He shook his head. "And now a missing person report's been filed."

"Do you, by chance, remember if she was wearing gloves while you guys were packing up?"

"Yeah." He waved it off, obviously not connecting the same dots Emma had. "Didn't want to break a nail or some such nonsense. Clearly, that wasn't the right job for her."

"No. Probably not." Unless she'd taken the job to get close to Broderick. But for what purpose? It made more sense that Aldridge's killer had done something to Arianna, then used her gloves to kill him. Or she'd set the gloves aside and left them there when she left. Either way, donning gloves and picking up a discarded lug wrench sure seemed more like a planned killing than an accident. Phillip popped into her head again. He'd have had access to anything on the property, including gloves, if they'd been left lying around, but how would he, or anyone else for that matter, have gotten into Arianna's trunk for the lug wrench?

"...feel kind of bad, though, that I had to give them Tiny's name."

Her introspection skidded to a halt. "What do you mean? What does Tiny have to do with anything?"

He averted his gaze. "I didn't say anything to you earlier because it was personal, and I like Tiny, so I didn't want to muddy his reputation."

Impatience with the whole situation shortened her tone. "What are you talking about, Eric? What does any of this have to do with Tiny?"

"One of the first few times he met with Aldridge about his new tiny home,

117

he was going over the plans with him, and Broderick got a call about an investment. He told Tiny about it, said what a great deal it was, and how they were going to make a ton of money on it. He asked Tiny if he wanted to invest, which Tiny did end up doing."

"How do you know?"

"Because Tiny told me about it and asked if I wanted in."

"Did you?"

"Nah. I didn't even understand any of it, just pretty much let him go on about what a sure thing it was and then said no thanks. I'm not into that kind of thing. I save my money the old-fashioned way, in my mattress."

Emma's gaze shot toward the bedroom at the back of the house.

Eric laughed. "Just kidding, Emma, I actually don't really have any savings to speak of, and what little I do have, I put in the bank."

"Haha."

"Sorry."

"Don't worry about it. I'm just in a mood over this whole thing." While she'd worried Broderick's murder might have some sort of impact on her business, she hadn't foreseen the toll it would take on Granny Rose, on her friends, on the whole community, and a wave of guilt threatened to drown her.

"Hey." He rested a hand on hers, which were clenched together on the table. "Don't worry about it. I'm sure it'll all get straightened out."

She nodded. What else could she say or do? "So, whatever happened with Tiny? Why did Detective Montgomery need to know about that?"

"Because the day Broderick was murdered, the investment tanked, and Tiny lost everything."

Her stomach somersaulted. "Ah, man."

"He was furious, called me screaming and carrying on. I've never heard Tiny like that."

"No, he's like a giant teddy bear most of the time."

"Exactly, which is why his behavior was so out of character. He swore Aldridge scammed him on purpose somehow." He picked up a pen, tapped it up and down in a staccato rhythm.

"Do you know if he ever talked to him?"

"I don't know if he found him or not, but when I talked to him, he was on his way over there and out for blood, that I can tell you."

All Emma wanted to do was escape. She needed a few minutes to order her thoughts, to take a step back from murder, to figure out what to do next. Wait, what was she even thinking? There shouldn't be a next. She was already too involved in this whole mess. What she should do is just walk away, leave the investigating to the police. They were so much better equipped than her to figure out who killed Broderick Aldridge.

But how could she walk away when her friends, the people she involved with Broderick in the first place, all seemed to be suspects in his murder? And for someone who was clearly not a people person, why had Broderick had so many visitors on the day he died? And which one of them did he push over the edge?

And then it clicked—a timeline. That's what she needed. "Do you remember what time you last saw Broderick alive?"

"Huh? The police asked me that too, but I really don't. It was later in the evening, but I couldn't give an exact time. I'd already finished another job and wanted to get home and eat. Why?"

"But you're sure you locked the container when you left?"

"Positive, because I was mad about the check," he said.

"What about Tiny? What time did you talk to him when he was looking for Aldridge?"

"I don't know. Later in the day. I was at the other job and stopped working for a minute, leaned against the truck to take his call because I figured maybe it was a problem with the Aldridge job."

"And you don't know if Tiny ever found him?" But she just couldn't see Tiny losing his temper like that. And how would he have gotten the lug wrench from Arianna's trunk?

"Nope."

But something wasn't adding up. Something about the timeline was definitely off. Unless someone was mistaken. Or, someone was lying. "Was Arianna with you when you went back?"

"Yeah, we left her car there to go do the other job, then she came back with me. We loaded up a few last-minute things and did a walk-through, double checked we didn't miss anything. Then I went to talk to Broderick and get a check. When I came out, Arianna was standing next to her car, staring at her flat tire. I was really aggravated, but I couldn't leave a young girl there with a flat and no one to help her, and she didn't seem to have a clue what to do, so I gave her a hand, then locked up the container and left."

"Was Arianna already gone when you left?"

He frowned, paused the pen tapping. "I don't know, actually. I put the tire and stuff in her trunk for her, locked up the container, and got into my truck. I didn't notice if she pulled away before me or not. Does it matter?"

"Probably not." But her mind was already racing ahead, because if she could figure out who was the last to see him alive, maybe she could figure out who did, or at least who didn't, kill Broderick Aldridge.

Chapter Fifteen

Emma strode through the door into Pocket Books and held up a hand. "No one talk to me."

Granny lifted a brow at Chloe.

Chloe only shrugged and returned to redoing the window display.

Emma worked to ignore them both. She needed a timeline, needed to know exactly who was with Broderick and when. She grabbed a pad and pen from beside the register, hurried to the back of the shop, and sat at a table facing the coffee pot, which was a mistake because now she wanted coffee. She jumped up, trying to order her thoughts, and poured a cup, then returned to her seat at the table and positioned the pad in front of her. She drew a line across the middle of the page. That wasn't going to work because she didn't know what came first. What she needed was a list, then she could try to put the visits in order. Setting aside the first page, she smoothed a clean sheet of paper and wrote Jade's name at the top of the page. "Okay, so, Jade went to see Broderick after I spoke to her, and that was after Granny and I ate dinner, which was fairly early but still evening."

"What are you trying to figure out?" Granny pulled out a chair and sat beside her.

Chloe leaned over her other shoulder. "You can't possibly think Jade had anything to do with Broderick's death."

"Of course not." So much for quiet to order her thoughts. That was all right, though. Who knew? Maybe Chloe or Granny Rose would see something she'd missed. Besides, Chloe had sparked another idea. She also needed a suspect list. "I figured I'd try to get a timeline of who saw Broderick on the day he was killed. Maybe then we can figure out who saw him last."

"Hey, that's not a bad idea." Granny got up and poured coffee for her and Chloe, while Chloe pulled up another chair and sat beside Emma.

"So, Jade went to see Broderick after she spoke to Whitney and saw him looking into the open storage container. Whitney went to have dinner with him after she spoke to Jade and made plans to go out." She couldn't tell from that whether Jade or Whitney had been there first. She was going to have to talk to Whitney and see what time she went to dinner. She said she'd seen the movers, so it must have been after they'd gone to the other job and returned, but she needed to know if the storage container was open or closed at the time and if the movers were still there when she left. That would actually work out okay, since she needed to find out if Whitney would be willing to sell the house in Mini-Meadows to Granny Rose.

"Whitney said the movers were packing up last-minute things when she was there, so I'm going to assume the storage container was still open while she was there, which means she was probably there before Jade." She squeezed Whitney's name above Jade's on the paper. "Eric says he closed the container and locked it before he left because he was angry about Broderick refusing to give him a check. He also said his fingerprints ended up on the murder weapon because—"

"Wait." Chloe splayed a hand over the paper. "What do you mean his fingerprints were on the murder weapon?"

Emma gave them a quick run-through of her conversation with Eric. "But he didn't know if Arianna was still there when he left, and he didn't know if Tiny found Broderick either."

"So, it's possible Eric was the last to see him alive," Chloe said.

"Not only that," added Granny Rose. "It's also possible he was the last to see Arianna before she disappeared."

"Great." She wrote Eric, Arianna, and Tiny below Jade's name. "This is not helping as much as I thought it would. The only one I've managed to eliminate as a suspect is Jade."

"And Whitney." Chloe pointed to her name above Jade's.

"If she's telling the truth. Besides, that timing's really only a guess on my part."

"True." Chloe propped her elbows on the table and cradled her chin in her hands.

Granny Rose clicked her dentures.

The three of them sat, silently lost in their own thoughts, and stared at the page as if the answer was going to jump out at them.

Not only couldn't she account for Eric, Arianna, or Tiny's whereabouts at the time just before and during the murder, but she had no clue where Mildred and Phillip were either. She jotted their names at the bottom of the page. "Whitney said Mildred was there when she was, but no one else said anything about seeing her. The only one no one seems to be able to place at the scene at any time during that day, after Eric saw him early in the morning, is Phillip."

"Don't sound so disappointed." Granny tapped his name with one long rhinestone-studded fuchsia nail. "Maybe he's the only one who was smart enough to make sure he had an alibi because he was the only one who knew he'd need one."

Hmm...she hadn't thought of that. "That could be true. What I really need to do is talk to Whitney again and see if I can pinpoint a more precise time from her, get in touch with Tiny and ask if he ever found Aldridge that day, and find out where Phillip was when his father was killed."

"Sounds like a plan." Granny Rose rubbed her hands together. "And after all of that, you can try to figure out who was taking pictures of me and Butch and your house and why."

Was that all? No problem. Wait a minute. Speaking of Butch... "Granny, where's Butch?"

She rolled her eyes. "I couldn't very well bring him to Chloe's shop with me, now, could I?"

"No." *Uh oh.* "So where is he?"

"I left him home. Why?"

"Alone?"

"Well, I certainly didn't hire a babysitter."

"With Ginger?"

"Oh...huh. I didn't think of that."

She didn't waste time massaging her temples. No doubt it would do nothing to ease the dull throb anyway. "All right, come on."

Granny Rose frowned. "Where are we going?"

"To check on Ginger and Butch, then I have to see a few people." Emma scribbled a quick plan—talk to Tiny, Whitney, Phillip—in the margin and ripped the page off the pad, then stuffed it into her pocket.

"You're not going to leave me alone at the house with a stalker, are you?"

Ah man, how could she have forgotten about the stalker? She needed to hit the brakes for about ten seconds and figure out a plan of action.

"Don't worry about it." Chloe glanced at her watch. "I'm just about ready to close up anyway. Why don't you go do what you have to, and I'll take Granny Rose home and check on Ginger and Butch, then stay with her until you get back."

"What about dinner?" Granny asked. "With what all's been going on, I haven't had time to cook."

"No problem." Chloe flipped over the Closed sign. "We'll ask Jade to pick up pizza and bring it over."

"Sounds like a plan. Thank you, Chloe." With that resolved, Emma kissed Granny Rose's cheek then turned to Chloe. "I'll tell you what, I'll stop by Jade's and ask her to get the pizza. I want to see if she'll call Whitney and find out if she'll talk to me anyway."

"Perfect, thanks." Chloe opened the register and lifted out a small stack of bills.

"Thank you for staying with Granny. I'm really not comfortable leaving her alone without knowing what's going on." At least, she wasn't when she remembered there was someone possibly stalking her. And to think she'd gone into Chloe's with the expectation of finding peace and ordering her thoughts.

Emma walked down the road toward Little Bits. So much for clearing her head. When she'd walked into Pocket Books with her mind whirling at a hundred miles an hour, she wouldn't have thought it possible she'd leave even more confused than when she'd gone in.

"Oh, hey, Emma." Max fell into step with her. "I was just on my way to see Jade."

"Me too."

His cheeks reddened. "Mind if I walk with you?"

"Of course not." Thunder rumbled as the sky started to darken. Wind picked up, kicking up a scattering of leaves that had fallen. "Were you able to find out anything more about Phillip?"

"Oh, yeah." He pulled a flash drive out of his pocket. "Plenty."

"Seriously? Like what?"

"I'll tell you and Jade together, so I only have to go through it once. If that's okay," he hurried to add.

"Sure."

He held the door open for her to precede him into the shop.

"Thanks."

Jade looked up from the register. "Hey there. Just give me a sec. I'm counting out the register."

Max's gaze stayed glued to Jade as he crossed the shop and tripped over a slight dip in the wood flooring. He stumbled, regained his footing, and practically fell into an armchair and crossed one leg over the other as if he'd meant to do exactly that. All the while, his attention never strayed from Jade bent over the register, lower lip caught between her teeth in concentration.

If Emma knew Jade would say yes, she'd encourage him to just go for it and ask her out. But, since she couldn't be sure Jade would accept, and she didn't want to see Max hurt, better to keep her mouth shut and mind her own business. Granny Rose could learn a lesson from her.

Jade dropped the last of the bills into a deposit bag, then wrote something down and tucked the paper into the bag with the cash. Once she was done, she put the bag into her purse, locked the front door, and flopped into a chair next to Emma's. "I'm exhausted."

"Busy day?"

"The busiest. Seems murder gives people the sudden urge to shop. Go figure." She stretched her arms over her head, arched her back. "So, what's going on?"

Emma gestured toward Max. "Max was just about to tell me what he found out about Phillip Aldridge."

"Oh, um, yeah, right." Max hitched himself up straighter and cleared his throat, like a school boy who'd been daydreaming when the teacher called on him. Hopefully, that would untie his tongue. He held up the flash drive. "Can I use your computer?"

"Sure." Jade pointed toward her laptop, which still sat open on the counter beside the register, but made no move to get up.

While Max hurried over to grab the laptop, Emma brought them both up to date on Eric's fingerprints being found on the murder weapon, Tiny's apparent investment loss and resulting tirade, and Arianna's flat tire.

"Has anyone heard from her yet?" Concern creased Jade's brow.

"Not that I know of." Emma's concern echoed Jade's. The fact that Broderick Aldridge was murdered just before she disappeared didn't bode well. Unless she killed him and took off, but what motive could she possibly have had? "And then there was the woman who was following Granny Rose and taking pictures of her and Butch."

Jade shot upright in her seat. "Someone's stalking Granny Rose? Is she okay?"

"Yeah, Chloe's with her now. I'm supposed to tell you to pick up pizza and meet them at my house for dinner, but since I'm here anyway, you can just ride over with me, and we'll pick up the pizza on the way. Chloe can drop you back off for your cart later."

Jade sank back into the seat and nodded, letting her eyes fall shut. "Sounds better than having to drive."

"Pizza, huh?" Max slid a small side table over and set the computer on it. "I wouldn't mind some pizza."

"You're more than welcome to come, Max." The least Emma could do was invite him for pizza, especially after he'd gone through the trouble of researching Phillip for her so quickly. Besides, who knew? Maybe it would be just the nudge Jade needed to open her eyes and see how he felt about her.

He glanced at Jade, and a smile lit his face. "Thanks."

126

"Any time."

"Okay." Tilting the screen down so they could all see it from their seats, Max pulled up the information he'd put on the flash drive.

Emma leaned forward. "That looks like a court document."

"That's because it is." Max rubbed his hands together, then started typing. A moment later, he pointed to the court website he'd pulled up. "See here. It seems Phillip Aldridge tried to have his parents declared incompetent and take over control of their finances."

"Are you serious?" Suddenly, Jade didn't seem so tired. "When?"

"Coincidentally, just after Broderick signed the contract for his new tiny home and presumably informed Phillip he'd have to get out." His fingers flew over the keys, and a list of numbers flashed on the screen.

"What's that?" Jade frowned at him.

"Broderick's bank account. One of them, at least. There could be more I haven't uncovered yet."

Emma surged out of the chair. "You can't do that, Max."

"Do what?" He looked up innocently.

"Hack someone's bank account."

"Of course, I can." He gestured toward the screen. "See?"

"Ah, man. I don't mean you're not capable of it, I mean you can't do it. It's illegal, isn't it?"

He shrugged it off. "It's not like I'm stealing any of the money, just taking a peek. Besides, there's nothing left to steal."

"What are you talking about?" Emma leaned over his shoulder to see the screen.

"See here." He pointed to the day Broderick died. "Emptied."

"Broderick emptied the account?"

"I mean, I can't say for sure it was him, and I can't tell what time the transaction was made, but someone withdrew more than ten thousand dollars on the same day he was killed."

"Well, dang." No wonder all the checks bounced. "Do you think Broderick did it on purpose so the checks he wrote for the move wouldn't clear?"

Jade shook her head, frowned at the screen. "Maybe it wasn't him. Maybe

Mildred didn't agree with him inviting a woman he fathered while married to her into her home, while he was pretty much dumping everything she owned and leaving their son out in the cold, so she helped herself to the money."

"Could be. But something was off when she pulled up the bank website while I was at her house." She wished now she'd been able to get a better look at the screen, to see what had put a hitch in Mildred's stride when she'd first pulled up the account.

"What do you mean off?" Jade asked.

"When she first pulled up the account, she seemed surprised, but then she turned the screen away, so I couldn't tell what was wrong. She did put enough money into the account to cover the bounced checks, though." She pointed to the transaction Mildred had made while Emma was there with her, transferring funds from a different account into the one in question. "So we know she had access to the account."

"And we know there's more than the one account I've uncovered so far," Max added.

"But we don't know who else might have had access to them." Eyes narrowed, Jade studied the information on the screen.

Emma couldn't find anything that seemed out of the ordinary before that one large deposit. Deposits went in, checks went out. Nothing hinky. Until, that is, Broderick or someone else who had access to the account withdrew one large lump sum on the day he was killed. "Possibly Phillip?"

"Did Phillip know about Whitney?" Max asked.

"Not that we know of. Phillip seems to have been conveniently missing in action that whole day." But where was he? He must do something all day, other than linger in his mother's hallway eavesdropping on her conversations. "Hey, Max, can you find out if Phillip has a job and what he does?"

He wiggled his fingers and hunched over the laptop.

"No, wait. Why don't we do it at my house after we get the pizza. I don't want to leave Granny Rose for that long when I don't know what's going on. Besides, I need to get in touch with Tiny and see why he hasn't returned my calls." Chloe had offered to take Granny Rose home so she could take care of her calls, and instead, she'd once again gotten caught up in talk of murder. "That reminds me, Jade, would you mind giving Whitney a call? I want to see if she's willing to sell the caboose house to Granny Rose."

"Sure thing." Jade stood and closed the laptop, then lifted a brow at Emma. "You don't really think Tiny could have been angry enough to kill Broderick, do you?"

"I don't know." He'd always seemed so calm and easygoing. Then again, if the rant Eric described wasn't exaggerated, there was clearly a side to him she didn't know. "Not really, I guess."

"Why not?" Max took the computer from her, plugged it back in, and slid it under the counter. "It wouldn't be the first time."

"The first time what?" Emma asked absently as she searched her phone for the pizza parlor number. They'd definitely need at least two pies. Maybe she'd get one with pepperoni.

"The first time Tiny killed someone."

Chapter Sixteen

Emma was speechless long enough for Jade to turn off the lights, questions ricocheting around her head, before she finally settled on the only one that made sense. "What are you talking about, Max?"

"Walk and talk, Merlin." Jade held the door open, waited for them to exit, then locked up behind them. "I'm starved."

After Emma called in the order and dug her keys out of her bag, she gestured to where she'd parked in front of Pocket Books. She glanced around to make sure no one was in hearing distance and kept her voice low. "What do you mean Tiny killed someone? You can't just blurt something like that out without elaborating."

"Sorry. I just figured it was common knowledge, so I assumed you knew."

Emma looked at Jade, who simply shook her head.

"What happened?"

"It was way back, before Mini-Meadows was even a thought. Tiny and I grew up right down the road in the same small town, went to the same schools, but he was a year ahead of me and a big-time jock, so everyone in the school knew who he was. I, on the other hand, was a computer geek and not even a blip on his radar." He said it in the matter-of-fact way of someone who'd accepted his role in life early on and embraced it. "When I first ran into him in Mini-Meadows, he didn't recognize me, but I knew who he was right away."

As much as Emma wanted him to hurry up and get to the killing part, she took a deep breath, filling her lungs with the scent of the coming thunderstorm, and waited for him to tell it his way.

"Anyway, at the time of the killing, Tiny insisted that he was walking home from practice one day when he got jumped by two guys, guys from a rival school who'd been known to torment our players from time to time. Supposedly, they went at him with a bat, broke a couple of ribs before he was able to take them down and get away. Unfortunately, one of them died on the way to the hospital."

"Was Tiny arrested?" She hit the button on the key fob, and they all piled into the car as the first fat raindrops splattered the windshield.

"Sure was, but he was found innocent. Self-defense." Max gripped the backs of both seats, pulled himself forward, and paused while they settled in.

Sadly, the one thing Mini-Meadows didn't boast was a pizza parlor. Good thing she had her car with her and not the golf cart she used to run around town, since they'd have to leave the development.

Once Jade had her seatbelt on, she motioned for Max to continue.

"That's about it. After the trial, he and his parents moved out of town, and I didn't see or hear anything else about him until I moved in here and ran into him. Like I said, he didn't remember me but seemed uncomfortable when I mentioned going to school with him, so I just let it drop, wished him a good day, and went about my business."

"Why do you think he was uncomfortable?"

He shrugged. "He'd made a life for himself here, ran his own business. I just assumed he didn't want his past running rampant through the gossip mill. Not that I blame him."

"No, me neither." But Emma was going to look him up first chance she got, make sure there wasn't more to the story than Max had heard or remembered. Tiny was a big guy, and if he had a short fuse, he could certainly inflict some major damage on someone like Broderick Aldridge.

"There's a spot." Jade pointed out a parking spot a few spaces from the pizza place, and Emma pulled in.

"Be right back." She made a mad dash for the front door, splashing through ankle-deep rivers of water as the rain pounded down on her. While she waited for the two customers in front of her on line to be helped, shivering in the air-conditioned shop, she glanced at the small TV that hung in one corner and was tuned to the local news station. A picture of a young woman, auburn hair spilling over her shoulders in waves, green eyes sparkling with her huge smile flashed on the screen. The caption underneath read, "Have you seen this woman?" It also gave Arianna Jenkins's name and a tip line number to call with any information.

For some reason she couldn't explain, Emma had a sneaking suspicion Arianna could shed some light on what happened to Broderick Aldridge, if she was still alive to do so. Was it possible whoever had killed Aldridge had also taken out Arianna? Had she witnessed something that made her a target? Or could it be possible she'd killed him? For what reason, though?

And wasn't that the million-dollar question.

"Next," the harried-looking cashier called out, intruding on Emma's train of thought.

Emma moved up in line, paid, and took two pies from the young man behind the counter. The aroma of cheese, sauce, and oregano wafted up to her, making her mouth water. She hadn't realized how hungry she was.

After putting the boxes in the back of the Jeep, she called Granny Rose to check in and let her know she was on her way. By the time she arrived home, Granny had already set the table, put out drinks, and fed Butch and Ginger.

Emma stepped out of her wet shoes by the door, then set the pizza boxes on the counter. She petted Butch's head and scratched behind Ginger's ears. Not even Butch's presence could deter Ginger from the scent of pizza. The thought of going back out in the storm did not appeal, especially after just coming into her cozy home, filled with friends and the aroma of good food, but she wasn't letting Granny Rose go out alone, especially after dark, until she had a better understanding of who'd been following her. "Did you walk Butch yet?"

"Yes."

"Granny, I don't—"

"Relax, Chloe came with me, and we just walked him right outside. It was starting to rain by then anyway." She handed Emma a paper plate. "Stop worrying and eat."

"Thanks." Emma set the plate on the counter. As much as she would have liked to change into dry pajamas before sitting down to dinner, she didn't want to be rude and leave her guests. She'd wait until everyone went home to change. But her email couldn't wait. She hadn't checked it all day, and she always made sure to return emails from customers within a few hours. "Just give me a minute to check my email. Everyone, help yourselves."

Since her breakfast bar wouldn't seat everyone, they all just grabbed slices and soda cans and made themselves comfortable, Jade and Granny Rose at the breakfast bar, Chloe and Max in the living room. Not that it mattered where anyone sat. In such close quarters, it was easy enough to carry on a conversation no matter where you were.

Even from her desk, Emma could keep up with the conversation—unsurprisingly a recap of Broderick's murder—while she scrolled through her email. Junk, junk, Gabriella Moreno asking if she'd gotten in touch with Tiny and letting her know she'd spoken to Jade and had set up an appointment with her. "Thanks for meeting with Gabriella, Jade."

"She sounded like a real sweetheart."

"She is. You'll like her."

"Probably better than the last client you sent me." Even as the words slid out, she winced. "Sorry."

"Don't worry about it." What could she say? Jade wasn't wrong. She hovered over an unfamiliar email address, almost hit delete, but the subject line read, *Urgent.* With a sigh and the expectation of more spam, she clicked on the email and opened it.

You're gonna want to stop asking questions.

What the... She clicked on the first attachment, and a picture of Granny Rose and Butch standing in front of Emma's house popped up. Emma gasped.

"Hey, what's wrong?" Jade set her pizza aside and stood. "Emma?"

"I..." No words would come.

"Emma." It only took a few steps for Jade to cross the room and lean over Emma's shoulder to see the screen. She gripped Emma's shoulder and squeezed. "Okay, Emma. It's okay. I'll call Detective Montgomery."

133

She gripped Jade's arm. "No. Wait."

"What do you mean wait?" Jade held her phone, ready to dial.

"I have to think for a minute." Anger crept in slowly to replace the shock. Bad enough, someone had made Granny Rose feel afraid in her own community, but now they had the nerve to threaten her?

"What's going on?" Max stood beside Jade, studied the email and picture on the screen. "Do you know who it's from?"

Emma shook her head.

"Here, get up." He held the chair back and waited for Emma to move, then took her place and started hammering on the keyboard.

"What are you doing?"

"I'm going to see if I can figure out who sent it and from where?"

"You can do that?"

He shrugged. "We'll see."

Emma turned to find Jade, Chloe, and Granny Rose watching her. Since Jade had already filled them in, it saved Emma the trouble. With her legs a little rubbery, but her nerves too jittery to sit still, she moved to lean against the counter. "What do you think we should do?"

"Call the police." Jade held up the phone. "What else would we do?"

Though she hesitated to voice her fears out loud, not wanting to frighten Granny Rose any further, sheltering her from the truth wouldn't do any good. Besides, Granny Rose was not one to be sheltered, at least, this new version of Granny Rose wasn't. "What if whoever sent the message is watching the house? If they see the police come, they'll know I called."

"They didn't say not to," Jade argued. "They'd have to assume you'd call the police if someone threatened your grandmother."

"Maybe, but I still don't want to do anything to anger anyone." She turned to Granny, gripped her arms gently, and pressed her forehead against hers. "I'm so sorry, Granny Rose. I never should have let you get involved in this. I don't even understand how I got involved, really, but I want you to do me a favor."

"No."

"I want..." She lurched upright. "Wait, what? What do you mean no, I haven't even told you the favor yet."

"You want me to go back home to your father's mansion where I can be locked up and protected." As usual, Granny could read her thoughts. Or, more likely, just knew how she'd react.

But Emma was not giving in on this. "Well, yeah. I love having you here, but if anything ever happened to you, I'd never forgive myself."

"First of all, honey, I don't run from trouble. And second, there's no way I'm leaving you here alone if there's even a remote possibility you could be in danger. Besides..." She turned to Butch, who stood at her side, and patted his head. "Butch here will protect us, won't you, boy?"

He barked once, and even though Emma didn't think he'd understood Granny's question and barked in response, it still helped ground her. Of course, you never knew. It seemed there'd been some kind of bond between Granny Rose and Butch pretty much since they'd met. "Okay. Let's just sit down and think for a minute."

"Here, drink this." Chloe handed her a glass of water and pulled a stool out from the breakfast bar. "Sit."

Emma nodded and did as she was told. "We need to figure out who sent that message."

"Working on it," Max called over.

Jade squeezed her shoulder in a gesture of support. "It would help if we knew who could have realized you were asking questions."

"It's not like I'm investigating the case or anything. Not really, anyway. Just curious and trying to figure out what could have happened." And now Granny Rose was in danger because she'd somehow gotten herself involved in this whole mess. She never should have taken the Aldridge job, should have walked away the first time he was rude to someone she'd suggested he hire. What a disaster. But there was no way she could back down now. At least not until they'd found whoever sent the message threatening Granny Rose and made sure they got locked away in a cell.

Granny Rose wrapped an arm around Emma's waist, Butch glued to her side at alert. While he might not understand exactly what was going on, he clearly sensed the tension.

"Well, you must have spoken to someone who thought you were getting a little too close to learning something," Granny Rose said.

"Huh." She hadn't thought of that. Maybe she'd gotten closer than she thought to the killer, stepped on his or her toes, so to speak. "Okay, so who did I talk to?"

"Eric, for one." Jade retrieved two plates, handed Max another slice, and sat down next to Emma with her own slice. "And Mildred."

"I didn't speak to Eric until after the pictures of Granny Rose were taken, so he'd have had to be nervous even before our conversation, but Phillip knew I talked to Mildred. And, uh." She'd also talked to Whitney, but she didn't want to mention that, considering she and Jade were friends.

"It's okay, Emma. Whitney's name has to go on the list too. I understand that." Jade took a bite of the lukewarm pizza.

"And it was a woman I saw taking pictures of me," Granny Rose added.

"Yeah, but that doesn't mean it was a woman who sent the pictures," Chloe said. "She could have been a photographer the killer hired to take the shots."

Shots. A shiver tore through Emma, and she leaned into Granny Rose. What if the photographer had been a sniper instead? Someone had already killed an elderly man, so they'd obviously have no problem killing someone else.

"Whoever she was, she may not even have known why she was taking them."

Chloe had a point. Emma fished the list out of her pocket, got up and kissed Granny Rose's soft curls, and grabbed a pen from her desk.

Merlin sat typing away, brow furrowed in concentration, so she didn't bother to ask if he'd found anything.

Instead, she returned to her seat and grabbed a slice of pizza. Granny Rose was safe for the moment, surrounded by friends and family. The best thing to do would be figure out who she'd spoken to, who they might have told, and how the information had gotten back to the killer. In a town the size of Mini-Meadows, where gossip spread like wildfire in a drought, it could well have come from anyone. Okay then, best to start at the beginning. So, who knew she was actively asking questions about the case?

Her gaze shot to Max Merlin, computer wizard. She'd spoken freely in front of him the day before, hadn't censored anything. Could he have repeated something to the wrong person? He had gone over to Libby's after speaking to them at Little Bits. Could he have gossiped and been overheard? She doubted he had anything to do with Broderick's murder. After all, as far as she knew, Max didn't even know Broderick Aldridge, and he'd seemed surprised to hear there'd even been a murder. But could he have been lying? She doubted it, but then again, she didn't really know anything about him.

Chapter Seventeen

A ll right, now she was being ridiculous. What would Max Merlin have had to do with Aldridge's murder? Nothing. But, at the end of the day, she couldn't dismiss the fact he might have innocently mentioned something in Libby's and the wrong person had overheard.

She slid the pizza boxes over, smoothed her timeline-suspect list on the counter, and studied the names written there in the order she suspected they'd visited Broderick the day he was killed. And it told her nothing new.

Butch propped his head in her lap and rolled his eyes up to stare at her.

"It's okay, Butch." She patted his head. "We'll figure it out."

He barked and danced backward, smacking into the side table beside the loveseat, rocking the lamp, and sending Ginger on a beeline for the stairway with a screech, then ran to the front door and spun in a circle.

"You have to go out, boy?" Granny Rose started for the door.

Emma stopped her with a hand on her wrist. "I'll take him out."

The fact that Granny Rose didn't argue told Emma she was more rattled than she'd let on.

Who could blame her? Emma took a bite of her cooling slice, then hooked the leash to Butch's collar and walked him out the door. As long as she stayed near the house and kept alert, they should be fine. At least the thunderstorm had passed, though the trees still dripped overhead. The floodlight beside her front door offered a small circle of light, but most of the neighborhood was bathed in darkness. The lack of streetlights had never bothered her before, but now she searched every shadow, listened intently for any sound that didn't belong, glanced up and down the road for any unfamiliar vehicles.

Her phone rang, and she practically jumped out of her skin. Laughing at herself, she pulled it out of her pocket. "You're going to have to hurry up there, Butch."

She glanced at the caller ID, then looked around nervously, hoping no one was watching her. Not that she planned on questioning Tiny about the murder. Not exactly, anyway. "Hey, there."

"Hi, Emma." Tiny's voice sounded strained. "Sorry I couldn't get back to you sooner. It's been a heck of a day."

Wasn't that an understatement. She allowed herself one moment to consider Tiny, a man she was friendly if not actually friends with. Another man she didn't really know. And yet, she just couldn't picture him threatening an old woman. Tiny was much more Teddy bear than grizzly. But still, she couldn't imagine him killing anyone either, even if it was self-defense.

"Emma?"

"Oh, what? Sorry, Tiny, my mind is all over the place."

"Don't worry about it. I just wanted to return your call and let you know the Aldridge check cleared this time."

"Oh, thank you. That's a relief." At least the people she'd recommended would be paid. Who knew? Maybe Mildred would even pay Emma's bill once she submitted the invoice. Although, it could possibly be in poor taste to ask for the final installment, considering she never actually moved Broderick into the house. Probably better to just let that go.

"Was that what you were calling me about?" A scattering of clicks came across the line. She'd better say whatever she wanted to say before she lost the connection.

"Oh, um," Obviously, he wasn't going to mention anything about the police looking for him. Unless he didn't know. Should she tell him? Maybe later. Definitely not while she was outside, where anyone could be lurking in the darkness, spying on her. A chill pricked the back of her neck as she searched the nearest shadows. "No, I, uh, wanted to see if you were interested in a job, not a tiny home, but a woman who's downsizing to a condo. She's having a baby and could probably use all those nooks and crannies you're so good at."

"Flattery'll get you everywhere." He laughed, the sound a relief. "Sure, I'll take a look. I suppose this is another rush job?"

"We-ell, actually." Seemed they were all rush jobs lately, everyone in a hurry to get where they were going.

"Don't worry about it. It's not a problem. Get in touch with her and set up an appointment, then shoot me a text and let me know when it is, and I'll meet you over there."

"Great, thanks, Tiny." Now, how could she bring up the police and the information Eric had given her discreetly? "So, anything else going on?"

He sighed. "I suppose you'll hear about it soon enough anyway, so you may as well hear it from me."

"Oh, what's that?" Her heart thundered in her chest. Probably not a bad thing, maybe it would drown out the sound of Tiny's voice if anyone was close enough to overhear him.

"I was questioned by the police a little while ago. That's why it took me so long to get back to you."

She chose her words carefully so as not to alert anyone to what they were discussing. Though, in her defense, she hadn't asked a single question. "It seems you're not the only one."

"Yeah, so I heard. Jade and Eric, too, right?"

"Mmm...hmm." Though, technically, Jade hadn't been questioned, she'd gone to the police with what she'd seen and heard. Maybe the fact that Detective Montgomery had questioned her in Little Bits rather than her going in to the station made it look as if he'd initiated contact. That could be a good thing. Emma had been so freaked out about Granny Rose being a target, she hadn't thought about who else might be in danger.

"Anyway." Tiny coughed, cleared his throat. "I got involved in a business deal with Aldridge and lost a substantial amount of money. I was pretty irate, to say the least, and I may have gone on a bit of a tirade about it, but I didn't kill the guy."

"Did you ever get ahold of him?" She kept her tone casual, not too interested, just a boring work-related conversation.

Butch pranced in a circle and headed for the door, but Emma wasn't quite ready to go in yet. Despite her fear of being overheard, this wasn't a conversation she wanted to have in front of a houseful of people, all of whom would undoubtedly be listening intently.

"Yeah, I found him."

"And what happened?"

"I yelled, ranted, threatened, and stormed off."

She waited. No way could she make "did you kill him?" sound like a casual conversation.

"But he was alive and well and thorny as ever when I left him." He blew out a breath. "Anyway, I just wanted to let you know what happened. I'm sorry, Emma. If you're no longer comfortable recommending me, I'll understand."

"Don't be silly. Of course I'll recommend you. You do amazing work. Besides, it's me who owes you an apology. It seems everyone I recommended for that job ended up having problems with him." Not to mention the police.

"Don't worry about it. It was my own fault I got involved with him financially. I should have known better. Did, really, he just made it sound so dang good."

"I'm sorry, Tiny."

"Nah. It's all good. So, we're okay?"

"Absolutely."

"Good. Just text me the info on the new job, and I'll be there."

"Thanks, Tiny." She realized her mistake the instant his name left her mouth, but it was too late to stop it. Besides, she was pretty sure she'd already said his name out loud at least once while they were speaking. She looked around, didn't see anyone—replayed the conversation in her head but didn't think she'd said anything that would let someone know they'd discussed anything other than business.

"See ya." He disconnected.

"Yeah, see ya." The instant she slid the phone into her pocket and started toward the house, Butch bolted, jerking hard on the leash, and she had to run to keep up. Her foot hit a slick patch of mud and went out from under her, sending her sprawling in the mucky puddle.

Butch stopped and looked back at her, then lowered his gaze and whimpered.

Keeping a firm grip on the leash with her mud-covered hand, she climbed slowly to her feet. She wiped the mud off her face and clothes as best she could. "It's all right, boy. It's not your fault."

He approached slowly as if gauging her mood.

She swiped her dirty hand over the back of her jeans, then patted his head. "Come on, let's go get changed."

This time, when she started to limp toward the house, her knee aching from twisting it when she fell, Butch walked sedately at her side.

She pushed the front door open, unhooked Butch's leash, and shut and locked the door behind her, then turned to find everyone staring at her.

Chloe jumped to her feet. "Are you okay?"

"What happened?" Granny Rose ran toward her with a dishtowel.

"It's all right, Granny, Butch just got a little overenthusiastic about coming back in. I'm fine. Only thing injured is my pride."

"Then why are you limping?"

"Okay, and maybe my knee." She gestured toward her computer. "Were you able to find out who sent the email?"

Max shook his head. "No, sorry, but I can tell you where it was sent from."

"Oh?" If he could determine where it was sent from, chances were good they could narrow down the sender. "Where?"

"E-Jitters. A small café right outside of Mini-Meadows."

"I know the place. I go in there for coffee all the time."

"Yeah, well, unfortunately, so do most of Mini-Meadows' residents," Max said.

"Oh." Disappointment surged. "Right."

"But…" He held up a finger, giving Emma the briefest rush of hope. "Since I can tell where and when it was sent, I'm going to see if I can access any surveillance cameras in the area. But I have to do that from home, so Jade's going to come with me, see if we recognize anyone going in or out."

Emma bit the inside of her cheek to keep from smiling and simply nodded. Maybe something good would end up coming out of this mess. "That'd be great, thank you."

He pushed back from the desk, stood, and pushed in the chair. "Will you and Granny Rose be okay here?"

"Yeah." She'd lock the doors as soon as Max, Jade, and Chloe left, and Butch would probably alert them if anyone was outside. Besides, Emma would be on the loveseat in the living room all night, and she doubted she'd get much sleep anyway. At the first sign of trouble, she'd just call 911. "We'll be fine."

Jade caught her lower lip between her teeth and glanced back and forth between Emma, Granny Rose, and the fairly flimsy deadbolt on the front door. "And you don't want to call Detective Montgomery?"

The last thing she wanted was a lengthy conversation with the detective, or anyone else. She was too exhausted to even think straight. And the air conditioning blowing on her soaking wet clothes raised goosebumps over her entire body. First, she needed a hot shower and warm pajamas, then she'd rest, clear her head, and start fresh in the morning. Hopefully, by then, Max would have found something. "There's not really anything he can do, at least, not yet. If Max is able to figure out who sent the email tonight, then we'll call him. Otherwise, why don't we wait until morning to give him a call?"

"Sounds like a plan," Jade said. "I'll let you know if we find anything."

"Thanks." She started to shiver, wrapped her arms around herself for warmth as her teeth all but chattered. "Why don't we meet up at Libby's for breakfast, and we'll talk more then?"

They all agreed.

"Okay, then, I'm going to get some clean clothes and take a shower." And clean up the mud she was now tracking through the entire house.

Ginger peeked at her through the railings at the top of the stairway, her tail flicking lazily back and forth. And, if Emma wasn't mistaken, she wore a very self-satisfied smirk.

"Before you do." Max pointed toward the laptop screen. "Two other things. First, there's a newspaper article here about Tiny's arrest when he was younger."

"All right, I'll take a look after I get changed. What's the other thing?"

"You wanted to know if Phillip Aldridge works, but as far as I can tell, the man's never worked a day in his life."

"Hmm…somehow, that doesn't come as any great surprise." Leaving her now cold pizza on the counter, she started up the stairs. Once she got cleaned up, and everyone was gone, she'd heat some up and sit down to eat. While she loved the company, the house was too crowded now for her to try to sort through the information she had and make any decisions. "Oh, Jade, will you get in touch with Whitney? See if she'll talk to me again?"

Even though there was no way Granny Rose was moving out and into her own house until this was resolved, Butch or no Butch.

"Sure thing," Jade said. She lifted her arms as if to hug Emma, eyed her up and down, then let them drop at her sides. "I'll see you in the morning."

Unless someone had overheard her talking to Tiny about the case, even though technically she hadn't asked any obvious questions, then maybe not so much.

Chapter Eighteen

When she reached Libby's the next morning, after a night spent tossing and turning on the loveseat without ever really falling asleep, Emma could barely keep her eyes open. Coffee. That's what she needed. A lot of coffee.

She hooked her bag over the back of her seat and sat between Granny Rose and Jade. While they usually took a booth, the addition of Granny and Max to their breakfast meant the need for one of the large round tables in the center of the room. Which, in turn, meant very little privacy and the potential for anything they said to be overheard.

As much as she hated to admit it, she was going to have to talk to Detective Montgomery about the threat to Granny Rose. Burying her head in the sand and pretending the problem didn't exist wouldn't make it go away. It might even make things worse, put Granny Rose in more danger. She should have dealt with it last night instead of just hoping the whole problem would go away.

She leaned closer to Jade and pitched her voice low. "Did you guys find anything?"

"Actually, we did. When they call Max 'Merlin,' they aren't kidding." She hooked a thumb toward a blushing Max. "The guy's amazing on a computer."

"Coming from the woman who's lucky she can work her cell phone," Emma said.

Jade grinned. Everyone, including Jade, knew technology wasn't her thing. Not that she wasn't smart, she was, but for some reason, she just couldn't grasp electronics and technology.

Emma figured she just wasn't interested, preferred a simpler life. Maybe she was on to something.

"Anyway," Jade whispered, "I have good news and bad news."

"Great." Searching for anyone who seemed at all interested in their conversation, Emma scanned the diner. When she didn't notice anyone overtly eavesdropping, she continued. "What's the good news?"

"Max was able to hack a security camera outside of the café the email was sent from."

"That's great." Her excitement only lasted a moment. "What's the bad news?"

"It's possible the email was sent on a time delay. And the surveillance footage is kind of grainy, making it hard to see people's faces clearly. Max is trying to clean it up some, but we think we saw Phillip, Eric, and Tiny all go in at different points throughout the day, all before the time the email was sent."

"So, it could have been any of them." Her hopes sank. "That doesn't narrow it down any. Did any of them go in with a woman?"

"No. The only woman I recognized that had anything to do with Broderick Aldridge was Whitney, but she wouldn't have sent you a threatening email."

"No." Probably. "Of course not."

"So." She gripped Emma's hand, squeezed. "Sorry that's not really helpful."

"Don't worry about it. It was a long shot anyway." Disappointed, Emma straightened and opened her menu. After three slices of pizza the night before, she wasn't particularly hungry, so she settled on oatmeal and fruit. "Did you get in touch with Whitney this morning and ask her if she could meet with me?"

"I tried, but she didn't answer, so I left a message." Jade studied her menu. "I'll text you as soon as I hear back from her."

"Yeah, thanks."

Libby arrived to take their order, not nearly as harried as she'd been the day before. She yanked a pen from amid her pink updo and held it over her pad. "What can I get you guys?"

Answers, to start, but Emma figured Libby didn't know any more than they did. Although, Libby was usually a good source of gossip, considering she spent all day long listening to rumors. Emma looked around. Even though the diner wasn't as crowded as the day before, a good number of customers lingered over breakfast and coffee. No way she could chance asking questions. Instead, she ordered a bowl of oatmeal with berries and let it go at that.

Once everyone had ordered, and Libby left them, Emma shook off thoughts of murder to concentrate on work. "Hey, Jade, when are you meeting with Gabriella?"

"This afternoon. Why? You want to tag along?"

"Maybe." Going through the house with the two of them would give her a good idea what Gabriella planned to keep, which would help her know what kind of space she'd need Tiny to create. Gabriella had seemed more than willing to part with things, but Emma had been down that road before. People usually ended up keeping more than they intended to, which was fine, but she'd have to find room for it all. "Can you give me a call on your way out, and I'll let you know?"

"Sure thing."

She pulled out a pad and wrote cubbies with baskets. If Tiny could build shelving into one wall, they could use some for bookshelves and partition others into cubes to put baskets in, or even better with a baby, fabric bins in colors of her choice. At first, they could be used for baby supplies, then as the baby got older, to keep toys organized. The bins could hold a lot, yet give a neat, clean, organized appearance. She'd like to run the idea past Gabriella, see what she thought.

Her gaze skipped to Granny Rose. She couldn't leave her alone.

Granny eyeballed her. "Oh, stop it, already. You're hovering like a mama hen. I'll be fine."

"Sorry, but I can't help worrying."

"You can't watch me twenty-four hours a day. You have to work. Plus, I'm still holding out hope one of these days you'll develop a social life."

Not likely. Desperate to avoid the "you need a husband lecture," Emma ignored the comment about her social life. But she couldn't ignore work.

"Will you stay with Chloe at Pocket Books until I get back?"

"Emma," she sighed, "I don't need a babysitter."

"Will you at least agree to stay home with the door locked until I get back? I'd feel better if you weren't alone." Maybe she'd call Detective Montgomery on her way, ask him to have a patrol car ride past the house a few times.

"I won't be alone. Butch will be with me. He'll take care of me just fine. And just in case he can't...." She opened her fanny pack and whipped out a small pistol. "This little beauty oughta do the trick."

"Yikes, Granny." Emma's gaze shot around the diner to see if anyone had noticed. She lowered her voice to a harsh whisper. "What are you doing with that thing?"

"What?" Granny studied the gun and frowned. "I knew it. I should have gone with the big one—that thing was like a cannon, like in those *Dirty Harry* pictures, much more intimidating than this little pea shooter. She pointed the gun across the table toward Max. "Go ahead, make my day."

His eyes went wide, and he lurched upright, but he stopped just short of shooting his hands in the air.

"Granny!" Emma gripped her wrist and lowered her hand.

Granny Rose studied the compact weapon. "See, not nearly as intimidating as the big one, but anyway, that hunky salesclerk talked me out of it, told me this sexy little number suited me just fine, then he winked. You know I'm a sucker for a good wink. It's a lost art if you ask me."

Emma sent the salesclerk, wherever he was, a silent but heartfelt thank you. "Put that thing away. Now. Before you hurt yourself or someone else."

She shrugged and dropped the weapon back into her bag. "I don't see what the problem is. A woman living alone should be able to defend herself."

Emma propped her elbows on the table, lowered her face into her hands, and prayed for patience. Not that she disagreed about protecting yourself, but still... "Have you ever fired a gun, Granny Rose?"

"Well, no, but how hard could it be? The winker at the gun shop said it was real easy to use, and I watched one of those YouTube videos that showed me how to load it, so all I have to do is point and shoot."

Emma jerked her head upright. "You're carrying around a loaded weapon in your purse?"

"Well, dear…." Granny scowled at her as if she had ten heads, then she used the haven't-you-a-shred-of-sense tone Emma remembered so well from her childhood. "What good is it going to do me if it's not loaded? What am I supposed to do if I get mugged? Ask the mugger to just hold on a sec while I load my weapon?"

The fact that she made a certain amount of sense didn't help Emma's argument. "Okay, Granny, but if you're going to carry a weapon, small, sexy, or otherwise, we need to go to the range so you can learn how to use it properly."

Her eyes widened. "That's a great idea. What better place to search out potential husband material than a nice, manly gun range?"

Jade covered her mouth with a napkin and lowered her gaze. Her shaking shoulders and the tears in her eyes gave her away.

Thankfully, Libby arrived with their breakfast just then, and Emma was saved from having to answer. She sat back and waited while Libby set her bowls in front of her, wishing she'd gone for the western omelet with home fries and a Kaiser roll slathered with butter. "Thanks, Libby."

"No problem." She leaned over so only Emma could hear her. "But please don't let your granny take that gun out again. I already had to soothe one couple after her Annie Oakley imitation."

Emma winced. "Sorry about that. She'll keep it put away."

"Thanks." Libby grinned. "She sure is a feisty one."

"You don't know the half of it." Maybe Granny Rose wasn't the one who needed Detective Montgomery's protection. She almost pitied the fool who tried to attack her. Once Libby left them, she turned to Granny Rose. "Until we can get you to the range, would you please stay with Chloe or inside while I go out to Gabriella's with Jade? Then if Whitney gets back to her, we can stop by on the way home to ask her about selling you the house."

"No problem. Butch and I will stay home. I want to catch up on my stories, anyway; I haven't had much time for daytime TV since the murder."

"Thanks." Knowing Granny would stay in the locked house watching soap operas for most of the afternoon freed her up to take a ride with Jade and see if she could get in touch with Whitney, though there was no way she'd let Granny Rose live alone until this whole mess was cleared up and the killer caught, even if Whitney did sell her the tiny home.

Jade's phone rang, and she looked at the caller ID and frowned.

"What's wrong?" Emma tried to see the screen over her shoulder.

She turned the phone toward Emma. "Mildred Aldridge."

"What do you think she wants?"

Jade shrugged, pushed back from the table, and stood. "I don't mean to be rude, but if you'll excuse me, I really need to know."

"Go." Emma really needed to know too.

Jade answered the call as she walked out the front door.

While she waited for her to return, Emma sprinkled cinnamon onto her oatmeal and took a bite. It was no omelet, but it was good, warm and creamy with a bit of honey.

"So," Chloe started. "Did you decide if you're going to call Detective Montgomery and report the threatening email?"

"Yeah, I'm going to give him a call right after breakfast. If nothing else, maybe he'll at least have someone ride by the house now and then to make sure no one's lurking."

"For what it's worth, I agree." Chloe bit into her Spanish omelet and sighed.

"Me too." Max dug into his meat lover's omelet. "Can't be too careful."

Not all that hungry, probably largely due to stress, Emma picked at her oatmeal, stirring it around more than eating it. When the front door opened, she glanced up.

Jade returned to the table, dropped her phone into her bag, and sat, her expression neutral. "She wanted to know if I'd stop by later and take the rest of Broderick's things. She says she'll give me a good deal on whatever he left; she just wants it all gone."

The fact she'd call Jade surprised Emma, especially after Phillip had accused her of stealing. "How does Phillip feel about that?"

"She doesn't seem to care."

"Are you going to do it?"

She shrugged. "Why not? I'll offer her a fair price and take it from there.

If she's interested, great, if not, so be it. Do you mind stopping on the way back from Gabriella's?"

"No, that's fine." Now that Max had told her he couldn't find any job Phillip held, she couldn't help but wonder what Phillip did with all his time. "I'm curious to see if Phillip's there."

"Hey!" Granny Rose lurched to her feet, tumbling her chair behind her, and pointed out the window. Everyone in the diner paused mid-bite to stare. "That's the car."

Before Emma had a chance to turn around, Granny took off running.

"Ah, man." Emma tossed her napkin onto the table and ran after Granny Rose.

Chapter Nineteen

Emma followed Granny Rose outside and found her standing next to the Jeep, one hand on the door handle, shifting impatiently back and forth from one foot to the other. "Granny Rose, what is going on?"

She pointed down the road into the development. "You have to follow that car. It's the one the woman who was taking pictures of me was driving."

"Are you sure?" Emma went to reach into her bag for her keys and realized she'd left the bag hanging over the chair back in her haste to follow Granny Rose outside.

"Of course, I'm sure." Craning her neck to see down the road, Granny bounced up and down as she tried to keep track of the retreating vehicle. "Wouldn't have said so if I wasn't. Now, hurry."

"Hang on. I forgot my keys, I'll be—"

"Hurry, they're getting away."

Emma whirled back toward Libby's.

Jade was already running toward her, holding Emma's bag out. "I thought you might need this. Chloe's taking care of the bill."

Max, who'd run out on Jade's heels, skidded to a stop beside Granny Rose and gripped the back door handle. "Was that the woman who was taking pictures of you?"

"It was, and she's getting away." Granny Rose yanked on the still-locked door handle.

Emma fished out the keys and hit the button to unlock the doors. "Get in."

They all piled in, Granny Rose in the front with Max right behind her and

152

Jade next to him in the back seat.

Emma fumbled the key into the ignition.

"What are you waiting for? Floor it. She's getting away." Granny Rose flung one hand in the direction the vehicle had gone as she slammed her door shut. "Burn rubber, baby."

While still trying to buckle her seatbelt, Emma checked her rearview mirror and hit the gas, spitting up gravel as she pulled out. Though she hadn't gotten a good look at the car, she had caught its rear end headed down Main Street and rounding the corner toward Emma's house. Hoping not to lose her, Emma took the turn a little too fast.

Granny braced herself against the dashboard and let out a hoot.

Max leaned forward between the seats. "I have to admit, if I'd realized how much fun you guys are, I'd have started hanging around a lot sooner."

"I know, right." Granny did a little bounce and shimmy in her seat. "I'm sorry for accusing you of being dull, Emma. I guess it really was just that you were busy with work when I first moved in. This is much better."

A quick look in the rearview mirror showed Jade grinning back at Emma and shaking her head. "Did you see which way she went?"

"No, but since I don't see her ahead of us, and the only other road leading out from back here is the dirt fire access road, I'm guessing they went that way." Since none of the houses on the block boasted a garage, Emma checked the driveways and carports for any unusual vehicles. Nothing. The woman had to have taken the access road, which meant she was probably familiar with the area. From watching Granny Rose? Or was she a local? Of course, there was a third option. There was always a chance Granny Rose was mistaken about it being the same vehicle. "Did anyone happen to get the license plate number?"

Of course, no one had. That would have made things too easy. They could have just handed it over to Detective Montgomery and been done with the whole mess. Now, she'd have to catch up, at least get close enough to read the tag number, if nothing else.

"Doesn't that road fork a little ways up?" Max slid back and buckled his seatbelt.

Thankfully, the four-wheel-drive Jeep wouldn't have any trouble navigating the dirt road. The last thing she needed was to get stuck in the middle of the forest with a killer. Emma hit the turn signal, even though there was no one around for miles. The back end fishtailed as she made the turn onto gravel, but she quickly regained control as the road turned to hardpacked dirt. "The fork is about a quarter mile up, leading out toward the main road or deeper into the forest. See if you can see a dust cloud or tracks to indicate which direction they went."

While the others kept a close eye out for clues to the car's whereabouts, Emma had a quick moment for an internal debate over whether or not she should be chasing a potential stalker-killer into the woods. Of course, she already knew the answer to that, but she couldn't think of any better way to stop the threat to Granny Rose. Besides, there was no saying she had to stop and confront whoever was driving, even if she did find them. She could easily follow her, see where she went, and then call the police and tell them where to find the vehicle. But if she lost her, she'd be no closer to finding out the truth. She'd have nothing, not even a description of the car or driver to give the detective. And Granny would still be in danger.

"There." Jade pointed toward the left, where a dust plume had already begun to settle over a fresh set of tracks. Towering pines spread in every direction. Swampy muck encroached, narrowing the road.

Emma turned left in pursuit. Leaving the road to turn onto the narrower trail, bordered on both sides by swampy brush and prehistoric-looking pine trees, brought a change from hard-packed dirt to softer sand, which was much more difficult to navigate. The Jeep bounced and slid as she struggled to keep it on the increasingly challenging pathway. "Are you sure that's the car that was following you, Granny?"

"Yup, pretty sure." She looked around the forest. "It sure is beautiful in here, in a creepy, horror-movie sort of way."

"No kidding." Emma loved the Florida wilderness—from a comfortable distance. While she enjoyed walks on nature trails throughout the numerous parks in the area, trapsing through the deepest forests, even in a four-wheel-drive vehicle, was a bit out of her comfort zone. "Do you think we should keep going?"

Max unbuckled his belt and slid forward again. He held his phone out in front of him so Emma could see. "I was able to get a map of the area."

When she reached a stretch of solid dirt roadway, she stopped and checked the map. "This trail goes on for about ten miles, winding through the forest with no apparent trails to turn off onto."

"At least none that are on the map," Max agreed. He pointed out a section of the map. "It shows an open field about a mile farther up with a scenic lookout that might offer a place to turn around."

"Do you think that's what we should do?" When no one answered, Emma shifted into gear and started forward. Some of her original urgency to catch the fleeing vehicle had begun to fade as they bounced and rocked over the increasingly rough terrain. Since there was nowhere to make a U-turn on the narrow road, with swampy ditches filled with murky water and probably an abundance of critters she'd do well to avoid, bordering either side of it, she pressed forward while considering her options. On the one hand—

"Stop!" Granny yelled.

Emma slammed on the brakes.

Granny lurched forward in the seat until the seatbelt tightened and yanked her back.

Emma's heart surged into her throat. "What's wrong?"

"Back that way. I thought I saw...." Granny pointed back in the direction they'd come and shook her head. "In the ditch."

A variety of possibilities pummeled Emma at warp speed—alligator, snake, bear, the vehicle they were in pursuit of—

"You have to go back." Tremors shook Granny Rose's hands as she unhooked the seat belt and reached for the door handle.

Emma lay a hand on her arm. "Wait. You're not getting out. I'll just back up. What did you see?"

Granny Rose sucked in a deep breath, her pale skin almost translucent.

Looking over her shoulder, Emma shifted into reverse.

Jade and Max had both unfastened their seatbelts and were staring out the back window, blocking Emma's view.

"Did you guys see anything?"

They both shook their heads.

"Wait. Stop." Apparently, having composed herself, Granny looked in the side-view mirror. "I don't think you should back up. I'm pretty sure I saw someone back there. In the ditch. But if so, it's probably a crime scene, and you shouldn't back up."

Emma braked.

"If it's a crime scene, we should do whatever we can to preserve it." Max scratched his head. "How sure are you?"

Granny kept her gaze on the mirror, squinting as if it would allow her to see what was there. "Sure enough that it warrants a second look, but not quite sure enough to call the police without double checking."

"Okay." Emma parked but left the Jeep running in case they had to make a quick getaway and opened her door. "You guys stay here with Granny Rose. I'll go back and take a look."

As she walked toward the back of the Jeep, she scanned the area, mindful of the fact they'd pursued a possible murder suspect into the woods. Could whoever was driving have dumped the body? Was she far enough ahead of them to stop, get rid of the body, and move on without them seeing? Probably. But what if the woman who was stalking Granny Rose was the one in the ditch? What if she hadn't been a body when they went into the forest but had been killed on the spot? If so, could she be alive and in need of help?

Emma picked up the pace, still surveilling the area, not only for killers but for any wildlife that might be lurking nearby, and screamed when a hand landed on her shoulder.

"Sorry." Max yanked his hand away and stepped back. "I didn't mean to startle you, but I didn't want you to go alone."

Emma pressed a hand against her chest to keep her heart from leaping out and tried to catch her breath. "What about preserving the crime scene and all that?"

"I won't go too far. I'll stay with you, but I'll just hang back and keep watch for anything dangerous."

Since he'd managed to sneak up on her without even trying while she was keeping a wary eye, she couldn't really argue. "Okay, fair enough."

With Max watching her back, she inched forward. The swampy odor gagged her. Mosquitos swarmed. The hot sun beat down on her, and sweat trickled down her back. What was she doing? Her hair stuck to her neck and face, and she used her wrist to swipe it back. Tiny gnats she couldn't do anything about swarmed her face.

An arm came into view first. A woman's arm, her pink, rhinestone-studded nails a vulgar contrast to the boggy surroundings. "Oh, no. Max, stay there and call the police."

With a quick glance over her shoulder to be sure he did as she'd asked, she hurried forward, trying to stay toward the harder ground at the edge of the path. While she didn't want to mess up any evidence, she couldn't very well wait for help to find them, even if Max could manage to give them decent directions. If there was any chance the woman was still alive and needed medical attention, Emma might be her only chance for survival.

Her foot slid down the muddy slope, and she went down on one knee in the muck. Catching herself at the last minute, she managed to keep from faceplanting in the swamp, barely. She crept forward more cautiously.

"Emma, wait." Jade moved past Max, coming toward her.

"Stay there, Jade," Emma yelled.

She paused for a moment, narrowed her eyes, then started forward, following the path Emma had taken.

Torn between getting to the woman and keeping Jade from coming with her, Emma paused. "Please, Jade, just go back and stay with Max for a minute."

Jade paused but stayed where she was.

Mindful of her footing, Emma reached the woman. Kneeling beside her, even though she could tell it was too late, she felt for a pulse. Nothing. Tears threatened. If she had driven faster, been able to catch up to the car, would she have been able to save her? Had she even been killed by the driver, or was it a coincidence the vehicle had driven right past her body? She finally lost her battle and let the tears fall. "Ah, man, Whitney. I'm so sorry."

Chapter Twenty

After another round of questioning with the increasingly suspicious detective—who at first had a hard time believing she and Jade had simply stumbled upon another body but looked at them with slightly less derision once they'd explained about the stalker and Granny Rose and why they were following the vehicle into the woods—Emma parked across from Pocket Books, and they all piled out of the car.

Jade's eyes were still red from crying, and Max held her hand in an offer of comfort, continually assuring her Whitney's death wasn't her fault. Despite knowing there was nothing she could have done to save Whitney, the guilt was a difficult burden for her to bear.

Unfortunately, with no license plate number, no clear description of the vehicle or the driver, and no real idea what direction the vehicle had fled, Detective Montgomery didn't hold out much hope they'd find the car or driver. Though he did promise to keep Emma informed about any progress on that front and to have a patrol car routinely drive past her house until the killer was caught.

Chloe whipped open the door and hurried out. "Oh, my gosh. Is everyone okay?"

Emma spared a quick look at Jade and lay a hand on her shoulder.

Jade gripped Emma's hand with an ice-cold one of her own. The smile she offered was shaky, but at least she'd smiled. "I'll be okay, thanks."

"Come in, come in." Chloe held the door for them to enter.

The blast of cool air felt amazing after standing in the hot, humid swamp for the better part of the last few hours. Emma lifted her hair off her neck and basked in the cool breeze.

"After you guys ran out in such a hurry, I had Libby pack up what was left of your breakfast orders. I put them in the fridge, so if you're hungry…" Chloe gestured toward the mini-fridge at the back of the shop.

The thought of food turned Emma's stomach.

"I could eat." Granny headed toward the back.

Max followed close behind. "Me too."

Jade just shook her head and went to sit at the table.

"Your names are on the boxes." Taking a seat beside Jade, Chloe patted her hand and turned her attention to Emma. "What happened?"

After apologizing for running out on her the way they had, Emma gave Chloe a quick run-through of the events that had transpired, beginning with Granny Rose's claim she'd seen the woman who was stalking her.

"I said I saw the *car* that was stalking me." Granny Rose popped her to-go box in the microwave, folded her arms, and leaned against the counter. "I never actually saw the driver, so there's no guarantee it was the same woman."

Honestly, knowing Granny Rose, there was no guarantee it was even the same car, but finding Whitney made it seem likely. A shiver tore through Emma, and suddenly the air conditioning that was so blessedly refreshing a moment ago had the cold seeping all the way to her bones. What if it had been Granny Rose they'd found in that ditch? She shook off the thought. Had to if she was going to function with the killer still on the loose. But she'd be sticking close to Granny until the killer was found and locked up.

Emma pulled the timeline she'd started out of her back jeans pocket, unfolded it, and spread it out on the table.

Max glanced at the page as he set his food on the table and sat between her and Jade. "What's that?"

"I started a timeline of who was where on the day Broderick Aldridge was killed." Of the names on the list, the only one she'd so far managed to eliminate with any degree of certainty was Jade. One, because she'd said Broderick was standing outside looking into the open container, and Eric said he'd seen Broderick alive before he'd closed the container. Two, she knew Jade, and the other woman was no killer. Besides that, if she had killed him in a fit of rage, she'd have been uncontrollably distraught afterward, and she'd have taken responsibility for her actions. She crossed off Jade's name. She'd only included it because she was hoping to figure out if Jade or Whitney had been there first, but with Whitney gone, there was no way Emma could think of to pinpoint the timing of her visit.

"So, who was with him?" Chloe set a cup of coffee in front of Emma.

"Thanks." Emma had been so lost in thought, she hadn't even noticed she'd gotten up to make it.

Max shrugged. "From what you've said, he wasn't very well-liked. How many people could he have seen?"

"Turns out, more than you'd expect. I know Whitney was with him, as well as Mildred, because Whitney told us that." A quick glance at Jade showed she was holding up at the mention of her friend. Of course, Emma would have to add Whitney to the victim list. Huh…maybe that would help her pinpoint or eliminate someone as a suspect, assuming whoever had killed Broderick had also killed her. "Eric and Arianna were there moving his belongings into the storage container earlier in the day, and they returned later to pick up a check, which Broderick didn't give Eric, and he locked the container. And Tiny said he found Broderick and had words with him over a business deal or something, but he didn't say when, and I forgot to ask."

"What kind of business deal?" Max pulled a napkin out of the holder on the table and grabbed Emma's pen.

"I don't know exactly, only that Tiny got involved in some kind of business deal with Aldridge and invested money, then lost it all."

"Hmm." Max jotted a couple of notes on the napkin, then handed Emma back the pen.

Not that she knew what to write. She still couldn't cross any names off and didn't understand where Whitney fit in or how she'd ended up dead, though the inheritance plus eliminating the shock of having a new family member to deal with were kind of glaring motives. "Who'd have wanted to kill Whitney?"

"Phillip," Jade and Granny answered at the same time.

Emma couldn't argue, since it seemed likely his mother would inherit now, and chances were she'd make a will of her own naming her son the beneficiary. A flicker of fear touched Emma. Could Mildred be in danger? Maybe. But even if Phillip wanted to get rid of his mother, he'd have to wait until she inherited and then made a will of her own. So, she should be safe for the moment. "And yet, Phillip is the only one whose whereabouts I can't confirm for that day. The last time anyone remembers seeing him at Broderick's on the day he was killed was early in the morning. If he really doesn't work, where could he have been?"

Max reached over and tapped the page. "It seems to me, this is who you've got to track down."

"Arianna?" Emma frowned at the name he'd pointed to, then looked up at him. "Why?"

"Because she's nowhere to be found, and someone reported her missing. That means someone expected her to be somewhere, and she didn't arrive. The way I see it, she's either a suspect or another victim." He pushed his plate back and wiped his mouth, then looked at Chloe. "If you have a computer I can use, I'll see what I can find out about her."

"Sure thing." Chloe pushed back her chair and stood, then led him into the back room, where she had a small office. Though boxes and stacks of books covered most surfaces, a pathway led to a desk that was surprisingly free of clutter.

While the others crowded around the desk, Chloe keeping a watch out front for customers, Max sat and cracked his knuckles. "All right. Let's focus on Arianna. We know she didn't go home, or she wouldn't have been reported missing. So, if you were in trouble, where would you go?"

Emma tried to imagine being scared, alone. Without knowing Arianna's situation or frame of mind when she'd left, it was hard to think what she'd do. If she'd killed Broderick, she'd probably be frightened. Same if she'd witnessed his murder. So where would Emma go if she was scared and in trouble? Easy, Granny Rose. Or Jade or Chloe. "Maybe a friend or family member?"

Max studied something on the computer screen. "Then why the missing person's report?"

"True. So, where would she have gone?"

Granny Rose snapped her fingers. "A tire place."

"Huh?"

"Well, last time I got a flat tire, your father sent someone to change it. A real looker, too." Granny winked. "Anyway, after he put the spare on, he put the old tire in the trunk and told me where to drop it off to be fixed. So, if Eric changed her tire, he probably did the same thing."

That was actually a good idea. "Okay, so where's the nearest tire place?"

Jade already had her phone out and was scrolling. "There's two within five miles of Mini-Meadows, plus Jeb's Garage."

Jeb's Garage was a small garage at the back of Mini-Meadows where most of the residents had their cars fixed. Jeb and his son could do all kinds of repairs from fixing flats to replacing engines. "We can try Jeb's in case she brought the tire back home with her and dropped it off, but since Arianna got the flat out at the Aldridge ranch, do you think she'd have brought it somewhere closer to there?"

Jade shook her head. "Probably not. She most likely would have had to leave the tire there. Why have to go all the way back out to Aldridge's to pick it up?"

"That makes sense. Okay." Emma stood and tucked the page back into her pocket. "I'm going to check out the tire places and Jeb's. Anyone want to take a ride?"

Granny Rose threw out her to-go box. "I'll go with you."

Emma already had every intention of taking Granny Rose with her, since she wasn't about to let her out of her sight, but she nodded. "Thanks. Jade?"

"I don't much feel like opening today, but I'm going to have to at least go put a note on the door at Little Bits. Then I think I'll hang around and see what Max comes up with." Her cheeks flared red.

Emma grinned but didn't say anything. Granny Rose was currently preoccupied with Broderick's murder investigation, but any reminder of an interest in men could nudge her back into full-on matchmaker mode. And Emma was pretty sure Jade had developed a liking for Max Merlin.

Jade rolled her eyes at Emma, a sure sign she was right.

Happy that Jade seemed to feel a little better, Emma let the matter drop and headed out to the Jeep with Granny Rose. As she emerged from Pocket Books, strode quickly down the sidewalk, and crossed the road, she constantly scanned everywhere for any sign of something amiss. But with no clue who she was even looking for, who might pose a danger to Granny, the gesture was probably useless. Still, she waited for Granny Rose to climb into the front seat and close her door before getting in.

"Listen, Granny—"

"Save it." She held up a hand.

"But—"

"We've already been over this." She sighed and put on hot pink sunglasses. "I'm not going back to your father's. Number one, this is my home now. With you for the moment, but even if I can't buy that adorable little caboose house, I'm going to buy a house in Mini-Meadows. I was thinking maybe I can get that fella Tiny to make me something shaped like a tiara. What do you think?"

Resigned to the fact Granny wasn't going anywhere, even for the short term, Emma contented herself with hoping the caboose house went up for sale. "It would certainly be different. And very uniquely you."

"I know, right." Granny grinned and turned on the radio, then bopped along to something with a lot of drums.

Emma drove out of Mini-Meadows toward the first tire place while she brooded over how to find Broderick Aldridge's killer. When her phone rang, she switched off the radio and picked it up on the Bluetooth. "Hey, Chloe, what's up?"

"I thought you'd want to know, the homeowner's association has scheduled a town meeting for eight o'clock tonight at the Community Center."

"What for?"

"To discuss the murders and address the security situation in Mini-Meadows."

"Hmm…" It wouldn't hurt to have extra security in Mini-Meadows, even with the patrol car Detective Montgomery had promised driving by now and then. "Probably not a bad idea. Are you going?"

"Yeah. Jade and Max are too."

"After I check out the tire places, I have to go home and take care of Butch and Ginger and maybe grab something to eat. Granny and I will meet up with you there." Would the killer show up at something like that? Would he want to see the fear he'd instilled in the community, want to hear what people were saying, maybe catch a clue about what the police might know? She had no idea, but she was all for anything that would keep Granny Rose safer.

Chapter Twenty-One

After hitting the jackpot at the second tire place they'd visited and a light dinner of chicken soup and rye toast, Emma parked her golf cart amid about fifty others, along with a scattering of full-sized vehicles in the gravel lot at the Community Center that served as everything from a party hall to a yoga studio.

"Seems most the community is here." Granny Rose got out of the cart and turned in a circle. "I didn't even realize this many people lived in Mini-Meadows."

"It's a fairly large community, comparatively speaking. I'm pretty much at one side of the development. It actually extends way over that way." Emma gestured the opposite way off Main Street, distracted by the number of vehicles and the small clusters of residents gathered outside the building and in the doorway. "Do you see Jade or Chloe?"

Granny stood on tiptoes and craned her neck to see past the lingerers, then fluffed the long waves draped over her shoulder. "Nope. But there's that handsome Tanner Reed."

Oh, boy. Here we go. Ah well, as long as Granny was focused on her own love life, maybe she'd leave Emma's lack thereof alone.

"Why don't you go find your friends while I say hello to Tanner?" She shooed Emma toward the entrance.

"I'm not leaving you alone, Granny Rose. We can both say hi to Tanner." Gravel crunched beneath her feet as they crossed the lot toward him.

"Thing is, dear." Granny furrowed her brow. "You'll kind of cramp my style. I don't want the man to think I'm not a modern, independent woman.

You know? Especially after he was nice enough to call the other morning to let me know a body had been found and you were at the scene of the crime. It sure was nice of him to be concerned about you and try to look after you."

Emma's interest was piqued. "That's how you found out about Broderick?"

"Yup."

"How did Tanner know?"

"Apparently, he enjoys an early morning constitutional. When he saw what was going on and you seemed distressed, he called me. And I wouldn't mind repaying the kindness with a homecooked meal one night this weekend...." She winced. "If, that is, you can find something to do elsewhere."

Ah, man. Emma sighed. She could probably hang out with Jade or Chloe one night. "I'll agree to that under one condition."

"Oh?" Granny Rose offered a finger wave at Tanner.

His smile widened as he waved back and started toward them, cardigan pulled tightly around him.

"What condition is that, dear?"

"Oh, uh..." Distracted by the sight of Eric and Tiny walking across the far end of the lot, seemingly in a serious discussion, Emma faltered and lost track of the conversation.

"The condition, Emma? You said you'd let me have the house for an evening with Tanner under one condition."

"Oh, yeah, right." She watched as Eric flung his hands wide, and Tiny leaned toward him. "I'm not leaving the house until after Tanner arrives, and you call me when he's getting ready to leave so I can come back. I don't want you alone at the house."

"Ugh." She sulked for a moment but then perked up. "Okay, fine. But you wait down the road until after he leaves. You never know. I might want to give him a goodnight kiss, and I wouldn't want to be interrupted."

"No, I agree. That's definitely not something I'd want to interrupt. It's a deal then."

"Good. Now..." She put on her warmest smile and held both her hands out to Tanner, then leaned toward Emma and whispered, "Make yourself scarce."

"Granny Rose, you look beautiful tonight, as always." Tanner gripped her hands in his and kissed both her cheeks.

She looked down at her ankle-length skirt and blouse, with her high-heeled black lace boots, then peered from beneath her false lashes. "Why thank you, kind sir."

Tanner, for his part, looked adorable and very professor-like in slacks and a tan cardigan complete with elbow patches, what Emma had come to think of as his signature look. As much as Emma hated to admit it, since she'd always see Granny Rose with Grandfather no matter how long since he'd passed, she and Tanner did make a cute couple. And Granny Rose seemed happier than Emma could remember seeing her in a long time. Maybe Mini-Meadows would turn out to be good for her once this whole killer business was straightened out.

"Why don't you two go ahead in and save some seats? I'm just going to take a look around and see if I can find Jade and Chloe." And try to get closer to Tiny and Eric, who, if Eric's wildly flailing hands were any indication, were in the middle of a full-blown argument.

Granny Rose smiled and hooked her arm through the elbow Tanner offered. "Of course, dear. If we see them inside, I'll let them know you're looking for them."

"Thank you." Angling herself so she could watch Granny Rose and Tanner walk into the building, she edged closer to the two men. Before she was near enough to hear their conversation, Max called out to her.

Dang. She stopped and turned toward him. "Max, hey. What's up?"

He gestured toward the front door of the community center. "Jade and Chloe are already inside. Granny Rose—she said I should call her that...."

For as long as she could remember, Granny Rose told everyone to call her that. Unless she didn't like you, which was rare, in which case she lifted her chin in her snootiest look and said, "That's Mrs. Wells to you."

The memory brought a smile.

"Anyway, Granny Rose said you were out here, and I didn't want you to be alone, so I figured I'd take a walk out." Hooking his thumbs into his pockets, he kicked at the dirt with the toe of his sneaker.

"Thank you, Max. I appreciate it." And she did. Very much. But she wished he'd have waited just a couple more minutes, since Tiny and Eric had finished their "discussion" and were now walking toward the building.

"No problem. I wanted to talk to you alone for a minute anyway, so it worked out for the best." He stuffed his hands all the way into the pockets of his fuchsia cargo pants and strolled with her toward the Community Center door. The multitude of earrings in his left ear clicked together as he shook his head and sighed.

"Is there a problem?"

"Well, yes…and no." He stopped walking and turned to face her. "I found something while you and Granny Rose were off at the tire places."

Emma had too, and she hadn't had the chance to share it with her friends yet, but something was clearly weighing on Max, so she figured she'd save her information for later and wait him out, give him a moment to work out whatever was bothering him.

"Okay." He stopped and faced her, his gaze lowered. "I'm going to tell you what I found, but only if you promise you're not going to go running off to confront anyone."

"Why would I do that?"

He lifted a brow and studied her. "Oh, I don't know, but the more questions you ask, the more danger you're putting yourself in, and I don't want to be the cause of you rushing into danger and getting yourself hurt. So you have to promise to keep it to yourself."

She nodded slowly, taking her time to figure out if she should agree to his deal. She wouldn't lie to him, so if she promised what he asked, she'd have to uphold her end of the bargain. No matter what. In the end, her nosiness got the better of her. She had to know what he had. "Fine. I won't talk to anyone about it. Unless it's something the police need to know, then I'll have to tell Detective Montgomery."

"Fair enough. But…" He lowered his head and ran a hand through shaggy hair that already stood up in tufts. "The police can probably access the same cameras I did, and…well…."

"You hacked into something you probably shouldn't have."

CHAPTER TWENTY-ONE

He shrugged and shot her a sheepish grin.

"Fine." She wouldn't go back on her promise, and she wouldn't give his name or do anything that would get him in trouble, so she'd have to decide what to do with the information after he dished. "Spill it."

"Okay, so." He held his hands out in front of him, gesturing animatedly as he spoke, obviously excited about something. "I got to thinking about the whole situation with the money being withdrawn out of Broderick's account and where it could have gone to. Did someone else transfer it online, did Broderick take it out so the checks wouldn't clear, or whatever?"

"And?"

"Then I started thinking about Phillip. If he doesn't actually work, where does he get money from?"

Emma had wondered that herself.

"So I did a little digging, and it turns out Broderick has been transferring about ten thousand dollars a month from the same account the money went missing from the day he was killed into an account in Phillip's name."

"You mean like an allowance?"

He shrugged and looked around the lot. "I can't say, but it seems that way. I went back about two years, and the withdrawals from Broderick's account post on the same day as the deposits to Phillip's account."

"Ah, man, Max." She took a quick look around to be sure no one could hear them and decided this was most definitely not information she could share with Detective Montgomery. "You hacked Phillip's accounts too?"

"Yeah, but..." He waved that off as if it was unimportant, and Emma had the fleeting thought that she might have created a monster asking him to help them out. "That's not the best part."

"Seriously?"

As people started moving from the parking lot to the building, he walked toward the door with her. "The money that disappeared from Broderick's account that day showed up in Phillip's."

"Okay." She was pretty sure there had to be a point in here somewhere, but it was lost on her. "So, that was normal, right?"

"Not exactly. The regular withdrawals and deposits always posted on or around the first of the month. Sometimes the second or third if there was a weekend or holiday, but never later than that."

"But Broderick was killed on the fourteenth."

"The very same day the money was withdrawn from Broderick's account and deposited in Phillip's."

Emma's mind raced. Had Broderick cut Phillip off? If he stopped paying his allowance and tossed him out of the house, what would Phillip have done? "At ten thousand dollars a month from his father while living home, Phillip must have had quite a nest egg set aside."

Max was already shaking his head, jingling the row of earrings adorning his left ear. "On the contrary, Phillip was on the verge of bankruptcy."

"Really?" Assuming he didn't have many expenses, since he was living with his parents, what could he possibly have done with that amount of money? "How could that be?"

"Phillip likes to play in the casinos."

"Gambling?"

"I found numerous trips to Las Vegas, with regular payments to one particular hotel." He grinned and spread his arms wide, rocked back on his heels. "And I was able to find and access IP security cameras showing the entrance of that hotel."

Having no idea what an IP camera was, Emma just stared at him blankly.

With a huff, he explained, "The cameras are hooked to the internet, so I was able to hack the footage."

Her interest shot through the roof. "And?"

"Guess who Phillip's date was on several occasions?"

"Who?"

"Arianna Jenkins."

For just an instant, Emma froze, not knowing what to think. Then, her thoughts took off in a free for all. "You're sure?"

"I'm positive it was her because I looked at her social media the other day, and when I recognized her in the security footage, I double-checked."

"So Arianna and Phillip were dating."

"Apparently."

So where was Arianna now? Emma's concern for the woman increased, because she didn't buy for one minute that Arianna just happened to go to work for Eric just in time for the Aldridge job when she was coincidentally dating the victim's son. There had to be more to it. But what? Did Arianna have something to do with his death, or would hers be the next body found?

Chapter Twenty-Two

The instant Granny Rose, Jade, and Chloe spotted Emma walking in the door with Max, they pounced, barely giving her a minute to wrap her head around the new information.

"Did you see...?"

"Do you think...?"

"Did you know...?"

The only thing she knew for certain was that Arianna had been alive the morning after Broderick was killed, because the guy at the tire place said she dropped off a tire with a large puncture in it to be patched. A tire she was supposed to pick up the following day and had never returned for. Had someone deliberately flattened her tire? Why? To keep Eric around long enough to have been one of the last to see Broderick alive? Not that a bounced check was a sufficient motive for murder, but it could have led to an angry confrontation that escalated to murder.

Could Phillip and Arianna have concocted a plan to kill Broderick and frame Eric for the crime? Because if his murder was planned ahead of time, they were looking at something completely different than the crime of passion Emma had suspected all along. It would certainly explain why they then had to get rid of Whitney, though. But that was a mistake, because Emma couldn't see a reason in the world Eric would have to kill Whitney... unless, of course, she'd witnessed him killing Broderick. But wouldn't she have called the police? Plus, she'd seemed sincerely shocked when Jade told her he was dead.

"Emma?" Granny Rose snapped her fingers in front of Emma's face. "Did you hear a word I said?"

"Oh, uh, I'm sorry, Granny Rose. My mind wandered for a minute." She scanned the room, looking for Eric and Tiny. She had to find Eric and ask him how he'd found Arianna for the job.

"I said…" She gave Emma's ribs a nudge with her elbow. "Did you see the hottie at twelve o'clock?"

She shook off all other thoughts to concentrate on whatever Granny Rose was going on about. "What do you mean? I was with you at twelve o'clock, dealing with Detective Montgomery."

"No, silly." She slapped her palm to her forehead. "Not the time, twelve o'clock, the position."

And with that, she grabbed Emma's shoulders and whirled her toward the front of the room, then pointed one salmon-colored nail at a guy standing about twenty feet straight in front of them. The same guy Emma had noticed at the crime scene.

"Well, ain't he a tall drink of water." Granny waggled her eyebrows with a grin. "Hubba, hubba."

Emma lowered Granny's hand and stepped into her line of sight, effectively cutting off her view of the admittedly handsome stranger. "Stop staring. And definitely stop pointing."

"Why don't you go over and say hello, introduce yourself?"

Flames flared in Emma's cheeks. "Absolutely not. Now you behave yourself. We're here to find out about any new security measures the council plans to enact, to hear any new details of Broderick's murder, and to hopefully find a way to keep you safe from the stalker. *Not* to pick up men. This isn't the time for that."

"On the contrary, dear, it's the perfect time. What good man wouldn't come to the aid of a damsel in distress?"

"I said, no."

That earned her another elbow nudge. If she kept this up, she was going to have a nice black and blue mark.

"What's the matter, Emma?" Granny narrowed her eyes at her. "Don't you want a husband?"

Did she? Eventually. Probably. But not nearly as bad as Granny Rose wanted her to have one.

When Granny's attention wandered, Emma breathed a sigh of relief. Her reprieve was short lived, when a moment later, she noticed Granny Rose's full focus on an elderly gentleman who'd just entered. "Here, honey, watch and learn."

"What?"

"You heard me." She boosted the girls up a bit to get whatever cleavage she could manage and did a little shimmy. "Watch. And. Learn."

Mortified, Emma did a quick scan of the room to see if anyone had noticed. "Granny, don't—"

But Granny Rose had already set a course for her target. She tucked her purse beneath her arm and sauntered toward the elderly man she'd honed in on.

He stood alone against the back wall, hands clasped behind his back, wearing wrinkled slacks and a button-up shirt with the sleeves rolled to the elbows. His loosened tie hung slightly askew. The instant he spotted Granny, he straightened away from the wall and smiled.

Granny pretended not to notice him as she scanned the room as if searching for someone. When she reached him, though Emma had no idea how she'd timed it so precisely, she nudged her bag from beneath her arm and let it drop.

The gentleman rushed to her aid, handed her the purse with a big smile, and the two started talking. Then he started patting his pockets.

Granny Rose batted her lashes and lay a hand on his.

"Hmm." Jade stared wide-eyed, then turned to Emma and shrugged. "She's not wrong. She might just be able to teach you a thing or two."

"Yup," Chloe added. "The woman is smooth."

A moment later, Granny Rose dug a pad and pen out of her purse and wrote something down, then smiled and turned back toward Emma, Jade and Chloe. When she reached them, she held up the phone number written beneath the name Marcus Weatherby and wiggled it back and forth before dropping it back into her bag. "And that, ladies, is how it's done."

Emma just stared. What could she say? Thankfully, the meeting was called to order before she had to respond.

"Oh, let's hurry." Granny Rose took her elbow and pointed toward a line of empty seats a few rows up. "Tanner is saving seats for us."

As she followed, Emma's gaze fell on the guy from the crime scene. Could it really be that easy? Just walk past and drop her bag, and a knight in shining armor would pick it up, hand it to her, and they'd ride off into the sunset together. Horrified at the thought, Emma quickly averted her gaze. Yikes! Who'd have thought her grandmother would turn out to be such a bad influence?

Granny Rose, Jade, Max, who'd reappeared out of nowhere, and Chloe preceded her into the row, so Emma took the aisle seat just as the president of the homeowner's association approached the podium at the front of the room and cleared his throat.

The short, stocky gentleman, all business in a jacket and bow tie, adjusted the microphone and began to speak. "Good evening, and thank you for coming."

A quick glance over her shoulder brought surprise at the number of people crowded into the large gymnasium-style room with streamers and banners still hanging from someone named Jim's fiftieth birthday party last weekend. Not only was every seat filled, but many latecomers stood against the back and side walls. A nervous hum rippled through the crowd.

"Good evening, ladies and gentlemen. For those of you who don't know me, I'm Ashton White, president of the Mini-Meadows Homeowner's Association, and I'd like to thank you all for coming. As I'm sure you're all aware, we've had a couple of..." he tugged at his collar, "unfortunate incidents over the past couple of days."

Boy, was that an understatement. Hopefully, it wasn't an indication the association was going to make light of the murders.

"In light of those recent events, we..." he gestured toward three men and two women sitting at a long table behind him. "We thought it might be a good idea to meet and discuss increasing security in the community."

"Have you spoken to the police?" a man shouted from the back of the room. "Do they have any idea who the killer is?"

He was already shaking his head. "No one has been apprehended yet."

Murmurs started through the crowd, and Emma could have sworn she heard Eric's name mentioned more than once.

"Please, everyone, calm down." He blew out a breath, clearly frustrated with the lack of silent cooperation. "We will give everyone a chance to speak if they'd like, but please, can everyone quiet down and listen? We have a few ideas to increase security in the community."

The mutters increased, turning to a dull roar the timid man had no hope of controlling.

One of the women seated behind him, slightly overweight, dressed in jeans and a T-shirt, with her hair pulled back in a ponytail, stood, approached the podium beside him, stuck two fingers into her mouth, and let out a sharp whistle. Then she grinned. "Good to know that skill comes in handy for more than just corralling my daughter's soccer team."

A hint of laughter rippled through the room, easing some of the tension. The woman stepped back and gestured for her compatriot to continue.

He thanked her and returned to his position, tugged at his collar as he cleared his throat. "First off, the police have assured us they will increase patrols through Mini-Meadows."

Emma had already gotten that much from Detective Montgomery.

"But we thought it wouldn't hurt to set up a neighborhood watch, maybe take turns patrolling with a partner or a small group. We were hoping Detective Jacob Bennett would take charge of that."

A few heads turned to look at the object of Emma's earlier attention.

So, he was a cop. Emma wasn't surprised.

The man she'd noticed at the crime scene that morning shifted but kept his gaze focused on the podium, didn't return a single look. It seemed to Emma he had no interest in coordinating the neighborhood watch. But at least now she knew his name. Somehow, it suited him, and she found herself wondering if he went by Jacob or Jake. Or maybe Jace. He looked like a...

"Hmm..." Granny Rose leaned close and pitched her voice low. "A cop. That's a pretty good catch, ya know. Benefits, retirement."

A nice reminder of two things Emma needed to look into but had been putting off this past year. Instead of letting herself get caught up worrying about the future, Emma simply groaned and pulled her attention away from her curiosity about Jacob Bennett. All she wanted was to go home, put on some comfy PJs, and curl up with a good book, a cup of herbal tea, and Ginger on her lap. Instead, here she was at a community meeting that clearly hadn't had much planning, with Granny Rose determined to marry her off at the soonest opportunity.

"Anyway." Ashton cleared his throat when Jacob didn't respond and moved on. "We've also heard a disturbing rumor that in addition to the two bodies that were found on Mini-Meadows' property..."

Huh, Emma hadn't realized the land at the back of the development where she'd found Whitney belonged to Mini-Meadows.

"...by Emma Wells..."

All eyes turned to Emma. Those who didn't know her followed the gazes of those who'd turned to stare. No doubt she'd be easy enough to pick out of the crowd; if the heat searing her cheeks was any indication, her face probably blushed bright red from her chin to her hairline.

"There was also a stalking incident inside the development in which Ms. Wells's grandmother was followed by a woman who was apparently photographing her. Can you confirm those rumors, Ms. Wells?"

Since everyone in the room was silently staring at her, and Ashton White didn't continue speaking, she figured they were expecting some sort of response. But how much should she tell them? Detective Montgomery hadn't said to not tell anyone about the email, but drawing attention to the implied threat in a roomful of people, any one of whom might be the killer, couldn't be a good idea. Plus, the threat had only been made toward Granny Rose, specifically to keep Emma from asking any more questions, so it didn't seem any of her neighbors or any Mini-Meadows residents should be in danger from the killer. Though she couldn't know that for certain.

"Umm." Her chair scraped back with a screech as she stood. "I don't know if stalking is the correct term. A woman followed my grandmother while she was walking her dog and took pictures of her, but she wasn't harmed.

Although, that being said, it couldn't hurt to be careful until this matter is resolved. The neighborhood watch sounds like a good idea."

She took her seat, hoping Ashton would move on and the attention would be diverted from her.

No such luck. "All things considered, would you be willing to take on the responsibility of coordinating with Detective Bennett to set up the neighborhood watch patrols?"

Jacob Bennett's attention finally shifted from Ashton, as he turned and hooked an elbow over the back of his seat. His gaze met Emma's and held. If she wasn't mistaken, a slight grin played at the corner of his mouth, just for an instant before he ran a hand over his goatee, and any hint of good humor disappeared.

She needed to shift everyone's attention away from her, and the quickest way to do that was probably to agree to do what he'd asked. Especially since, though he hadn't outright accused her of causing the current situation by finding first Broderick's and then Whitney's bodies, he'd certainly implied it.

Granny Rose jumped to her feet. "She'd love to."

Granny's elbow in her ribs—again—had her blurting a response without any further thought. "Sure. Uh, yeah, I guess I could do that."

"Okay, then. Thank you." While Ashton continued to outline whatever ideas they'd come up with, Emma tuned him out.

What had she done? The killer demanded she stop asking questions, and instead of hunkering down at home with Granny Rose and locking the doors, she'd just agreed in public to take charge of the civilian patrol tasked with keeping the neighborhood safe from him.

Chapter Twenty-Three

When the meeting concluded, Emma curbed the desire to make a beeline directly for the door. Whether she liked the idea or not, she'd agreed to help coordinate the neighborhood watch, so she at least had to make an effort.

"Emma." Delia Sanderson, owner of Tantalizing Temptations and member of the homeowner's association board of directors, hurried toward her, waving a clipboard. "Here you go. I figured you could get started gathering names for the neighborhood watch while everyone's here. You can use the table and chairs by the podium."

"Oh, right, thanks." Emma took the clipboard with a stack of looseleaf papers clipped to it. Someone had written Volunteers across the top of the front page. "I'll get started."

But Delia wasn't about to let her off the hook that easy. She lay a hand on Emma's back, gestured toward the table where a small group had already gathered, and strolled at Emma's side. Probably to make sure she didn't escape. "It was difficult enough to believe you found that man's body in the moving container, but then to find another out in the woods behind Mini-Meadows…well, that's some coincidence."

"I know, right." Emma picked up her pace. The sooner she reached the table, the sooner this conversation would be over.

"So, what were you doing out there, anyway?" The intensity of the unblinking gaze Delia pinned her with belied the pretense of aloofness. "It's not often anyone uses that road. Where were you going?"

As Emma looked around, searching for any excuse not to answer Delia's question, she spotted Jacob Bennett quietly moving toward the door. *Oh, no, you don't, buddy.* "I'm sorry. Would you excuse me, please, Delia? I have to catch up with Detective Bennett before people start to head home."

"Oh, right, of course. We'll talk more afterward."

Not if I can help it. Emma just smiled, nodded, and bolted for the door. "Detective Bennett?"

He stopped and turned, waited for her to reach him.

"I'm Emma Wells." She stuck out a hand to shake. "It's nice to meet you."

His rough, calloused hand enveloped hers. "Pleasure. It's Jake."

Jake. She knew it. Okay, now what? She couldn't just stand there awkwardly shaking his hand, smiling, and hoping he'd approach the subject for much longer, although she couldn't deny the warmth of his strong grip comforted her. She extricated her hand from his and tapped the clipboard. "So, um, Delia said we could use the table at the front of the room to sign up volunteers for the neighborhood watch."

He studied her a moment before speaking, pursing his full lips. "And you think that's a good idea?"

Uh, oh. The sinking sensation she was on her own with this endeavor threatened to drown her. "You don't?"

"Okay." He lowered his gaze, raked a hand through his shaggy hair. When his gaze returned to hers, she stepped back, knowing he wasn't going to help her. He gripped her shoulders and turned her to face the crowded room, adjusted his grip, so he still held both shoulders as he stepped up behind her, leaned close to speak in her ear. She inhaled deeply as the woodsy scent of his aftershave lingered. "Look around this room and tell me what you see."

She shrugged, a little too comfortable with the intimate way he'd closed them off from the rest of the room. "A group of Mini-Meadows residents?"

"Look closer. Give me some observations about the crowd. Just off the top of your head, just between us."

How was she supposed to observe anything with him so close, his warm breath tickling the back of her neck? Trying to ignore the sensation, she did as he'd instructed. What was he trying to show her? How did he see the crowd? Eric stood in the far corner, talking to a few men she recognized as friends of his. Tiny sat in a chair toward the back, alone, his bulky arms folded across his chest, long legs stretched out in front of him crossed at the ankles, appearing to sulk. She'd have to remember to try to talk to him before he left, make sure he was okay.

"Well?" Jacob asked.

Granny Rose tapped Chloe's shoulder, lifted her chin in Emma's direction and grinned.

Emma barely resisted the urge to squirm out of Jacob—Jake's—grip. And it hit her. Most of the residents in attendance were closer to Granny Rose's age than Chloe's. "I never realized how many of Mini-Meadows' residents were older."

"And do you think it's a good idea to have these elderly men and women out at night chasing after a killer?" He waited for her answer as if he hadn't already decided what it would be if she had an ounce of common sense.

"No," she had to admit. "Probably not."

"And what if one of them stumbles across this killer while on patrol?"

He had a point. "Maybe we could—"

"And what else do you see? What can you tell me about their collective state of mind?"

And it hit her, the undercurrent of fear that pulsed through the room like a live wire, shocking everyone it touched. He was right again. "They all look scared."

"And rightfully so." He finally stepped back and released her, giving her some breathing space.

She turned to him. "So, what do we do?"

"My suggestion would be to forget about it and go home, leave the investigating to the police."

She thought of Granny Rose, how stubborn she could be when she got something in her head. If these people, who all seemed to be waiting around even though the meeting had ended, were half as tenacious as Granny Rose, there would be no deterring them. They'd simply figure it out for themselves if Emma and Jake walked away. "What if we let people sign up to volunteer, list times that are convenient for them to do patrols along with their contact information, and tell them we'll be in touch as soon as we figure out a schedule? Hopefully, the killer will be caught before we have to move forward on that."

He lifted a brow.

She bristled. At least she was trying to come up with a viable option. "That way, no one else will take it on themselves to start up the patrols."

Finally, he nodded. "That could work."

She breathed a sigh of relief. He was right. Most of the residents here didn't belong patrolling the neighborhood in the dead of night with a killer on the loose. "And in the meantime, if we get any volunteers we think could handle themselves, we can schedule them first."

With a noncommittal shrug, he lay a hand on the small of her back and gestured for her to precede him toward the table. "We'll see."

"What about you?" She weaved her way through the crowd toward the front of the room. She should have seen what he did sooner, the fear, the determination, the fact that these people were not police officers. "Will you volunteer?"

Because Emma would sleep a whole lot better knowing Detective Jake Bennett was outside keeping watch.

"No, ma'am."

That put a hitch in her stride. "What do you mean?"

"I mean no. I'm here in Mini-Meadows for a reason, and it's not to get involved in a murder investigation."

"Oh." And with that, since he obviously had no intention of elaborating, she promptly ran out of conversation. But he'd definitely piqued her curiosity.

She'd placed the accent easy enough, New York, so what was a detective from New York doing in Mini-Meadows? He seemed way too young to be retired. Undercover? If that was the case, she could see why he'd want to keep a low profile. But what would he be investigating in Mini-Meadows, a small, quiet, peaceful town in a rural area of Central Florida where the most exciting thing that ever happened was the six-foot alligator that came up out of the lake and spent an hour basking in the sun on Main Street?

Until Broderick Aldridge was murdered. Could his presence have something to do with that? She'd found it odd she'd never noticed him before the morning of Broderick's murder, especially since he was—as Granny Rose would say—easy on the eyes. But he'd been at the crime scene where she'd found Broderick. He didn't make it from New York to Florida in less than an hour from when Emma found Broderick in the container to when she saw him standing in the crowd. Huh…seemed Detective Jacob Bennett might need a little looking into.

"I'm ready to sign up." Granny Rose was the first on line at the table when Emma set out the volunteer list. She set her purse on the table and grabbed a pen.

Jake sat back in his seat, folded his arms, and settled in for the show. At least he had the good grace to hide his smirk with a cough.

Emma sent him a scathing look, and he laughed out loud. Ignoring him, she returned her attention to Granny Rose. She could only deal with one problem at a time. "Do you really think signing up for the neighborhood watch is a good idea, Granny Rose?"

"Why not?"

Because you're the one I'm trying to protect from the killer. Instead of voicing her opinion, Emma tried to reason with her. "What would you do if you found the killer somewhere."

She huffed out a breath. "That's what Ole Betsy's for."

She shouldn't even ask. "Ole Betsy?"

She whipped the handgun out of her purse. "So I can hold him for the police."

That perked Mr. Smarty-pants right up. "Ma'am, do you have a license for that weapon?"

"Put the gun away, Granny," Emma hissed, hoping not to draw attention to the situation.

In true Granny Rose fashion, she ignored Emma and propped a hip against the table, focusing her full attention on Jake. "The guy who sold it to me said I didn't need one."

Jake stood and gently took the weapon from her hand, then slipped it back into her purse. "You don't need a license to own the weapon, but you do need one to carry it concealed in your purse."

"So where am I supposed to keep it?" Her eyes lit up like a child in a candy shop, and she snapped her fingers. "Maybe in a pink or gold rhinestone studded holster on my hip. What do you think?"

"I think." Jake's gaze jumped to Emma, probably for confirmation she wasn't pulling his leg, then back to Granny Rose. "Home in a gun safe with a good lock is the best place."

Granny's mouth fell open in her most appalled expression. "What good is it going to do me there?"

"While you have a valid point," Jake scored a few points for patience. "If you want to carry the weapon with you, you will need to get a license."

Emma interrupted before Granny Rose could push it any further. Could a Detective from another state make an arrest in Florida? Who knew? But she didn't want to find out. "We'll take care of it, thank you."

"Sure." He let it drop. Then again, he could afford to, considering the entire incident only worked to prove his point.

She should have realized organizing patrols wouldn't be as easy as gathering a list of names and sending people off to do their thing. Without the proper training and guidance from law enforcement, the neighborhood watch idea might actually end up getting someone hurt. She turned the clipboard toward her and added a row. In addition to name, contact info, and preferred schedule, she added *Training*. That ought to help. Then she turned the clipboard back toward Granny Rose for her to sign up.

Once Granny Rose was done, with firm instructions from Emma to stay inside, she wandered off.

Chapter Twenty-Four

When Tiny approached the table, a glimmer of hope tried to surface. It didn't last long, though. Emma didn't need Detective Downer to tell her a suspect, no matter how far down the list in Emma's mind, wouldn't make a good candidate for the neighborhood watch. "Hey, Tiny, what's going on?"

"Eh." He shrugged. "Not much. What about with you?"

"Nothing new, really." Unless you counted trying to keep Granny Rose somewhat under control while searching for a killer who'd now dumped two bodies, one the friend of a friend and the other a client, where Emma would find them. "Have you had a chance to come up with any ideas for Gabriella Moreno's condo yet?"

"Actually, yes." After jotting his name and information on the page, he moved to the far end of the table to allow room for others to continue adding their names to the list. A shortage of willing participants was definitely not a problem. "I've gone over a few of them with her. We're going to do a wall of cubbies, like you suggested. We're also going to do a built-in toy box and bench seating with storage underneath in the kitchen. And since she has a great oversized garage space, we'll do another wall of cubbies in there for shoes and whatever else she might like to store."

"That sounds great."

"It is, and she sure is a sweetheart to work with."

"I'll say. And best of all, she fully understands the meaning of downsizing. She's selling, consigning, or donating most all of her furniture, then using the money to buy a crib with drawers built in for the baby and a captain's bed with two rows of drawers underneath for herself to eliminate the need for dressers." Working with someone who understood and listened to suggestions on how to make good use of the limited space was a pleasure.

"The fact that she's in a hurry and doesn't have much time to mull over each decision doesn't hurt either," Tiny added.

"Very true." Since no one seemed to be paying particularly close attention to them, Emma smiled and risked a question. "I was going to say hello earlier, but you and Eric seemed to be having some sort of disagreement."

"Eh." He waved it off. "No big deal."

"Are you sure?" While she didn't want to appear nosy, Eric and Tiny both had business dealings with Aldridge, and she couldn't help but wonder if their altercation had anything to do with his death. "You seemed pretty upset."

He sighed and shrugged one broad shoulder, and Emma was struck, not for the first time, by his size. He could certainly do some damage if he hit anyone. Even without a tire iron. "Yeah, well, you know Eric. Sometimes he can be tough."

"In what way?" She'd always found him to be pretty laid back and easygoing. Then again, she mostly dealt with him on a business level. "I only know him from work, so I don't know what he's like on a more personal level."

"Yeah, that easy-going charm he exudes when it suits him is a direct contrast to what's hidden underneath." He blew out a breath and ran a hand over his bald head. "Heck, that's not really fair. It's not his fault the deal went south. I guess I'm just mad at everyone involved. Mostly myself."

Emma checked to be sure the sign-ups were going smoothly, then propped a hip against the table's edge and scooted closer. "What are you talking about? What deal?"

"You know. We talked about it on the phone. The deal...business arrangement...scam, whatever I got involved in with Broderick Aldridge."

"What does that have to do with Eric?" Since Eric had specifically told her he hadn't been involved, even joked around about keeping his money in his mattress where it belonged.

"He's the one who told me about it in the first place. Said Aldridge had some sure thing going." He shook his head. "Serves me right for trying to make a quick buck. I know better, know the best way to make money is to work hard for it."

Emma couldn't argue with that, though her own family had made a small fortune in investments along with their hard work. "I didn't know Eric had any involvement in that."

"Involvement is probably not the right word, but he did let me in on it, said he'd put in a good word with Aldridge if I wanted him to, so I thought, what the hay? Ya know?"

"Sure." She nodded her agreement, but her mind raced. Had Eric deliberately left out that he was the middleman? No wonder Tiny had gone to Eric when he was on the hunt for Aldridge the night he'd been killed.

"Anyway, I gotta get going, got an early meeting tomorrow, but this here neighborhood watch is a good idea." When he gestured toward the clipboard on the table, where a nice line had formed to sign up, she turned a smirk on Jake.

Too bad Detective Know-it-all was looking the other way, frowning at whatever he'd noticed that was lost on her.

"Sure, Tiny. Good to see you."

"Yeah, same goes. And I'll keep you up to date on any changes on the Moreno job."

When he started to walk away, she called him back. "Sorry, Tiny, I meant to ask, did you happen to run into Phillip Aldridge when you caught up with Broderick on the day he was killed?"

His expression twisted into a grimace. "Didn't have no run-in with him, but I saw him out at the house, skulking around as usual."

Hmm...she hadn't thought of it that way, but the observation sure did fit. Especially on the day Emma had gone to see Mildred with Granny Rose. The instant they'd started talking about money, Phillip had materialized out of nowhere. Skulking was a good word for spying on his mother's conversation. Had he done the same with Broderick?

Tiny frowned. "Is that all you wanted to know?"

"Oh, yeah, great, thanks."

"Later, then."

"See ya." But by the time he walked away, her attention had already shifted to thoughts of Phillip. Had he overheard his father giving Tiny investment advice? Had Phillip invested and lost a fortune as well? Not if Max Merlin's hacking skills were half as good as he claimed they were, which she had no reason to doubt. According to Max, the younger Aldridge was on the verge of bankruptcy, had no income aside from the allowance from his father.

And what about Eric? She tried to replay the conversation with him in her head. He'd told her Broderick had offered him the opportunity to invest, said Aldridge offered the deal to Tiny when they were going over plans or blueprints or something, but Eric had turned him down, and Tiny had invested. Had Eric lied? And if so, why? To cover up his own involvement? Or did he simply forget exactly how the events had unfolded? Possible. She scanned the room in search of him. Surely it was just a misunderstanding, and she could get to the bottom of it with one quick conversation.

A hand on her shoulder startled her, had her jumping, whirling, and coming face to face with Detective Bennett. "Sorry, didn't mean to startle you, but I wanted to say goodnight before you got involved in another conversation."

"Goodnight?" She glanced at the people still lined up to join their cause.

He followed her gaze and leaned his mouth close to her ear. "A neighborhood watch, done right and with proper guidance from a police officer, can be a good thing. And you certainly have a gung-ho group ready to protect and serve. But having the homeowner's association just 'decide' and send people out to patrol isn't enough. It might not be a bad idea to go through the proper channels and get it done for the future. When it's not a killer you're after. It will deter crime in the neighborhood."

"Aren't you a police officer?" She couldn't help the retort, though he'd already made it clear he wasn't going to help.

"Not anymore." He stuffed his hands into his pockets and strolled off through the crowd.

No way could she let that comment go without digging deeper, which he probably knew since he'd tossed it out there and walked away. She briefly considered asking Max Merlin to look into his past, but somehow it seemed more intrusive to conspire with someone else to study up on him than it did to research him herself. At least if she ran her own background check she could tell herself she was just being safe checking into the past of a man she might be interested in pursuing. Whoa! Yikes. Where had that thought come from?

She choked on that and glanced around to make sure no one was looking. Not that anyone could read her thoughts, but still…

Shifting gears as the line at the sign-up table started to dwindle, she realized Eric must have already left. Too bad. She'd been hoping to ask him about the business deal between Tiny and Broderick, see if he'd fess up he'd been the one to approach Tiny with the deal. Of course, she couldn't be sure that was the way it had happened. Could be Tiny didn't remember correctly. Or, though it made her skin crawl to admit it, lied to her about it. But what purpose would that serve?

Whatever. It was past time to set all of this aside for the night, go home and get a good night's sleep. With that in mind, she started across the room toward the back row of chairs, where Chloe and Jade sat talking. "Hey, guys, what's going on?"

"Nothing much, just waiting for Max to come back."

"Where'd he go?"

Jade shrugged and looked around. "He didn't say, just said to wait here for him, and he'd be right back."

Emma didn't see him in the room, so she started to sit and wait with her friends but stopped and jerked abruptly upright. "Where's Granny Rose?"

Chloe jumped to her feet and scanned the room. "Where did you see her last?"

"She was signing up for neighborhood watch detail."

"Granny Rose?" Jade lifted a perfectly sculpted brow.

"Yeah, I'll tell you later." It was easy enough to see through the thinning crowd that Granny Rose was no longer in the room. Who else was missing? Jake Bennett. Eric. Tiny. Max. Her heart thudded wildly against her ribs. "Have either of you seen her since the meeting ended?"

"No, but I'll check the ladies' room." Chloe patted Emma's arm on the way past.

Jade stood on a chair and did a slow circuit, scanning every inch of the open space, then jumped down. "Don't worry, Emma, we'll find her."

"Where could she have gone?" With her insides in knots, she looked around again. "The last thing I said to her was don't leave the room."

She should have kept an eye on her, should have insisted she stay right next to Emma or with Jade and Chloe. And beating herself up wasn't going to find Granny Rose. The self-recrimination would have to wait for later.

"Okay, stop and think. Who would she have left with?" Jade asked.

"I don't know." Emma rubbed her temples, as if the massage would bring answers to the forefront of her brain. "Tanner Reed, I suppose."

"Do you have his number?"

Emma handed her phone to Jade as she scanned the room in search of him.

"Lose something?"

Emma whirled and came face to face with Jake Bennett, holding an indignant Granny Rose by the elbow.

"Granny Rose." Emma threw her arms around her, held her close, inhaled deeply the scent of the perfume that had comforted her since childhood, then gripped her upper arms and set her back. "Where were you? I told you not to leave the room."

Granny Rose lifted a brow. That look held memories from her childhood as well, though not as fond as others. "I'm not a child, dear. I know how to be careful."

Reigning in her temper, Emma silently counted to ten before holding a hand out to Jake. "I don't know how to thank you for bringing her in. I was worried sick."

Ignoring her hand, Jake took her elbow and led her outside the door, then stopped. "Keep her close."

Emma nodded, unable to force words past the lump in her throat, lest she start blubbering in front of the whole neighborhood.

"I found her standing in the parking lot with this." He held a sticky note by one corner, shifted it out of the way when she went to take it. "I'll wait around for Detective Montgomery and give it directly to him."

"Detec...? I need to call the police? Why? What is it?"

"I've already called, and Montgomery is meeting me in the parking lot where I found Granny Rose." He held the note up again, giving her the chance to read the message scrawled in what looked like black Sharpie. *Meet me out front, I have a nice surprise for you.* It was signed with a heart.

Emma gasped, and her gaze leapt to Jake's. "Where did she get that?"

"She said someone bumped into her in the crowd, but she didn't see who, and then she found the sticky note stuck to her purse."

"Who do you think wrote it, and what does it mean?" The possibilities pounded rapid-fire through her mind, but she had no hope of ordering her thoughts just then.

He shrugged, but the intensity of his dark eyes belied the offhanded gesture. "It could be your Granny has a secret admirer."

Since his gaze held no sign of the amusement she'd seen earlier, she had a sneaking suspicion he didn't buy into that theory. "Or?"

"Or it could be someone decided to have a talk with her, maybe try to ascertain how much she, or you, know about the killings."

Emma didn't dare think about what else someone might have wanted with Granny Rose, but this case needed to be solved, and fast. "Thank you so much for looking out for her. I can't tell you how much I appreciate it."

"Well, if you want to repay the kindness, once Detective Montgomery is done questioning her, take your Granny home and tend to her. Keep her out of harm's way while the police investigate."

"I sure will. Thank you, again."

He nodded and started back toward the building, then paused and looked back over his shoulder. "By the way, I found her standing under a broken streetlight, and she just smiled and batted her lashes, even when I took her elbow to lead her inside."

The image of Granny Rose standing in the dark, trusting whoever walked up on her, made Emma's heart ache. Then another image formed, and she smiled. "You're lucky she didn't shoot you."

He laughed, smooth, deep, the kind of easy laughter that made you feel like everything was right with the world. "That's probably true."

Chapter Twenty-Five

The instant Emma unlocked the front door and pushed it open, Butch scrambled to his feet. He reached her in two bounds, leaped up, and planted a nice wet slobber on her cheek. "Yes, Butch, I missed you too."

Granny Rose patted his head as she trudged toward the kitchen.

As if he understood something was bothering her, Butch whined and looked to Emma for answers.

"I know, Butch. She's been like that since Detective Bennett brought her back inside at the Community Center."

Since Granny Rose stopped in the kitchen and pulled out a container of milk and the box of cocoa from the pantry, Emma figured she'd have a quick minute to walk Butch before Granny headed off to bed. "I'll be back in a minute, okay, Granny Rose?"

She waved over her head.

"Come on, boy." Emma clipped the leash to his collar and walked out, being sure to stay in the puddle of light from her porch lamp. Thankfully, Butch was quick, and they hurried back inside. During the minute or two she was out there, no patrol cars cruised past. Then again, neither did any other vehicles, so she supposed that was a plus.

The instant she unhooked Butch, he padded to where Granny Rose slumped on a stool at the breakfast bar, her hot chocolate obviously forgotten.

A quick survey of the room didn't show any damage or mess, so Emma figured things had gone okay between the new roommates. She took a moment to scratch Ginger's belly, where she lay spread eagle on the back of the loveseat. Ginger purred and twisted for Emma to pet her head. "Good girl, Ginger. Have you and Butch been getting along?"

Ginger continued to purr and rubbed her head against Emma's fingers.

Needing some small victory, Emma took that as a yes. With a sigh, she left Ginger curled where she was and washed her hands. She poured the milk Granny Rose had left on the counter into a pan, turned the burner on low, and got two mugs from the cabinet.

Granny Rose wrung her hands, her gaze fully focused on the task.

Emma walked up behind her, wrapped her arms around her, and rested her chin on Granny Rose's shoulder. "Are you okay?"

She shrugged and gripped Emma's clasped hands in her own. "What am I doing, Emma?"

"What do you mean?"

She shook her head.

Emma turned a stool to face her and sat, gripped her cold hands. "Talk to me."

A tear tipped over her lashes and rolled down her cheek. "What was I thinking coming here? Thinking I could start a new life, a life I would enjoy, at my age?"

"Granny Rose—"

"No, please. You don't have to say it." She wiped the tear. "I'm going to go back to your father's."

"What?" Emma's gut cramped. As much as she wanted Granny Rose safe, she'd come to love having her. She hadn't realized how much she'd missed her, missed living with her, missed her company.

"I'm just a foolish old woman."

"Granny Rose, look at me."

She lifted her gaze. "I'm sorry, Emma. I never should have come here, intruded on your life, gotten in the way."

"Are you kidding me?" She gripped her grandmother's hands tighter, held them as she looked her in the eye. "I love having you here. I'm so happy you came to live with me, and I'd be happy for you to stay forever. Before you came, I didn't even realize how lonely I was, but having you here, having Butch too, it makes me happier than I can ever tell you."

Granny Rose petted Butch's head. "I don't think your father will let me keep him."

"It doesn't matter what father thinks, because you're not going back there."

She tilted her head to study Emma and frowned. "I don't understand. I thought you wanted me to go back home."

"I want you to be safe, but I don't want you to leave. This is your home, Granny Rose. Not only do I love having you, but I admire you."

Her eyes widened. "You do?"

"Absolutely." With all of her heart. "And for the record, you are about as far from a foolish old woman as you could get. It couldn't have been easy for you to move out of the house you've lived in most of your life, to decide what would make you happy and go out in search of it. That takes courage, Granny Rose. And we're not going to let anyone get away with taking your independence away from you."

"We're not?"

"No. We're not." When the milk boiled over and sizzled on the stove, Emma jumped up and shifted it off the burner, and mopped up the spill. "I want you to promise me you'll stay put, though. I want you to stay with me or Jade or Chloe at all times until the killer is caught."

"I'm sorry I walked out tonight. I figured the note was from Tanner or that nice Mr. Weatherby." Propping her elbows on the counter, she cradled her face in her hands. "It seemed playful, not like something a killer would do."

"I know, Granny Rose, but you can't know what a killer would do. And it's not because you're a foolish old woman. You are one of the smartest women I've ever met." With one of the biggest hearts. Granny Rose rarely saw bad in anyone, and that innocence made her so special, but it also made her naïve and trusting. "The police will find out who killed Broderick and Whitney, but until they do, we have to do whatever we can to stay safe. Both of us."

"And you're sure I'm not a nuisance?" She lowered her hands and finally lifted her gaze to meet Emma's.

Emma started a fresh pot of milk, added the cocoa. "Are you kidding me? I've had more fun since you've been here than I did the whole year after I moved out."

"Okay, then." Granny Rose sat up straighter, her customary smile returning. "It's settled then. I'll stay. At least until this is all over, and we can get me a house of my own. Not that I don't love living with you, and I definitely want to stay close by, but I want something that's mine, something that's all me."

"And that's exactly what you'll have." Emma rounded the breakfast bar to kiss her cheek. "And even though we won't live in the same house, we'll still be neighbors."

"And I can cook for you every night."

She managed to resist groaning out loud.

"Just because we aren't living in the same house doesn't mean we can't eat dinner together. Unless, that is, you have a date with that handsome fella who took care of me tonight."

Emma started to offer up the usual protest, then changed her mind. Jake Bennett did seem like a nice guy, if a little less than forthcoming about his personal life. But there was nothing wrong with wanting a little privacy. Unless, of course, it was because you were hiding something dangerous.

"He sure is a looker, that one." With a grin, she waggled her eyebrows up and down.

Emma slung an arm around Granny Rose's shoulders and squeezed. "He sure is."

"You know, I could find out where he lives, maybe take him a nice lasagna to thank him for looking out for an old lady." She gave Emma a half-hearted elbow nudge. "I could maybe even put in a good word for you."

"Thanks, but no thanks." Emma laughed. It was good to see Granny back to her old self again, more or less, even if that did include matchmaker mode. Leaving her to it, and hoping that would end the conversation about Detective Jake Bennett, Emma returned to the stove and poured the hot chocolate into two mugs. "Now, bring your hot chocolate over to my desk so we can research while we drink."

"Research what?" Even as she asked, she stood, lifted her mug.

Emma grabbed a chair and set it next to hers at the desk, then brought her own hot chocolate and set it aside on a coaster. "I want to see what I can find out about all of the players."

"I thought you were staying out of the investigation?" Granny Rose frowned as she took her seat.

"I am. Mostly. I'm not asking any questions, simply doing a bit of research from my own computer from the safety and in the privacy of my own home."

It was Granny Rose's turn to laugh. "Keep telling yourself that, honey."

Apparently figuring they planned on staying put for a bit, Butch padded over and settled at Granny's side with a groan. Ginger clawed a comfortable spot on the rug on the other side of Emma, careful to keep the two chairs between her and Butch, then flopped over and began to wash. All in all, it was a comfortable scene, one Emma could get very used to. She smoothed her timeline-suspect list, crumpled from being in her pocket all day, on the desk and grabbed a pen.

Granny Rose leaned close and studied what she'd written. "Okay, so who are the players? And who's at the top of your list?"

"You know what, that's a good idea." She ripped a sheet of paper off the legal pad in her desk and folded it into four columns. At the top of the first column, she wrote *Suspect*. After a moment's thought, she topped the other columns with *Motive, Opportunity,* and *Alibi*. She tapped the pen against the desk a few times, then squeezed in a fifth column and wrote *Whitney*. The first name she added to the suspect list was Phillip Aldridge. She put a checkmark beneath Whitney's name. Of everyone on the suspect list, he had the most to gain from her death.

Granny frowned at the page. "Why Phillip first? Because you suspect he killed his father, or because he was mean to me, and he's just plain unlikeable?"

She'd asked herself that same question numerous times. She filled the columns as she thought it through out loud for Granny Rose. "In the end, I don't think it matters. He definitely had motive, since his father was tossing him out of his home with nothing, after apparently cutting off his only

197

source of income, his allowance. According to Max, he'd already tried to have his parents declared incompetent and take over control of the family finances. I can't confirm any alibi, but he had the opportunity, since Tiny placed him at the crime scene the day of—"

"True." Granny Rose held up a finger. "But you have to keep in mind, Tiny's a suspect too, so it could benefit him to say Phillip was there."

Hmm. She was right. However much Emma didn't want to accept it, if she was going to figure out who posed a threat to Granny Rose, she would have to be honest with herself, no matter how difficult. She put the word yes with a question mark after it in Phillip's *opportunity* column and added Tiny's name on the next row. "We know Tiny had the opportunity, since he admitted to being there and having a confrontation with him, and we know he had motive, though a bad business deal seems like a flimsy motive for murder."

"People have killed for less," Granny Rose said absently as she blew on her hot chocolate and studied the list.

Emma couldn't argue that. She left a second alibi column blank. "As far as an alibi, I don't know where he was at the time Broderick was killed. And I can't see any reason he'd have had to kill Whitney."

"Unless she was in the wrong place at the wrong time, or maybe they were involved with each other somehow." Granny Rose frowned. "What about Mildred? She'd have motive to kill Whitney."

Emma added the name and put a check in the Whitney column. "She would have had the opportunity for sure. And the motive, since her husband was selling or consigning everything she owned, selling her home out from under her, and leaving the bulk of his estate to an illegitimate daughter born out of an affair he engaged in during their marriage, a daughter he brought into her home and expected her to accept."

Granny Rose sat back and crossed one leg over the other, sipped her hot chocolate. "Seems like a heck of a motive to me."

"I agree, but I'm not sure she's strong enough to have killed him with a blow to the head. And even if she managed that, I don't see how she could have wrapped him in plastic and moved him into the storage container by herself. A partner, maybe?" Maybe the man she'd seen leaving the Aldridge house was working with her? Could she have hired a hitman? She put a plus and wrote partner with a question mark after Mildred's name.

"You never know, though. Killing her husband in a fit of rage might have sent adrenaline rushing through her. Enough to get rid of him, anyway, before she came to her senses."

"Could be." Which brought her to Eric. Reluctantly, she added his name in the next row. "Eric had the opportunity, especially since he supposedly locked the container when he left, which would mean no one else could have gotten Broderick inside it."

"Theoretically."

"True. I guess someone else could have had a key. Mildred for sure, if Broderick had a second key made. Or Phillip even." She jotted a note on a Post-it to ask Eric if Broderick had a key or could have had one made for the lock.

"Or, he could have thought he locked it, and either the lock didn't catch right, or he forgot." Granny Rose grinned. It was good to see her getting back to her old, new self. "Trust me, I do it all the time. I'm positive I did something, only to find out later I forgot."

And again she had to leave the alibi column and the Whitney column blank. She scribbled alibis under the note to talk to Eric. If she could narrow down the time Broderick had been killed, she might be able to at least figure out who couldn't have killed him. Which brought her to her next list. Halfway down the page, she wrote *Unknown*. Because there were other people who, while not necessarily suspects, could have some involvement in how events unfolded.

With a sigh, she wrote Jade's name.

Granny Rose jumped to her feet, tipping the chair behind her. "You can't possibly think—"

"No. Of course not, Granny." Emma stood and righted the chair for her. "This is a list of people who somehow could have played into how things happened that day, unknown catalysts that could have determined how things played out."

Granny plopped down with a huff.

Emma added Whitney's name under the unknown column, because she somehow factored into the situation, even if she hadn't killed Broderick. Arianna's name followed. As far as Emma knew, she was still missing. She did know she was alive after Broderick's murder, because she'd dropped off her tire to be fixed. The fact that she never returned to pick it up could simply mean she hadn't gotten time, which Emma could certainly relate to, or something more sinister. She turned on her computer, intent on checking to see if Arianna had been found, though surely she'd have heard if she was.

Then she added Jacob Bennett and balked at Granny's lifted brow. "What?"

"What could Detective Dreamy have had to do with Broderick's murder?" Granny Rose asked.

"I have no idea if he could have had anything to do with it, but again, he's an unknown factor. He said he's no longer a detective and didn't want to get involved in the case, but could he have been covering something up? He was at the crime scene that morning."

"So was half of Mini-Meadows." Granny shrugged. "Seems like a waste of time to me, but by all means, research him if you want. Who knows? You might find something interesting."

Emma let the conversation end there. She'd probably be lying to herself if she didn't admit some level of personal interest in the enigmatic detective, so better not to look too deeply into her reasons for adding him to the list. When her internet browser opened, she shifted her attention back to the matter at hand and typed Arianna's name into the search engine. A list of news articles popped up, none of them saying she'd been found, but Emma clicked on the most recent one to see if there had been any news. Arianna's picture popped up with *Missing* underneath.

"Hey, that's her!" Granny Rose tapped Arianna's image on the screen. "That's the woman who was following me and taking pictures."

"You're sure?"

"Positive. I told you I thought I'd recognize her if I saw her again. And that is definitely her."

Emma studied the picture—long auburn hair, green eyes, a thin face with sharp angles and contours—committing the details of Arianna's features to memory so she'd be sure to recognize her if she saw her anywhere. The woman had been present at the murder scene, by Eric's account had been one of the last to see Broderick alive, and had access to the murder weapon. She also had a relationship with Phillip Aldridge, as well as a fleeting work relationship with Eric. Though Emma had no clue what motive she might have had for killing Broderick or Whitney, she bore looking into. Now to figure out why she'd been following Granny Rose, what involvement she'd had with Broderick Aldridge or his killer, and where she'd disappeared to after his murder.

Chapter Twenty-Six

After spending another two hours the night before trying to research her suspects and coming up with nothing new, Emma had given up and spent another fitful night curled on the loveseat. Actually, thinking she hadn't found anything wasn't quite accurate. Her search of Detective Bennett had turned up an article about him being injured in the line of duty a few months before. So she had learned that. Oh, and she'd also learned that even his picture managed to send her heart all aflutter. But that was a problem for a different day.

Today's problem; she had a meeting with a client in about an hour and had yet to determine whether to take Granny Rose with her or see if she wanted to stay with Chloe at Pocket Books. She was trying to decide how best to ask without making it sound like she thought Granny Rose needed a babysitter when Granny walked in dressed for the day in olive green cargo pants with a men's khaki button-up open over a black tank. She'd left her work boots untied with the laces tucked inside. It was a good look, and Emma had a momentary flash of envy she could pull it off.

Granny Rose spread her arms wide and turned in a circle. "Well? What do you think?"

"It's a great look. Young and chic."

"That's exactly what I was going for."

"Umm…Granny Rose, there's something I need to talk to you about."

"What's that, dear," she asked, distracted as she unbuttoned one cuff and rolled the sleeve to her elbow, revealing pale, paper-thin skin with a network of veins running underneath. "What do you think? Better?"

And still… "I like it. But Granny—"

"Does it scream I'm a hard worker, and I know my business."

Emma tilted her head and studied her grandmother. "Actually, I think it does, but—"

"Good." She started on the other sleeve. "I was aiming for that."

"Well, you definitely pulled it off. Now, if you—"

"Have you walked Butch yet?" she asked.

Frustrated, Emma sighed. "Yes. He's fed and walked."

"Oh, good, thanks." She petted his back and dropped a kiss on the top of his head, which she didn't have to bend far to reach. "Then let's get out of here."

"But, I—"

"Come on. We'll talk on the way. I told Jade I'd be there by ten, and it took longer than I expected to find just the right look." She opened the bathroom door and looked in the mirror, smoothed her hair back into a long wavy tail, and tied it with a leather band. "There. Much more efficient."

A dull throb began at her temples, and Emma massaged them between a thumb and forefinger. Half past nine in the morning, and it was already turning out to be a long day. "But I'm trying to tell you, I have to work this morning. I have to meet Mrs. Carmichael. I promised her I'd get to her decluttering job this week, and since I don't have much going on today, I told her I'd be there by ten."

Swinging the bathroom door shut, Granny Rose glanced at her watch, a gold Cartier with a distressed brown leather band. "Then we'd better get going."

With a quick look down at her own boring jeans, oversized T-shirt, and white sneakers, Emma slung her bag over her shoulder and grabbed her keys from her desk. "I can drop you off at Jade's on my way, since Mrs. Carmichael lives right in Mini-Meadows, but how long do you want to stay? I figured you could come with me to the Carmichael job if you want. Or, I could take a break and come back for you, or drop you off at Chloe's if you'd prefer?"

Granny Rose waved her off. "Actually, I start today, so I'll be there until closing."

Emma locked the door behind them, scanned the neighborhood in what was becoming an ingrained habit, and double-checked the door. "What are you talking about? Start what?"

"My new job. Didn't I tell you?"

"What?" Emma stopped short in the driveway. "No. What new job?"

"I'm going to be working for Jade at Little Bits." She puffed up her chest, lifted her chin. "My first ever job."

"Your first what now?" Realizing they were sitting ducks out in the open, Emma hit the key fob to unlock the Jeep's doors. No way was she cruising around town in the golf cart. May as well paint a target on her and Granny Rose's backs. She opened the passenger door for Granny Rose, then hurried around and slid into the driver's seat, closing the door as quickly as possible.

"Yup." Granny climbed into the passenger seat with a bounce and a grin from ear to ear. "I've never had a job of my own before. Of course, I was a wife and mother, which is full-time work in its own right, but I went from my father's house, to my husband's house, to your father's house. I've worked on plenty of committees and boards and stuff like that. You know how it is, the kind of nonsense that's expected from a wealthy man's wife. But I've never had an honest-to-goodness job where I got to go to work every day and get paid and everything. I must have forgotten to tell you after the incident last night. And I was so excited when Jade asked if I wanted to go to work for her, but then I felt foolish after that nice detective—who you really should go thank properly—found me outside. I can't believe I fell for that whole surprise thing, but what with the new job and all, I kind of figured it was just a special day. So then I got a little down on myself for being naïve and all, and I must have forgotten to tell you."

Emma laughed, and just like that, the stress she'd felt only a few minutes ago melted away. She lay a hand over Granny Rose's. "You're not naïve, Granny Rose." Not much, anyway. "You're just innocent and kind. And they are two amazing qualities I wouldn't trade for anything."

Granny turned her hand over to grip Emma's for a moment, then released it so Emma could shift into gear. "Thank you, dear. That makes me feel a little better, but I promise I'll try to be more careful."

"Promise me you won't go out of the shop alone?" She glanced over to be sure she hadn't hurt her feelings. "It would make me feel so much less stressed knowing you were safe."

"I promise, dear. That's a mistake I won't be repeating any time soon."

Or ever, Emma hoped. "Thank you, Granny. I appreciate it."

"Look, there's Jade." Granny Rose pointed toward the sidewalk where Jade stood with her head tilted back, so the warm morning sun beat down on her face. "She must be looking for me."

A quick glance at the dashboard clock showed they still had fifteen minutes until Granny's start time. Emma pulled into the parking slot out front.

"See ya later." Granny Rose hopped out of the car, then glance back in. "Oh, and I was thinking we could go to Libby's for dinner, maybe celebrate my new job."

"That sounds great, Granny Rose. I'm looking forward to it."

When Jade spotted them, she waved to Granny Rose and approached Emma's window.

Emma rolled it down. "I don't know how to thank you, Jade. I've never seen Granny Rose so excited."

"I'm glad." She grinned at Granny Rose. "The door's open, Granny Rose, if you want to go ahead in and take a look around, start familiarizing yourself with the space and the merchandise."

"Of course, thank you." She waved to Emma. "See ya."

Jade shifted her hair behind her shoulders. "It just happened to work out perfectly. I mentioned at the meeting last night that I was going to run a help wanted ad, and Granny Rose said she'd love to have the job, so it saved me the trouble of looking for someone and then hoping I could trust them."

Emma chewed on her lower lip. Jade was Granny's employer now, but she was also a friend. Plus, she was fully aware of the situation with the killer.

Jade laughed and punched Emma's arm. "Stop fretting, Mom, she'll be fine."

Emma laughed.

Jade's smile faltered. "There's a memorial for Whitney tonight."

"Are you going to go?"

She heaved a sigh. "Yeah, I'll go."

No way would she make Jade go alone. "Okay, then, I'll tell you what. As soon as I'm done at Mrs. Carmichael's, I'll go home and take care of Butch and Ginger, then I'll pick you and Granny Rose up, and we'll all go together."

"Thanks, Emma. I really appreciate it. I wasn't looking forward to going alone." With a quick check over her shoulder to be sure Granny Rose had gone inside, Jade lowered her voice. "And I promise I'll keep an eye on her, make sure she doesn't wander off."

"Thanks, Jade. I don't want her to be a burden—"

"Burden? Are you kidding me? When we talked last night, she had some amazing ideas I'm really looking forward to exploring with her. She's an intelligent, fun, caring woman, exactly what I want in an employee and a friend. She could never be a burden." She leaned in and hugged Emma. "You just worry about you. Don't forget, Granny Rose might not be the only target."

How could she forget? A quick look around as she backed out showed nothing out of the ordinary. Nothing she could see anyway.

Chapter Twenty-Seven

Moss swayed from the branches of towering oaks in the gentle breeze. The lake on Emma's left rippled softly, reflecting the sun's rays as well as the blue sky and clouds that looked like giant piles of cotton. A beautiful day. For just a moment, she considered calling Mrs. Carmichael and rescheduling, then spending the day at the park. Butch would probably enjoy a good run if she could find a dog park nearby.

She dismissed the idea just as quickly. Granny Rose, Jade, and Chloe were all working, so she'd work today, but the next day they could all take off together she'd see if she could talk them into a beach or park picnic.

With that in mind, she pulled into Mrs. Carmichael's driveway. A porch swing piled high with boxes that looked like they were about to topple over greeted her as she climbed the steps to the front porch and rang the bell. The outside of the tiny home was fashioned much like Tanner Reed's, a mini version of a Victorian cottage. Beautiful, traditional, complete with stone façade and wrap-around porch. A white picket fence, lined with azaleas, surrounded a postage stamp lawn.

Although Mrs. Carmichael didn't plan on moving, she'd accumulated too much clutter over the years for such a small space. Since her daughters both worked full time and didn't have time to get over to help her clean the place out, they'd chipped in and hired Emma to help her go through and organize the mess. Emma had a sneaking suspicion it probably had less to do with their lack of spare time and more to do with the fact they didn't want to be the ones to argue with her over what she should and shouldn't keep.

The door opened wide, and Mrs. Carmichael smiled and stuck out a hand.

"Good morning, Emma. Thank you for coming."

Taking the proffered hand, Emma grinned back, then gestured toward the boxes stacked askew on the swing. "Looks like you already got started."

"Oh, that." She waved a hand dismissively and shoved a few errant strands of gray hair that had fallen out of her bun behind her ear. "They're just boxes of Mr. Carmichael's old newspapers. I never could figure out why he collected them. Other people read them and either throw them out or use them for lining bird cages or some such thing. But Otto kept every last one."

Emma couldn't figure it either. Then again, she'd grown up in a time of computers, where any information you wanted could be accessed instantly. And, since Mr. Carmichael had been gone for more than five years, she figured his wife had held onto them for sentimental reasons. "Are you okay with getting rid of them? If you wanted, we could maybe go through, cut out the front pages or headline stories, and make a scrapbook out of them. Then you'd be able to hang onto a piece of them without them taking up so much room."

Tears sprang into her eyes as she led Emma through a maze of boxes, clothing, various assorted pieces of furniture, and equipment and gestured toward one of only two empty seats at the kitchen table. All the others were covered with something. This was definitely going to be more than a one-day job. "Sit, please, would you like some tea?"

Since she already had the teapot and cups laid out, Emma accepted. "Sure, thank you. How long have you lived in Mini-Meadows?"

"Oh, I guess about ten years now. Once my husband retired, and the girls got married and moved out, we didn't see the need to upkeep a big house and yard. But we didn't want a condo where we'd be right on top of our neighbors. This place suited."

Ten years. It was difficult to believe anyone could have accumulated so much in ten years. But beneath the clutter, it was a beautiful home. Old fashioned, with its dark wood wainscotting, what appeared to be reclaimed barn wood floors—where they peeked through the mess, at least—and wood ceiling beams angled up the cathedral ceiling. A few solid pieces Emma was sure were antiques held a hodgepodge of piles. A stone fireplace, its mantel crowded with knickknacks threatening to knock each other off to claim an inch of space, stood sentinel on one wall. "Well, it's a lovely space, and once we get it cleared out a little, it will suit again, I'm sure."

"I can tell already my girls did the right thing by hiring you on." She poured tea, set out a plate with a variety of little frosted cakes on it. "You obviously get it. They look around and see a cluttered mess, but I see pieces of my life. They don't understand it's difficult for me to part with my Otto's things. I keep telling them once I'm gone, they can do whatever they want with the mess, sell it, toss it all, burn it down… I don't care one way or the other, but in the meantime, I like having Otto close."

Emma shifted her teacup aside and reached across the table to hold Mrs. Carmichael's hands. While she understood Mrs. Carmichael's dilemma, she could also see her daughters' points of view as they'd been concerned for her safety when they'd called. Not only was the clutter a fire hazard, they were worried she'd trip and fall over something and not be able to get help. "I understand completely. And I'll do whatever I can to help you preserve your most special memories while helping you clear a little more room for yourself."

"That would be wonderful, dear. I have to tell you, I was worried about you coming over here, telling me to get rid of all my stuff, but now I'm relieved to see it's going to be okay." She looked around the room, where every inch of flat surface was covered with something or another, as if the woman couldn't bear to look at empty space. "So, where do we start?"

"Well, Mrs. Carmichael—"

"Angie, please."

"Angie, would you mind showing me through the house, maybe pointing out some of the things that are most important that you'd like to keep?"

"Sure thing. You finish your tea and have a piece of cake, and then we can get started."

Emma made small talk while she ate a delicious lemon cake and sipped her tea. She figured Angie was about Granny Rose's age and thought the two would get along wonderfully.

When Angie finished her tea, she set her empty tea cup down in a saucer.

"So, I hear you're the one who found Broderick Aldridge's body. Nasty business, that."

Emma barely kept from choking at the unexpected shift in topics. "Yes, it was. Did you know him?"

"Enough to dislike him, but not really. Knew his wife more. Didn't much care for her either."

"Mildred?" Angie was the first person Emma could think of who admitted to knowing Mildred. It almost seemed the woman dwelled in her husband's shadow.

"Yup. Her son, Phillip, that no good scoundrel, went to school with my eldest daughter."

Not knowing what to say to that, she just went with, "Small world."

"It is indeed." Angie nodded. "I had to go over to their house one day, speak to her about her son's behavior."

Emma perked up. "Why? What did he do?"

"Stole my girl's lunch money. That bully." She sat up straighter, pointed a finger at Emma. "Did he steal lunch money from one of the big boys? Nope, not Phillip. He stole money from a petite, shy little girl. He'd done it four times before I finally realized something was wrong because she was coming home from school starving. Got it out of her, I did, then marched myself right on over there to his big ole sprawling ranch. And I thought to myself, what all would this boy need with my little girl's lunch money? That's when I realized he didn't need it. He was just bein' mean."

That sounded about right to Emma. "Were you able to speak to Mildred about it?"

"I meant to, and I did eventually." She leaned forward, rested her elbows on the table, and settled in to dish. "But while I was sitting there, parked across the street, wondering why this obviously well-to-do boy was pickin' on my baby girl, the front door opened, and Mildred peeked her head out and looked all around. Then, she kissed some man—and I'm not talking a peck on the cheek, I'm talking full-on tonsil hockey. I figured it was her husband, even though, for a moment, maybe they were so wrapped up in each other they didn't have time for their boy, and he was looking for attention. Sometimes, ya know, when kids are starved in that area, even negative attention will do."

That made sense to Emma, but she was still hung up on Broderick, and Mildred Aldridge locked in such a passionate embrace. She just couldn't picture it. But who knew? People changed. They could have been different when they were younger. Maybe he was less jaded, she less bitter.

"Anyway, once the fella left and I finally worked up the nerve to knock on the door, she invited me in, and I saw the painting over the mantle and realized that was not her husband she'd been playin' around with."

"Are you sure?" Mildred having an affair? She'd seemed so loyal to her husband, ridiculously so. Enough that she'd give up everything she owned because he said to. Emma couldn't wrap her head around that same woman cheating on him. Then again... She suddenly saw the man sneaking across the Aldridge property in a new light. Maybe he wasn't Mildred's attorney or Phillip's spy after all. What if he wasn't there for any nefarious reason, like getting paid for the hit on her husband? Could he be Mildred's side piece? If she had one years ago, why not now? Maybe the two of them had conspired to get rid of Broderick and then had to off Whitney after he left everything to her.

"Positive." Angie stood and started to clear the table. "I ran into them at functions and whatnot over the years and never saw her with that man again. Did see her with her husband, though, and that man always looked down his nose at me every time he saw me."

Emma stood and set her empty saucer and cup in the sink. "Did Mildred stop Phillip from stealing your daughter's lunch money?"

"Well, something stopped him. Right after his mother insisted he couldn't have done it, went the 'not my precious angel' route. But I saw him then." She frowned and looked off in the distance, lost in some memory of the past. "At least, I'm pretty sure I did."

"Saw who? Phillip?"

She shrugged and refocused on Emma. "Like I said, I can't be sure, but I did see movement in the shadows in the hallway right outside the room when I was talking to his mother, and the little hairs on the back of my neck stood straight up at attention. If I was a bettin' woman, I'd say for sure that boy was out there skulkin' around in the shadows. So I told her if it happened again, my Otto would come on over there to speak to her husband about it. I doubt the boy was ever punished for it, doubt she even believed it was true, but I'm pretty sure that little brat got the message, and it did stop, which is all I cared about." Once the dirty dishes were in the sink, Angie gestured toward the hallway. "I'll wash those up later. Now, one of the most important things I want to keep is my girls' baby clothes."

Emma couldn't get the conversation out of her mind, though. Had Mildred really been cheating on Broderick? Emma found it hard to believe the meek, do whatever Broderick wants woman could have been having an affair. But Angie seemed really sure of it.

While Emma was distracted by thoughts of Mildred straying, Angie stopped at an accordion-style door Emma assumed led to a small bedroom space. She slid it open, and Emma barely refrained from squeaking out loud. The entire bedroom space, but for a pathway through the boxes to the bed, was filled with storage bins and boxes.

The woman must have saved every stitch of clothing the two girls had ever worn. And she must have brought it all with her when she moved in, since the girls were already grown and on their own by then. Ah well, if she could tolerate Mr. Carmichael's newspaper obsession, he'd probably been able to deal with her hoarding baby clothes. Who knew? Maybe he agreed with holding onto that part of his daughters' childhood. "Are these all clothes?"

"Mostly. I know..." She let out a nervous laugh. "My girls keep telling me I need to find a hobby other than hoarding. But do you think we can find something to do with them all?"

A hobby. That's it! "Have you ever considered quilting as a hobby?"

"Actually, I love the idea. I've thought of giving it a try before, but I've never gotten 'round to it."

"Well, if you wanted, we could take out the most special pieces and keep them in a trunk at the foot of the bed." If they could unbury the foot of the bed. "Then we could donate, sell, or consign some of the less meaningful items. I can give you a business card for a consignment shop right here in

Mini-Meadows for that and have Jade come out and collect the stuff."

She looked around the room, wringing her hands. "I don't know."

Better to keep right on going. Because the girls were right, this was a dangerous situation. "Then, the stuff that's left, you can cut up and use to make a quilt."

Her eyes lit up. "That's a thing?"

"Sure. You cut the fronts out of the shirts and dresses, then sew them together, and it makes an awesome quilt. You could even do more than one." She winced. She probably shouldn't have suggested that. If she wasn't careful, she'd be back here trying to talk her into getting rid of all the quilts. "Then you could hang a quilt on the wall, drape a few of them over a ladder in the corner, throw one over the back of the couch, and snuggle up with it every night while you watch TV or read a book."

"Oh, my." She clasped her hands together. "I love that idea."

"Since we have a few good ideas about what to do with this stuff, why don't we start here today. I can even throw a bunch of the stuff you want to consign or donate in the back of my Jeep and take it with me later, since I'll be stopping by Little Bits on my way home to pick up my grandmother." She handed Angie Jade's business card and sent her to call Jade and work out the specifics while she tried to count the boxes, then gave it up as a lost cause. However many there were made no difference, they'd all have to be gone through. She dug into the first cardboard box, emptying the clothing onto the bed and crushing the empty box.

While she worked, her mind wandered back to Mildred. If she'd had one affair, why not another? Could she still be seeing the same man? Or a different one? Had she finally gotten fed up with Broderick and gotten rid of him so she could be with her lover? Had he found out, confronted her about it, leading to the altercation that had ended in his death?

The only thing she was sure of in the whole situation was the fact that Phillip had stolen the poor little girl's lunch money. An image of him holding Granny Rose's arm came unbidden. Once a bully, always a bully, she supposed. But had he stepped up the ladder to killer?

Chapter Twenty-Eight

True to her word, Emma had gone home and tended to Butch and Ginger, then picked Granny Rose, Jade, and Chloe up to attend Whitney's memorial. Thankfully, she still had some family living in the area, and the memorial was held locally, saving Emma a trip up to Jacksonville when she was exhausted from the Carmichael job.

Although, she'd left Angie's with a wonderful sense of satisfaction that boosted her mood. They'd actually accomplished a lot in the bedroom area, Mrs. Carmichael sorting through bins of old clothes, Emma piling those she was willing to part with in the back of her Jeep to drop off at Jade's when she picked them up.

Emma sat in a small seating arrangement against the back wall of the crowded room with Jade, Chloe, and Granny Rose. Though the police hadn't released Whitney's body yet, several of her friends spoke kindly of her as they reminisced about the past. From all appearances, Whitney was a kind, well-liked woman who'd had the misfortune to find out her true identity and get involved with the Aldridges. Emma's good mood began to waver.

"We'll go soon," Jade said. "I just wanted to come and pay my respects to Whitney's mom, tell her how sorry I am for her loss."

"I'm not in a hurry, Jade. Take your time, but it looks like the crowd around Mrs. Jameson has thinned out a bit. If you'd like to speak to her, now might be a good time."

Jade stood, blew out a breath, and smoothed her black skirt. "I guess it's now or never."

"I'll walk over with you." Emma stood, too, and looked around the room in her ever-growing habitual scan for danger. Would that habit ever die? Would she always be on the lookout for trouble now? Always be just a bit frightened and looking over her shoulder?

A hand on her shoulder had her screeching and whirling around.

Jake Bennett simply grinned, amusement dancing in his eyes. "Sorry, didn't mean to startle you. Although it is good to know you're on your toes."

"Fancy meeting you here." She lifted her chin, scraped together what was left of her dignity, and ignored the fact that he'd nearly scared her to death—again. She was beginning to think he did it on purpose. How had he managed to sneak up on her without her seeing him? So much for being aware of her surroundings. While she waited for her heart rate to plummet back down to normal, she had a moment to wonder what he was doing there. "Did you know Whitney?"

"No, I didn't." He held her gaze, his dark eyes intent on hers, caging her, sucking her in. "Did you?"

"I did, actually." *Sort of. In an I met her once kind of way.*

He grinned as if he could read her mind.

She shook off the attraction, had to if she was going to have an intelligent conversation with him. And figure out why he was there if he wasn't involved in the investigation and didn't know Whitney personally. "So, what are you doing here?"

Smooth, Emma. Maybe she should take Granny Rose's offer to teach her a thing or two to heart.

He shrugged it off and took a step back, releasing the sense of intimacy he'd created by being so close, much to her disappointment. "Same as you, I imagine. Just checking out who shows up."

A smile tugged at her. "I thought you didn't want to get involved in the investigation."

"Let's just say I have an invested interest in some of the players." He grinned, and her heart rate shot back up. Then he glanced over his shoulder at Granny Rose, who grinned back at him and gave a little finger wave. When he returned his attention to Emma, he sported a big smile. "How's she doing?"

Emma's heart melted. "She's okay. She was a bit shaken last night, but we talked, and she was feeling better this morning when she started her new job."

"Good, I'm glad." His gaze shifted over her shoulder. "I have to run, but keep an eye on her, okay."

"I will, thanks."

But his attention had already moved on, and he started across the room, hands in his pockets. He might even have pulled off the casual, uninterested observer, if not for the intense look in his eyes.

Once the crowd swallowed him up, she turned back to Jade. "Sorry, I—"

Jade's answering grin said it all, so she didn't even bother finishing the sentence. Instead, not ready to discuss her apparently way too obvious attraction to the detective, she hooked Jade's elbow. "Come on, let's speak to Mrs. Jameson."

Jade's smile faltered as she nodded and fell into step beside Emma. "You don't have to come with me, but I sure do appreciate it."

"No problem. I'll hang back while you speak to her, though, give you some privacy."

Jade nodded and swallowed hard, tears shimmering in her eyes, catching in her dark lashes. "Thanks."

"Sure." As promised, when they reached Mrs. Jameson, Emma simply offered her condolences and then stepped aside to wait for Jade. As she did, she caught sight of a man lingering in the shadows at the front corner of the room. She might not have noticed, since the room was packed with mourners, but the clandestine nature of the man skulk—

Skulking. Hadn't that been the term both Tiny and Angie had used to describe Phillip Aldridge's behavior? And Emma had agreed. The day she'd visited Mildred, she'd been sure someone was outside the room, lurking in the shadows, before Phillip stormed in and demanded his inheritance. An inheritance, it turned out, that didn't even belong to him.

And now, here he was again, lingering in the shadows at the corner of the room. He probably thought he was unobtrusive, invisible, but his sneaky nature actually made him stand out. To Emma, anyway. With a quick glance that showed Jade still in deep conversation with Mrs. Jameson and another woman, Emma approached him.

"Hello, Phillip." And that was as far as she got. When he simply stared back at her wide-eyed, she had no clue what else to say, didn't really even know why she'd approached him. Maybe just to show him he'd been noticed. "I'm sorry for your loss."

He frowned. "My loss?"

She gestured at a board filled with pictures of Whitney, from the smiling little girl she'd been to the striking woman she'd grown into. "The loss of your sister."

Anger flashed in his eyes, just for an instant before he recovered himself and feigned surprise. "Sister? What are you talking about?"

But he was lying, and she knew it. Even if he hadn't known about her before his father's death, there was no way he didn't know now. If nothing else, the police would have told him when they questioned him after her murder. Unless they hadn't questioned him. But why wouldn't they? He had to be a suspect, considering his father had been murdered, then the woman who'd inherited his entire estate had been found dead as well. "Whitney Jameson, your father's daughter and beneficiary."

"Not anymore." He shrugged, stuffed his hands into his pockets, and leaned a shoulder against the wall. "And as far as that woman being my father's daughter, that was never proven."

"Oh, I uh…."

"But…" He jerked upright, snapped his fingers, and pointed a finger at her. "Speaking of my father's estate, since Ms. Jameson passed away before claiming her inheritance, it's now reverted to my mother and me. Mother will inherit half, and since I'm his only offspring, I'll inherit the other half. So, that tiny home you were so keen on getting your hands on is once again on the market."

Shoot. Now what? On the one hand, Granny Rose really wanted that little caboose house. Not only was it perfect for her, it was only four lots down from Emma's. And, with the addition of Aldridge's house and Tanner Reed's house, the last of the free lots on Emma's side of the development were now filled. Even if Granny Rose did choose to buy a different house or have her own built, it would be on the other side of Mini-Meadows.

On the other hand, did she really want to do business with Phillip Aldridge, a man who by all accounts was a sneak and a bully, a man who might well have murdered his own father and sister? No, she didn't. She'd much prefer to have Granny Rose, and even Butch stay with her, no matter how crowded things were, no matter that she had to sleep on the loveseat every night. She could always get a more comfortable loveseat.

But Granny Rose really wanted her independence. And she had loved the house.

What did it really matter who sold it to her as long as the deal was legal? And she'd get a good lawyer to look it over, be sure Phillip wasn't scamming them somehow. "How much do you want for it?"

With a smirk, he shrugged and leaned his shoulder back against the wall. "I'll let you have it for the price my mother agreed on with your grandmother. Now that I'll inherit half of everything my father owned, I can afford to be generous."

The fact that he made "be generous" sound like he was donating to charity prickled Emma's nerves, but she let it go. Once Granny was happily settled in her new home, none of it would matter anyway. Of course, she wouldn't be going anywhere until Broderick's killer was found and apprehended, but she'd at least have the house, and they could spend their time together fixing it up just right for when she could move in. "I'll take it."

He straightened. "Good. I'll have my lawyer draw up the contract. Come out to the ranch tomorrow evening, say around seven, and we'll go over everything."

Though it took everything in her to force the words out, she managed a "thank you" without choking on it.

He started to walk away, then turned back to her. "Oh, and come alone."

Fear shot through her, stiffening her spine.

"I don't need the old lady pawing through my things again." And with that, he walked away.

While some of the fear dissipated, some remained. Though he'd said come alone, she figured what he really meant was don't bring Granny Rose. But how could Granny sign the contract if she didn't come? Then again, Emma had wanted to have a lawyer look over the paperwork anyway, and that would give her an excuse to take the contract home with her. Fine. She'd go meet up with Phillip. Maybe she'd hold off on telling Granny Rose until after the lawyer gave the go-ahead, that way, she wouldn't be disappointed if the deal fell through. One thing she did know, though, she wasn't meeting with Phillip at his house alone. But who could she take with her?

Chapter Twenty-Nine

While she'd toyed with the idea of asking Jake Bennett to accompany her, he'd already been gone by the time she'd finished talking to Phillip and reconnected with Jade. Besides, what kind of first date would that be? Plus, she'd have had to ask him, and she was kind of hoping he'd ask her out at some point when this whole mess was over. In the end, she'd given in and told Granny Rose about the deal, asked her, Jade, and Chloe to go with her and simply wait in the car.

Of course, Granny Rose spent much of the next day chattering about area rugs and curtains. But it was good to see her so excited, first with the new job, then with her new home.

Now, she just had to make sure Phillip followed through with his end of the bargain. Instead of pulling into the driveway, she parked along the road in front of the Aldridge house but behind a mature moss-covered oak that would provide some cover, and shifted into park. Since the night was cool enough, she turned the Jeep off but left the key in the ignition, just in case. "Remember, stay slouched down and try not to let Phillip know you're out here."

The way she figured, it didn't hurt to have backup. If nothing else, if things went smoothly and the contract looked good, maybe she could cancel the lawyer appointment she'd scheduled for the next day and let Granny Rose sign and be done with it.

"Don't worry. We'll be fine. Now," Granny Rose shooed her. "Go get me my house."

"You bet." She grinned as she hopped out of the Jeep and grabbed her bag. Then, just as a precaution in case Phillip tried to deny he'd sold her the house or pulled anything else she couldn't anticipate, she flipped on a mini recorder, then positioned it so it sat atop everything else in her bag, and left the bag slightly open. She knew it would record, because she and Granny Rose had tested it earlier. "Here goes nothing."

Careful not to jog the recorder, she hurried up the driveway, rang the bell, and waited. When no one answered right away, she checked her watch. Seven on the dot. Maybe Phillip had been pulling her leg about selling her the house? Just one more way to bully someone. A sinking feeling in her gut had her ringing the bell a second time.

Phillip opened the door, looked up and down the road, then stepped back and gestured toward the living room. "Come on in and sit down."

She did as instructed, noting the family portrait hadn't been returned to its place of prominence above the fireplace. She figured Mildred—

Her thoughts faltered when she noticed a woman sitting in an armchair, legs crossed, the look in her eye that of a much more calculating woman than the innocent girl Eric had painted her as. "Arianna Jenkins."

She nodded to Emma. "It's Arianna Aldridge, actually."

Arianna Aldridge? How could that be? Did Broderick have another child born of an affair?

Arianna tilted her head, studied Emma for a moment, then pointed to the sofa. "Sit. Let's chat."

Emma did as she said. The coffee table had been moved, a plastic drop cloth, much like the one Broderick had been wrapped in, spread in the center of the room, a pile of unopened paint cans stacked on the corner along with trays and rollers. She swallowed hard. "Doing renovations?"

Phillip sat on the arm of Arianna's chair, draped his arm across its back. "Arianna wants the house painted, something bold."

"Blood red." Arianna gestured toward the paint cans. Her smile made Emma's blood run cold. "What do you think?"

Emma had no clue what to think, and her mouth had gone too dry to answer anyway, so she simply nodded.

"So." Arianna shifted forward, rested her elbows on her knees. "Phillip says you want to buy Broderick's tiny home."

She nodded again.

"Well, he's had the contract drawn up." When she slapped Phillip's leg, he jumped up and ran to the desk, retrieved a stack of papers, and handed them to Emma, then sat next to her on the sofa.

She tried to relax as she flipped through the pages, read over the terms, which seemed fair to her and exactly as Mildred and Granny Rose had agreed. So why was her anxiety level through the roof? Why was her internal alarm system blaring at her full volume to get out of there? And what in the world was Arianna Jenkins, a.k.a. Aldridge doing there when she was supposed to be missing?

As much as Emma wanted answers, she figured it best to just take the paperwork and go. Whatever was going on here, she didn't want any part of it. And she most certainly didn't want Granny Rose getting antsy and walking in on it. She stood. "Okay, well, thank you. I'll take these home and have Granny Rose sign them all and get back to you."

"We're not done yet." Arianna stood, smiled a viciously cold grin. "Sit."

Emma plopped back down.

"Was there a reason you followed me out of Mini-Meadows the other day, Ms. Wells?" She paced as she spoke, back and forth, back and forth, like a caged tiger searching for escape.

"I don't know what you're talking about." But, of course, she did. Arianna had been driving the car she'd followed into the woods, right before she'd found Whitney dumped in the ditch.

"Come now. I'm not stupid." Her pacing took her past the doorway leading to the front door, effectively blocking Emma's escape in that direction. "You had to have been following me for a reason, since no one uses that back road out of Mini-Meadows. Come clean now."

She could try to make a run out the other doorway, but if she remembered correctly, that only led to Broderick's study, no means of escape in that direction. Unless she could get a window open and get out before Arianna or Phillip could reach her. Although, if the confused look Phillip currently sported was any indication, he may not know what Arianna was talking about. Maybe she hadn't shared the incident with him. Maybe he had no clue Emma was onto them, since she actually hadn't been before now. Although, in her defense, she'd suspected Phillip right from the beginning.

Emma swallowed the lump in her throat. "I didn't know it was you. My grandmother thought she recognized the car as one who'd been following her, taking pictures."

She nodded, thoughtful. "That's because it was. I hoped I could warn you off, but apparently, I was wrong."

Phillip shot to his feet. "What are you talking about, Arianna?"

Emma turned to him and was surprised to find he seemed genuinely baffled. Had he even known Arianna had followed Granny Rose?

"Why were you over in Mini-Meadows, and why would you need to warn Emma off?"

She paused and faced off with Phillip. "Because she asked too many questions, her and that nosy grandmother of hers."

"What are you talking about?" He propped his hands on his hips, anger coloring his cheeks. "You told me to sell the old lady the house, so I did. You said to make Emma come out here for the paperwork alone, which I also did. No questions asked. But now I want...no, I demand answers. What is going on here?"

Arianna shrugged and shot him a scathing look. "I suppose it doesn't matter now anyway."

Eric sauntered into the room from the hallway Emma'd been hoping to escape through. Keeping an amused eye on Phillip, he slung an arm around Arianna's shoulder, kissed her temple, and smirked. Then he turned his attention to Emma. "I'm sorry, Emma, I really am. I wish it hadn't come to this."

"I demand to know the meaning of this." Phillip took a step toward Eric. "And get your hands off my wife."

"Wife?" Emma couldn't help it blurting out.

Phillip stopped, eyeing Arianna and Eric, fists clenched. "Yeah. We were married in Vegas a few weeks ago."

Right before Broderick was killed. She'd been after Phillip's inheritance all along. And, unless Phillip was as good an actor as Eric apparently was, he hadn't known.

Phillip's mouth fell open. "You killed him? You killed my father."

"Of course I did." Arianna's already vicious smile turned predatory. "But you couldn't even get that right, didn't inherit a dime after all my hard work and sacrifice, and I ended up having to kill his daughter."

"How dare you!" Rage propelled Phillip forward again.

Arianna reached behind her back, came up with a handgun, aimed dead center at Phillip's chest. "Not another step, Phillip."

"But...but...you..." Phillip stuttered as he stopped short.

Emma willed herself invisible, edged slightly to the side. If she could at least get behind the sofa, maybe she'd have some cover. But Eric's gaze kept her pinned where she was.

"Who is he?" Phillip demanded, taking another stride toward Eric. "What is he—"

Arianna didn't even flinch when she fired, when the bullet hit Phillip's leg and he went down hard on the plastic drop cloth. "Quit your whining, Phillip. You should be grateful. The fact that your sister inherited the bulk of your father's estate kept you alive a little longer than planned. But now, well, no real need to keep you around, since you've already gotten your share, which I will conveniently inherit once you're gone."

Arianna had just admitted to murdering not only Broderick Aldridge but Whitney Jameson as well. And she'd shot Phillip. There was no way she'd let Emma walk out of there.

Tremors tore through her. "Eric, please."

"I'm sorry, Emma. I'm sorry I ever recommended you to Broderick for this job." He lifted his hands to the sides. "But it's out of my hands."

"I don't understand." Eric had recommended her to Broderick? And to think, she'd felt bad about involving him in this mess, had felt guilty when he'd been questioned by the police, had even considered giving him the money to cover Arianna's paycheck. "Why would you recommend me?"

"Because you do good work, of course." He shook his head. "Well, that, and having you coordinate everything put everyone I needed in place."

If she could just keep them talking. If she could stall for just a little while, maybe Jade and Chloe would realize something was wrong. Arianna hadn't put a silencer on the gun, maybe they'd heard the gunshot. *Granny Rose.* Surely, they'd make her stay in the Jeep. Keep her safe. Hopefully, they'd realize there was a problem and call the police, get Granny Rose out of there. Okay, she just had to keep it together, keep her wits about her long enough for Jade and Chloe to sound the alarm. Hopefully, before Phillip could bleed out. "Why, Eric? What does any of this have to do with you?"

He glanced at Arianna. Then, at her nod, he settled back on the arm of the chair.

Emma sat back down on the sofa. If she didn't, her rubbery legs would only betray her and give out anyway.

Arianna continued to pace. If she would just get close enough, maybe Emma could attack, take the gun from her. Of course, she'd have to contend with Eric too, but fear and adrenaline sometimes did crazy things to people, and she definitely had enough of both coursing through her. A quick glance at Phillip moaning on the floor and clutching his leg told her there'd be no help from him forthcoming.

"Broderick Aldridge scammed me out of everything I had." Eric's jaw clenched. He balled his fists in his lap.

Emma struggled to switch gears and follow what he was saying. "What are you talking about? I thought you didn't get involved in that, only Tiny did?"

"That time." He launched himself from the chair. "Before that, there was another sure thing, an investment guaranteed to net me a fortune."

"But I don't understand." Keep him talking, but try not to make him too angry. Just until help came. She could do that. She had to do that. "How did you know Broderick?"

"I moved a pal of his, and Broderick was there, rambling on and on to this guy about a sure thing he had a heads-up on, guaranteed to make anyone who invested a quick profit. Scammed me, the two of them, after I invested everything I had."

"But what about Tiny? He said you were the one who told him about Broderick's last money-making scheme." Sweat poured down her back. If

225

what Eric was saying was true, he'd purposely set Tiny up to lose money.

"And I was sorry to involve him. Really. But I had to do something. Arianna and I had this planned for months, had every intention of framing Phillip for his father's murder, but there was always the possibility the police wouldn't buy Phillip killed him, so we needed someone else, a plan B, so to speak. Then Tiny happened upon a conversation I was having with Broderick. Knowing about his violent past, I figured he was the perfect red herring."

"So this was the plan all along?" Phillip sobbed from the floor, clutching his leg, staring at Arianna. "You never loved me?"

Emma actually felt sorry for him.

"Oh, please." Arianna rolled her eyes and laughed. "Seriously, Phillip. I honestly couldn't wait to be rid of you. You have to admit, your whining and sniveling is a bit hard to take."

"But—"

"But nothing. Enough of this. Come on, Eric, let's be done with it and get out of here." She aimed the gun at Phillip.

Emma jumped to her feet. "No, wait!"

The front window imploded.

Arianna whirled toward the crash as a large garden stone flew through the window and into the room.

Three faces peered through the broken glass as Granny Rose screamed. "Freeze, or I'll shoot."

When Arianna lifted the gun, Granny Rose fired, hit her in the shoulder.

Arianna stumbled back, fumbled the gun as she grabbed her shoulder.

Emma lunged, grabbed the gun from her, and kicked the side of her knee as hard as she could, then danced back out of her reach as Arianna went down. "Don't move."

"Stop her, Eric," Arianna screamed.

When Eric started toward her, Emma jerked the gun toward him, her hand shaking violently. Could she pull the trigger if she had to? She wasn't sure. "Please, Eric. Don't make me shoot you."

He must have seen something in her eyes he believed, because instead of coming at her, he dropped to his knees beside Arianna and put his hands on his head.

Sirens screamed in the distance.

"The police are on their way," Jade yelled in through the broken window. "Are you okay, Emma?"

"I'm fine. I'll be okay until the police get here. Just please get Granny Rose away from the window. And call an ambulance. Phillip's been shot."

Jade reached inside, unlocked and pushed open the window, and climbed through, Granny Rose's gun held out in front of her. "Chloe took Granny Rose out to the Jeep."

Emma had never been so grateful to see anyone.

Jade moved to stand beside her, still keeping the gun aimed at Arianna.

Emma wished she could steady her hands, stop the tremors, but it wasn't going to happen. Probably not for a while.

Jade gestured with the gun toward Phillip. "Who shot him?"

"Arianna." Which didn't surprise her, though she still couldn't wrap her head around Eric's involvement. She'd thought he was her friend. Looked like another tiny home would be going up for sale in Mini-Meadows.

Chapter Thirty

Emma loaded the last of Granny Rose's things into the back of the Jeep, then ran back to the front door and looked around to be sure she wasn't forgetting anything. Of course, even if she had, she could just run it down the four lots to the little caboose home Mildred had sold her.

Granny Rose moved to stand beside her and peered inside. "Is that everything?"

"I think so." She put her arm around Granny Rose's shoulders, pulled her close. "I'm going to miss you, Granny Rose."

"Aww, dear." She hugged Emma tight, then stepped back and swiped tears from her cheeks. Ever since the incident with Arianna and Eric, she'd been prone to crying, her nerves frazzled. "I'll miss you too, but it's time to put all this behind us and move on."

Emma had to agree, hoping that doing so would help Granny Rose heal.

Butch barked, and Emma turned to find Jacob Bennett strolling up the driveway.

When he reached them, he smiled and took Granny Rose's hands in his, kissed her cheek. "How's my favorite hero this morning?"

Twin patches of crimson blossomed on her cheeks. "I'm doing okay. How are you?"

"Doing well myself, thank you." He looked up at the brilliant blue sky. "It's a fine morning for a walk."

"Why don't you come on in and have some tea? I was just about to pour some. It's hot work, moving." With a wink at Emma, she made herself scarce.

228

Emma couldn't help but smile. Seemed even moving wasn't going to stop Granny Rose's matchmaking. And that was just fine with Emma. "So, what are you doing here?"

He shrugged. "Seems I've developed a soft spot for your feisty grandma." Emma laughed.

"And I just wanted to check in, see how you were both doing."

She looked after Granny Rose. "We're doing okay, about as well as could be expected, all things considered."

"Good, I'm glad." He shook his head. "I spoke with Detective Montgomery today."

So much for staying out of the investigation. "And?"

"Seems they believe they have enough to convict both Eric and Arianna, especially since she rolled right over on him as soon as they got her into interview." He reached out, tugged a strand of hair that had come loose from her ponytail. "Though she tried to shove all the blame onto him, that recording you had of the entire incident will help them know what to look for, even if it's not admissible in court."

She was glad of that. She'd forgotten about the recording until she'd gone to get her cell phone out of her purse and saw the recorder still going. "And Phillip?"

He shrugged and leaned back against the house, took off his sunglasses and tucked them into the collar of his T-shirt. "He'll live. And since he's furious with Arianna for taking advantage of him—"

"But not for killing his father?"

"Apparently, not as much."

"Huh."

"So," he continued. "He spilled everything he knew."

"And he really had no involvement in any of it? I figured he at least had something to do with the ten thousand dollars taken out of Broderick's account the day he was killed."

"Not that he's admitted." He squinted toward the road. "And I'm pretty sure Arianna or Eric would have ratted him out if he'd been involved. According to him, Arianna had pushed him into getting Broderick to give him the money. This isn't quite the way he said it, but my take is he whined and goaded the old man into giving him one last allowance before throwing him out."

"Makes sense, I guess."

"How about Mildred? How's she taking it all?"

"Pretty good, it seems. She came by last night with a gift basket for Granny Rose as a housewarming gift." She'd come hand in hand with the same man Emma had seen leaving her house, who it turned out was her attorney as well as her beau. And for the first time Emma could remember, the woman had smiled as she'd thanked Emma for everything she'd done. Who knew? Maybe she'd be able to put all of this behind her and finally find happiness. Emma certainly hoped so.

"Anyway." Jake stood and pulled his sunglasses off his shirt, then used them to gesture toward the road. "Seems your friends are here to see Granny Rose off. But before I go, I was thinking, once you get Granny Rose settled into her new home, maybe you'd like to go out to dinner one night?"

She smiled as heat crept up her cheeks. "I'd like that, thank you."

"It's a date, then."

"And maybe you'll share with me how you ended up in Mini-Meadows." Because after finding out he was injured in the line of duty, she'd given up researching him. As far as she was concerned, it would be much more interesting to hear the story from the man himself.

"Maybe I will." With that, he slid his sunglasses on and strolled down the driveway, stopping to say hello to Jade, Chloe, and Max as he passed them.

Since Granny Rose appeared before he even made it to the road, Emma figured she'd been watching from the window. "Aww…he left already?"

"Yeah, but don't worry. He'll be back."

Granny Rose let out a hoot.

A wave of anticipation surged through Emma at the thought of unraveling his secrets, delving into his mysterious past, learning more about why he left the police force, how he'd been injured, and how he'd gone from New York City to a tiny home community in Central Florida. She had a feeling it was going to be an interesting story.

Emma and Granny Rose waited for their friends to make it up the driveway. Granny Rose would be living right down the road from her, she had amazing friends, and now a potential date with Detective Tall, Dark, and Dreamy. Emma couldn't help but think all was right in her world.

Acknowledgements

This book would not have been possible without the support and encouragement of my husband, Greg. We've built a wonderful life together, and I can't wait to see where our journey will lead next. I'd like to say a big thank you to my children, Elaina, Nicky and Logan, and to my son-in-law, Steve, for their understanding and help while I spent long nights at the computer. My husband and children are truly the loves of my life.

I also have to thank my best friend, Renee, for all of her support, long conversations and reading many rough drafts. I still wouldn't know how to use Word without her help. I'd like to thank my sister, Debby, and my Dad, Tony, who are probably my biggest fans and have read every word I've ever written. To my agent, Dawn Dowdle, thank you for believing in me and for being there in the middle of the night every time I have a question. And a very special thank you to Shawn Simmons for giving me this opportunity and for her wonderful advice and assistance in polishing this manuscript.

About the Author

Bestselling author Lena Gregory grew up in a small town on the south shore of eastern Long Island, but she recently traded in cold, damp, gray winters for the warmth and sunshine of central Florida, where she now lives with her husband, three kids, son-in-law, and four dogs. Her hobbies include spending time with family, reading, and walking, and now that she's living in the Sunshine State, she enjoys long walks in nature all year long, despite the occasional alligator or snake she sometimes encounters. Her love for writing developed when her youngest son was born and didn't sleep through the night. She works full time as a writer and a freelance editor and is a member of Sisters in Crime.

SOCIAL MEDIA HANDLES:

Newsletter http://lenagregory.us12.list-manage.com/subscribe?u=9765d0711ed4fab4fa31b16ac&id=49d42335d1

Facebook page: https://www.facebook.com/Lena.Gregory.Author/?fref=ts

Facebook profile: https://www.facebook.com/lena.gregory.986

Twitter: https://twitter.com/LenaGregory03

Pinterest: https://www.pinterest.com/lenagregoryauth/?etslf=2219&eq=lena%20gregory

Goodreads: https://www.goodreads.com/author/show/14956514.Lena
_Gregory

TikTok: https://www.tiktok.com/@lenagregoryauthor

AUTHOR WEBSITE:

http://www.lenagregory.com/

Also by Lena Gregory

Bay Island Psychic Mysteries:
  Death at First Sight
  Occult and Battery
  Clairvoyant and Present Danger
  Spirited Away
  Grave Consequences
  A Spirit Seeks Asylum
  With a Spirit of Vengeance

All-Day Breakfast Café Mysteries:
  Scone Cold Killer
  Murder Made to Order
  A Cold Brew Killing
  Whole Latte Murder
  A Waffle Lot of Murder
  Mistletoe Cake Murder

CPSIA information can be obtained
at www.ICGtesting.com
Printed in the USA
BVHW031836140423
662291BV00026B/209